Seven Oaks

Kaitlyn Johnson

Copyright © 2019 Kaitlyn Johnson

All rights reserved.

Cover designed by Jessica DeLucchi

Formatted by Andrew Clayton

I'd like to thank my friends, old and new, for being such an incredibly positive force in my life; you can bet some of the great characters in this book are based off of these friends. Andrew Clayton, you, as usual, have saved me from the brink of insanity with formatting this book. I'd also like to thank my parents for being so supportive, and, as always, my cat, Fe, for being the best darn cat in the world.

Chapter 1

After leaving Seven Oaks for the first time twelve years ago, I did not expect to return. I expected to leave it all behind, an unvisited part of the past, memories and all. The beaches, the forests, the shops, all of those pieces moved with me to Vancouver; the only thing missing was the small-town feel. I guess it was nice, spending my first few years in a town where I felt safe, where I could run around without a care in the world. Strangers often don't exist in places like Seven Oaks, to my limited knowledge.

I didn't think I would be coming back here. I didn't plan on taking this five-and-a-half-hour bus ride from the airport to get to a new school in an old small town. Hell, I didn't even anticipate attending post-secondary, but here we are.

A few years ago, the mayor of Seven Oaks made a rather odd announcement. I don't think I ever watched his press conference, because I could not have cared less at the time, but he said something along the lines of, "We are opening a fancy elitist school where the young residents of Seven Oaks can continue their education without having to sacrifice their town. The classrooms will be smaller, and our children will get the education they deserve!" He went on to explain how it's such a pity that so many people have to leave their town because they can't get the education they want and end up moving away. It's some tactic to keep people living in the tiny town of Seven Oaks. I'm not even sure if it's all that small, but it's definitely smaller than the Vancouver area. Mr. Mayor kept saying that it would be a little campus, and would work kind of like a high school, turning me off the idea even more. He said it would be like a private high school, but with furthering education, with some of the best instructors in the country.

Anyway, a couple years went by, and halfway through my first semester of my last year of high school, I found out that, wouldn't you know it, the university would open the fall of my first college year. After Mr. Mayor's announcement of opening a post-secondary school to prefer people who live in the town, assuring us of the transferable credits if needed, Mom insisted that I apply. I'd already been accepted into two other universities, neither of which I wanted to attend, nor had I any plans on applying to a third. After a long argument, I caved and applied with my B average grades to the beautiful new school of the East coast. I was from Seven Oaks, sure, but I didn't think I stood a chance. I was so confident that I even told my mom I would attend if they let me in.

Imagine my surprise when the letter came in the mail.

It's hard to believe that a year ago, I was getting ready for my final year of high school, and now it feels like I'm reliving it all over again. High school itself wasn't the worst for me; it wasn't good nor bad. It just happened. The people I'd met in high school, however...

The bus bumps once again, and I briefly hop out of my seat. I don't know if the roads are shit or if the bus is just sensitive, but I'll be surprised if my luggage survives the trip. I peer out the window and catch a sign mentioning my new school, aptly and uncreatively named *Seven Oaks University*, but I don't see how far away we are. We've been driving on this forest road for at least twenty minutes now, and before that was the wonderful strip of shops and all the local business in central Seven Oaks. Most of this place is nature, which I love, except for a few square kilometers that is just stuffed with whatever businesses will fit. I remember I heard a few years ago that there was a wild storm, and a bunch of the shops closest to the ocean were flooded and partially destroyed. Today, it didn't look like it at all.

I face forward to the back of the seat in front of me; after the flight here, I keep expecting a TV to be there, telling me our altitude and how much longer it takes until we land. The bus is still an immense upgrade from the cramped plane.

I should mention that I am the only one on this bus, other than the bus driver. Mr. Mayor made it clear that the university prioritizes students from Seven Oaks, and all others will be considered after the home-town residents. I wouldn't be surprised if I was the only one who hasn't spent their whole life on this sandy rock. I'm not entirely sure if that's legal or not, to deny admission based on location, but then I think about how students from other countries are charged double the admission price for universities here, so maybe it's not all that different. Still weird to me, but something that has been accepted as "normal."

My few memories of Seven Oaks are doing things that most kids do; riding my bike, going to the beach, playing with a friend or two. I remember crying when we had to move away, because I would miss my best friend, but I don't even remember her name now. I'd be shocked if she remembers me.

I hear some kind of mumbling, and I glance up to see the bus driver desperately trying to make some eye contact with me in the rear-view mirror. I remove my headphones.

"Sorry?" I chime.

"You're a freshman, right?" the bus driver asks, his voice as thick as the trees flying by.

It takes a moment for me to register, but then I nod. "First year, yeah."

"All right." He mumbles to himself a little bit, and I cautiously put one earbud back into my ear.

Through the forest, I can see the plunging cliff that will eventually lead down to the rocky ocean. I hadn't even noticed that we've been slowly going up a hill all this time. The experience itself has already been unsettling enough; revisiting the main city, seeing all the identical shops, it's like I walked right into the postcard that I have in my room back home.

I wipe beneath my eyes for the thousandth time today, something that becomes habit after I've been crying. I cried on the way to the airport and at the airport, and so did my mom. It wasn't a good time for either of us, and we attracted an awful amount of attention, but I couldn't help it. I stopped crying immediately after she left, with the distraction of figuring out my first flight alone, but I have been wiping my eyes ever since. I don't want any stray mascara leaving any clue that I was sobbing just this morning. Added to the time change, it's been a long day.

The bus slows to a halt, and the bus driver announces, "Freshman campus!"

I hop to my feet, a little surprised, and make eye contact with the driver. "Freshman campus?"

"Yeah." He chuckles, swinging his legs to dangle off the tall driver's seat, smiling. "Aren't you a freshman?"

First year. "Yeah, but we have our own campus?"

The man laughs again and takes off his hat to wipe the sweat from his forehead. He has a gold tooth in his warming smile, something that makes me uneasy. "Yes, ma'am. The other years are further along the road." *What kind of school has different campuses for different years? How does that even work? How do I know so little about this school?*

"Oh, okay." I throw my backpack over my back, ensuring I have all my belongings with me. I step past the driver, hiking down the lofty steps. "Thank you for driving me."

"Not a problem, ma'am. Do you need help with your bags?"

I glance outside, spotting the open side compartment of the bus. "No, I'm good, but thank you."

"All right. Give me a wave when you're done."

I skip out of the bus, my legs feeling wobbly. A humid summer heat strikes my skin, and I stretch my arms high into the sky.

Then I look at the campus.

I don't know what I envisioned, but it wasn't this. There's the parking lot, where the bus and I are loitering, and following up the steps before me leads to a huge brick building. It looks rustic and classic, like it was built decades ago but has retained its boastful colours and gleam. It's stunning. Along the sides of the first building are white columns, leading up to the roof past the three other floors. Trees surround the first building and begin to stray into different patterns that must lead to other departments. The pictures don't do it justice, I thought it would be a lot smaller.

I turn back to the bus and lug my suitcase out of the echoing dome inside. I prop it onto all four wheels, and then dive back in for my duffel bag. I have to shimmy inside the bus, but I manage to draw it out and throw it over my shoulder. I tried to pack light, but I am being weighed down from my past years of hoarding. I shut the hatch, patting it twice to make sure it's fully closed, and reappear at the side doors of the bus. I tap on the glass and smile, offering a small wave. The driver tips his hat to me and grins, bearing down on the gas to get the guzzler going again. I catch him briefly check in his rear-view mirror to make sure everything is shut, and then he begins to maneuver through the lofty lot.

"Hi!" I nearly jump out of my skin at the sound of another person, and I return to the gorgeous landscape to find a girl planted in front of me. "Are you Kim?"

"Yeah," I reply cautiously. She looks about my age, which makes sense considering I'm going to university with people who are all the same age as me, thanks to the strange separated campuses. Her red hair is parted to the right, tumbling down into a messy braid over her shoulder.

"I'm Carolyn, your Resident Advisor."

"Oh, right." *Here at Seven Oaks University, we offer all new students a tour by their very own Resident Advisor!* "Hi, yeah, I'm Kim. Nice to meet you."

"You too!" Carolyn bares her teeth, her brown eyes tightening. "I'll show you to your room?"

I tug at my suitcase, carrying the awful weight up the twenty steps to the main level of the campus, and I'm nearly out of breath when I'm done; I have *got* to get in better shape.

"So, this is SOU!" Carolyn claps her hands together at the top of the steps and faces me. Her hair bounces when she walks and talks, the braided curls loosening with each step and word. "This is the main building with your more basic courses, languages, math 101, history, that kind of stuff. Further to the left you have the science building and the creative arts building, and just to the right, I'll show you to your room."

I take in my first university experience, breathing in the fresh pine air, looking at the freshly vintage buildings that I will be spending the year living in. As I'm gazing around, something on a bulletin board catches my eye.

"What's that?"

Carolyn follows me, narrating, "That's the bulletin board. It's where people can post stuff, like, about clubs, tutoring help, courses..."

She probably thinks I'm an idiot for asking what a bulletin board is, but I shake my head and point at the only thing not related to school on the board. "I meant this."

I press my index finger in the middle of the paper, in the middle of a printed picture of a girl who doesn't look all that much different than me. Dark hair, blue eyes, except she has a stellar smile, slimmer nose, clear skin. Beneath the picture are the words, *Missing, Veronica Keating, 18.* Tiny script near the bottom of the poster reads, *If seen, please contact local authorities.*

"Oh, yeah, that's Veronica. We shouldn't even have these up." I turn to Carolyn who blushes, clutching her clipboard closer to her chest. "I know, that sounds bad. It's been months now, and it was just after graduation. She always talked about leaving and not looking back, so..."

"Did you know her?" I ask, returning to the photograph. It hits me that I've never seen one of these posters in real life. Not for a human, anyway. It's eerie, to look into the eyes of a woman whose fate is unknown.

"Everyone did. She was the valedictorian at Seven Oaks High." *Another spot-on name.*

The poster looks worn and wrinkled, like it's been here a while, despite the campus just being built. "Hello, Laura Palmer," I mutter, the small-town chills creeping on my back. Being confronted with a missing poster of a girl my age isn't exactly the welcome I'd hoped for with my return to Seven Oaks.

"What?" Carolyn prompts.

I turn back to her, cutting focus with Veronica. "Just from a show." It may be from the jet lag, or the fact that I haven't slept in almost a full day, but I decide that I have to keep pushing. Next to the bulletin board along the stairs are two concrete blocks, where two boys just happen to be sitting. I approach the one closest to me, grinning from ear to ear. "Damn fine coffee you have here."

He looks up at me, bewilderment in his hazel eyes. "What?"

"Best coffee I've ever had," I press. His friend doesn't look very impressed; if anything, he looks a little freaked out. I extend my arm past both of them, sweeping over the forest leading down the mountain. "And these trees, what do you call these magnificent trees?"

The two boys remain silent, but the one I'm speaking to produces a wide smile.

"Um, let me show you to your room," Carolyn says, and even takes me by the arm. I guess she, and everyone else, probably know everyone here. They all went to high school together, they've possibly spent their whole lives together. I'm the weird new girl, and this probably isn't helping.

I grab my suitcase and trail after my resident advisor, but not before hearing one of the two boys yell, "Douglas Firs!"

I giggle to myself, craning over my shoulder to see which one of the guys had yelled, but they're both looking my way. I'm not making a very good first impression, but at least I found my audience.

"So, the building there is the cafeteria and study hall, along with The Rec," Carolyn drags me back to focus, ignoring my attempts at humour. I follow her extended arm towards the cafeteria, and just attached to it is *The Rec*, apparently. "Behind it is the auditorium, which is in the same building as the arts classes. Keep forgetting that."

"I'm sorry, The *Rec*?" I've never heard that word used so liberally before, as if everyone knows what that is.

"The Rec. It's like our recreational room. It has the gyms, a lounge upstairs, has the pool downstairs, it's just for unwinding."

I had no idea that universities had that kind of stuff. "That's really cool."

Carolyn laughs. "I guess. Didn't your high school have one?"

"Uh, no. We had…a field." My faithful high school couldn't even afford to keep English Lit on the course list, not to mention we had the slowest internet in the district. I wish I was kidding.

"Oh. Then yeah, I guess it's cool." There's a sparkle in her eye, and she seems to be genuinely enjoying this tour. I like her.

There aren't very many people hanging around campus right now; there's a big grassy field behind the first building, where a few girls and guys are lounging in their unnecessary sweaters, and the sporadic student wandering around, but it seems pretty dead. Some crows caw and circle around the few trees planted in the patch of grass, prompting my next question.

"Are there any animals around here? Like, bears or anything?"

"Oh, no." Carolyn stops in her tracks and holds out her hands towards me. She seems terrified by the very notion. "No bears, just mostly deer. An occasional cougar."

My grip wavers on my suitcase and it almost tips over from all the one-sided weight. *A bear is outrageous, but the occasional cougar is fine?* "I've never seen a cougar in the wild," I confess, taking a step forward.

Carolyn quickly returns to her pitter-patter, guiding me along. "I've only seen one once, most people have never seen one around here. We get lots of racoons feeding from our garbage bins, but that's kind of expected. Just stay away from the dumpsters, and you'll be fine."

"Got it." Another thing to add to the list.

"Here's the girl's building." Carolyn stops once again and points to the building before us, reaching the end of the path. "The boy's is right there." She points to a nearly identical brick structure immediately next to our own building. "We usually try to keep it pretty separate. Boys in your room is fine, just don't loiter in the halls." I find it a little amusing how Carolyn knows so much about this school that has been running for all of four days. Amused and impressed.

"Won't be a problem," I joke, my heart stinging a little. I was not even close to popular in high school, and that is not going to change now. I didn't mind very much; my mind was preoccupied with survival more than anything.

"Tell me about it!" Carolyn giggles and takes me up the few steps into the girl's building. She holds the door open for me and ushers me in first. "The boys here are ridiculous. Don't get me wrong, there are a lot of hot guys, but they are so immature."

"Maybe University will fix that," I mumble, taking in the hall. From the floor to about three feet up is painted a subtle brownish pink, with a white wooden frame dividing the rest of the white wall. Before the hall veers off to the right, I can see twenty doors lining along, each a vibrant wood colour, along with small tags to the left of each door. I check the tag to my left; Cindy. My name must be on one of these rooms.

"Well, spending the past thirteen years with them hasn't done much," Carolyn states, crossing her arms over her chest. "Hey, where are you from again?"

"Technically, here. I was born in Seven Oaks, but we moved to Vancouver after kindergarten."

"Oh, so that's how you got in." I give her a strained glance, but Carolyn doesn't notice. *Am I really the only one who didn't grow up here?* "Vancouver, wow. Big city compared to here, eh?" We both chuckle politely, and she continues, "I'm sure you'll love it here. Lots of parties."

My eyes widen; the barely operating school is already known for being a party school? "Really."

"Oh, yeah. All the time." A blush rises onto Carolyn's cheeks and she straightens her arms out once more, taking a deep breath. "Anyway. Here," she signals to the first door to our right, "is our mail room. Mail key is in your room, along with your room key. Your mailbox is the same as the number on your door. Which is pretty close…"

I follow behind Carolyn past a few doors, until she finds one on the left. She points to my typed name on the tag and opens the door. "Welcome to Kim's!"

Before entering, I gaze down the connecting hall, finding it leading to a stairwell upstairs. There definitely has to be more girls living in this building, despite how quiet it's been since I've stepped foot inside.

I face my room once more, and I am floored. I rush inside, too shocked to believe it; it's huge. On TV, the rooms were always tiny, and the roommates quarreled, but this isn't like that at all. I have a double sized bed along with a dresser and desk, and a fully built bookshelf just waiting for me to unload my knick-knacks onto it. The floor is a fresh carpet, and there are two doors along the left side of the wall, near the heater, just below my window overlooking one of the many walkways.

I drop my duffel bag on my bed and slip out of my backpack, and then go check the doors. One is a closet that's even bigger than mine back home, and the other is…

"I get my own bathroom?" I turn to Carolyn. "I thought we would all have to share."

She snorts, rolling her eyes. "God, no. That would be awful. And thank god for no roommates."

I observe my new room, shocked by the magnitude of it. I saw pictures online, but I didn't believe the rooms would be this spacious and private.

"This is amazing," I laugh, forcing myself to stay standing. With my current level of exhaustion, if I sit down, I won't get back up. "The mayor built this, right?"

"Yeah. He really cares about the community." Carolyn rolls her eyes and leans against my doorframe. I didn't catch her sarcasm until then. "He has a kid who goes here, probably just didn't want him to move away. He's kind of a tool anyway."

"The mayor?"

"No, his kid. He's a douche." She clears her throat, blushing again, and stands up straighter. "Anyway. Oh, here." Carolyn unclips something from her clipboard and hands it to me; a pamphlet. On the front it shows a majestic picture of the school and reads, *Welcome to Seven Oaks University!*

"Thanks," I mutter, wondering if it's the same one I read online.

"All your info is in there, course locations, a map, everything you'll need here. Cafeteria is open from six to ten, buffet style. There are a few coffee shops that are twenty-four-seven, great for studying and hanging out. Your sheets are fresh from today, but there's a laundry room down the hall where you can exchange your sheets for clean ones, and of course, do your laundry. Upstairs from here there's a common room for the girls, with couches, a TV, some vending machines, your basic Netflix binge night in." I'm not sure I would call this place basic, considering it has the amenities of a hotel, but this is a rich town. Things are different here. Despite the fact that Mom had been saving for my college fund since the second I was born, I still don't understand how this could be within our price range...

"It also has my phone number!"

I stand there dumbfounded, forgetting what Carolyn was even talking about, until she plucks the paper from my hand and flips it to the last page. She holds the page up to me where a beaming photograph of her is on display, along with the words, *Resident Advisor*, and Carolyn's phone number.

"You can call or text me anytime," she adds.

"Wow, thanks!" I smile, blushing a little. "I will probably take you up on that."

Carolyn forces one last smile, and then it slowly begins to break, until her entire body deflates. "How was that?"

"...what?" My mind dances in a panic, wondering if I missed something important from my dazed state.

"My tour. I mean, I did it for everyone else here too, but I know them all, you know?"

"Oh. Right." My feet tango back and forth, begging to be set free of my thick boots, but I remain upright. "You did great. It's like you've been doing it for years."

"Okay, good!" Carolyn, in a poorly timed decision, tempts me by sitting down on my bed. "I know it's a lot to take in, but it's really exciting to have someone new here. Don't get me wrong, I love knowing everybody, but it's so refreshing to meet someone who I haven't grown up with. Honestly, I didn't expect anyone else here, other than the Seven Oaks High graduating class."

"I'm surprised too." My knees twitch at the sight of the fluffy bed, but instead, I lean my body against a wall; a compromise. "Is there anyone here who you didn't graduate with? Other than me?"

"Not that I know of." Carolyn neatly folds her hands on top of her lap.

"It's kind of a weird set-up," I say, drawing Carolyn's gaze.

"What do you mean?"

"I mean...this feels more like a high school than a college. Like, a really fancy private school." I'm curious to see how the classes work.

Carolyn scrunches up her nose and shrugs, glancing around the bare room. "I guess so. I like the idea of living on campus, though, means I don't have to drive to school." She smirks wickedly. "Means I get to sleep in an extra two hours."

"Tell me about it." Busing to school every morning was the norm, sure, but I will be able to have infinitely better sleeps knowing that I am a five-minute walk from my classes.

My RA stands up and straightens out her checkered skirt, a retro choice in this day and age. She smiles and places her petite hands on her solid hips. "Anyway, I'll let you get to unpacking. We're really excited to have you."

"I'm really excited to be here." My heart flutters, knowing that she will soon be leaving my room and that this will all suddenly become real. It's scary and exhilarating; a new milestone. It hasn't fully sunk in yet. "And Carolyn, thanks for the tour. I really appreciate it."

The girl beams and swats her hand at me, and I've even managed to draw a small blush from her. "Oh, it's no problem."

"And I will probably...*definitely* be texting you if I have any questions."

"That's what I'm here for!" Carolyn reaches for the door and lets herself out but stops just beneath the doorframe. "Oh, also, your keys are in your desk drawer."

I follow her directions and check the desk near my bed, finding two keys inside. Both are brass, but one is half the size of the other, presumably the mail key.

"I'll see you later. It was nice to meet you, Kim."

"You too, Carolyn."

I smile in her direction, praying that I'm not coming off too desperate, and she soon disappears from my sight, shutting the door behind her.

I lay my suitcase down on the floor and step over it, accessing my fallen duffel bag. I dig around inside, locating the item that gave me hell during the security check. I grip my baseball bat firmly in both hands, something that always comforts me. I played baseball all throughout middle school and high school, and I wasn't even very good at it, but I liked it. I didn't see any mention of a baseball team for Seven Oaks on the website, but maybe they'll have one in the spring.

I place my bat gently onto my bed, and feeling the sheets, I know it's all over. I kick off my laced boots and immerse myself in the puffy comforter, snuggling up with my bat beside me. I reach over to my backpack, never wanting to leave the luxury of this bed. I can feel it's still warm from the dryer. I rifle around in my backpack until I find my hidden friend, the one friend I could take with me from Vancouver.

A little brown bear with a red satin bow.

I bring him to my chest, my eyes drifting shut. I graze the slick bat on top of my covers, recalling the time; it's evening now, so if I sleep a long time, I might just be able to get up early and start the year right. Early to bed, early to rise.
What a concept.
I try to wrap my head around all the info Carolyn gave me during our short tour. Laundry room, cafeteria, boys suck, lots of parties. Maybe I'll actually go to a party for once.

I want to say that I didn't have friends back in Vancouver, but that's not entirely true. I had casual acquaintances who I sometimes saw, and for a while, I did have friends. At least, I *thought* that I had friends. I take comfort in the fact that I am a nobody here; this is the fresh start that I've been waiting for, that I've been yearning for. This is the new potential to make friends and be who I want to be, I can finally restart and leave the past where it belongs.

My mind, running a mile a minute, slowly starts to jog, my senses slipping away.

University is supposedly the time of self-discovery, and I am more than eager to take on the post-secondary stereotype.

I am finally here.

Chapter 2

The first week at Seven Oaks seemed to fly by in a blur. I was so nervous before my first class that I nearly threw up, but after five seconds in the classroom, I was instantly calmed. That fear of the unknown disappeared in a heartbeat when I realized that nobody else knew what to expect either.

I have two classes on Tuesday, two on Thursday, and one on Friday. I have to hand it to the school, they have the schedules on lock; I have my five classes in three different buildings, and they're organized by time and building to be the most convenient for me. It's like the school is catering to me, rather than me being purely lucky to even be here.

My course load is pretty light, but I guess that's what happens when my passions all lie within arts and language, as opposed to intellectual studies. The classes don't feel much like work, and only feel like practicing for my future potential career.

I haven't made any new friends, but I occasionally chat with my classmates. More than that, I've gotten the chance to watch how these people who have known each other all their lives interact now that they're in university. It feels like a giant family, and all the good and bad that comes with it. Everyone at least knows of each other, and I'm the perfect little wrench to throw into that equation. I have gotten a decent amount of attention, mostly from curious natives who can't help but wonder who the outsider is. I'm no stranger to the elongated stares. I'm not sure how many times I've been asked where I'm from. I started to keep a count, but after ten, I lost track.

Of my five classes, my last one of the week, this one, has got to be my favourite. It's Writing 101, comprising of the four main elements; fiction, non-fiction, poetry, and script. I was expecting a structured and harsh curriculum, but hearing Mr. Ace, our shockingly relaxed professor, explain the course outline, it sounds pretty chill. It sounds like a free-for-all more than anything. He said we would have one writing assignment a week and would spend the following class going over different techniques to correspond with those assignments.

"As budding writers, I want you all to be free to express your own unique style to the world," Mr. Ace says, sitting on the edge of his desk. The course only has about eighteen kids, something that continually surprised me throughout the week, so his voice echoes through the classroom. Despite my interest in what he has to say, my mind keeps wandering to the people sitting in the lecture hall. There's one girl, Georgina, who I share four classes with. The only one I don't have with her is my elective of the semester, Ornithology. I don't share any other courses with the kids in that class.

Georgina seems quiet, her head always down, and now that I'm thinking about it, always wearing headphones. She doesn't even try to hide it; her perfect blonde hair fails to disguise the shiny black plastic devouring her ears. Most of the professors said that their notes are all available online in case anyone "can't make it to class," so it's not like she's missing out on anything.

All my teachers in high school told me that university is different than high school, and that no one is going to spend their time holding my hand through a class. They clearly didn't know about Seven Oaks.

Mr. Ace stands up straight in front of the desk, raising one hand, but the clock on the adjoining wall diverts his attention; he's already five minutes overdue.

"If any of you have any questions, my door is always open to you. I am eager to read your papers next week about your first impression of our new school." I couldn't even believe that our first assignment was about what we think of the school. Mr. Ace said the dean, Mr. Wolfe, wanted a general consensus of the school from our class. We are basically the surveying population.

I don't even realize that Mr. Ace has dismissed us until all the students begin to scurry out of the classroom. I scramble to shove my notebooks and pens into my backpack, throw it over my shoulder, and I head towards the back door.

"Ms. Clay?" Mr. Ace's voice echoes, even louder with us being the only two people in the classroom. I turn to him and he waves his hand towards himself, inviting me over.

I walk to the front of the class, hand gripping one of my backpack's straps. Mr. Ace uncrosses his arms as I approach, and I take it as a good sign. It's ironic that his head is nearly completely bald, but his beard and moustache are thriving.

"How are you doing, Kimberly?" He looks gruff and rough around the edges, his voice surprisingly calm and even.

"I'm good," I respond confidently.

"You've been adjusting okay?"

I nod, gazing at the platinum band around his finger. He mentioned his family today, his wife and two kids, and I think one of them is just starting high school, if I recall correctly. Mr. Ace himself can't be younger than fifty.

"Yeah, I have." I smile knowingly, praying for this interaction will end. I tend to get nervous around authority figures, despite how friendly they may seem.

"Well, I am glad to hear it. I know you didn't go to school here, so the education system may be a bit different from what you know..." Mr. Ace stands up straighter before circling back to his chair, sitting down. "If there's anything you need, please don't hesitate to ask."

"Thank you, I appreciate that." I slowly release my tight grip on my bag, and I look Mr. Ace in the eye. "What exactly do you mean, the education system being different?"

The man chuckles, lacing his fingers together on his lap. "The small-town reputation of Seven Oaks holds true. Because of this, the school experience is a lot more personalized to each student. I've only ever taught around here, but I've heard it's a little different in bigger cities."

I blink a few times, processing his words; he's not exactly wrong. When I graduated, I didn't know a solid sixty percent of the people graduating with me. I had never even heard their names, and there is no doubt that I was part of that sixty percent to someone else. It's not like that here. Here, it's like some wild daycare facility.

"Yeah, I guess so," I conclude, unsure of how else to respond. I can't tell if he's insulting my education or not. "I guess it's hard not to be personally involved when you watch all these kids grow up."

Mr. Ace smiles, nodding slowly. "That's exactly right." He smiles gently, something I've started noticing more and more in the professors here. Almost like nostalgia for the present, and how the town is continuing to develop. "Anyway, I'm sure you're eager to go enjoy your weekend, so I won't keep you any longer. I hope you like it here."

"Thanks, Mr. Ace."

Mr. Ace offers one last gleam before turning to his computer. Despite the beautiful classrooms of sturdy desks, somehow tasteful marmoleum, and blanketing windows with views of the impeccable greenery, Mr. Ace's computer looks like it's almost two decades old. The start-up sound flashes me back to typing games and math exercises in elementary school, learning how to use a new-fangled com-pu-ter.

I skip out of the classroom, proud of myself for getting through my first week. So proud, I crash right into a perfect stranger. A broad shoulder catches my neck, and I resist the urge to dry heave in the hallway, and I instead stumble backwards.

"Oh, I'm sorry," I apologize, slowly gazing my way up to the person's deep green eyes.

"No worries," the boy replies, chuckling, and steadies his half-fallen backpack from his shoulder. He grips onto one of the straps tightly. "The doorways are pretty hazardous."

I laugh. "They really are. You'd think there would be warning signs, students crossing."

The brown-haired boy laughs at my joke, and after giving up another smile, I start to skirt past him. Until he calls behind me, "hey, you're *Twin Peaks* girl, right?"

I stop in my tracks, half impressed that he remembered me when I clearly forgot him, half embarrassed that my title has shifted from "new girl" to "*Twin Peaks* girl." I turn around, my mind sparking. "You knew the trees."

He nods, and I retrace my steps, standing in front of him once again. "I'm Owen, by the way."

"Kim," I chime back.

"It's nice to meet you." His voice is friendly, as is his warming face, and it draws a smile out of me.

"You, too."

He quickly glances behind me and then stretches his arms out, relaxing in his stance. "So, I don't think you're from here..."

"Technically, I am." His eyebrows pop up and I explain, "I was born here, and lived here until I was six. Then moved to Vancouver."

"Oh, wow, big city." *When you're living there, it doesn't feel like it.* "Is it weird coming back here?"

I shrug, glancing at the few students roaming the halls. I learned there are only a handful of classrooms per building, and they are each huge, so there are never many people trying to get from one place to another. "Yeah. The weirdest part is how everyone knows each other." It's like coming into the second act of a movie when all the characters have already been established, and I'm trying to figure out what the story is in the first place.

"That's what happens when the same families live here for actual centuries," Owen half jokes. "I've never really traveled anywhere, but I'm guessing Vancouver wasn't like that."

"Not even close." My mind jumps back to the bustle of Vancouver, the unpredictable transit system, the downtown dispensaries, the million sushi joints. It's a trendy city.

I catch Owen checking behind my head again, and I can't help but turn to see what he's looking at; a clock.

"Sorry, I'm just running late," he says, cheeks flushing.

"That's okay. It was nice meeting you."

"You too." His feet stay firmly on the ground, but I take a step back.

"And sorry again for bumping into you," I add, taking another step behind me. Owen hasn't moved, despite his urgent expression.

"Oh, yeah, it's fine. Don't worry about it. I'll talk to you another time."

After a single parting smile, I strut back down the hall feeling better than before; I actually talked to someone. I have a potential new friend! He even said the words, he will talk to me another time. It could be mindless chatter, but I'm choosing to run with it.

It's exciting to me, knowing that people here are friendly enough to strike up a conversation. It's exciting to know that my track record of friendships might not always be so shitty. I have hopes.

I exit the Language Arts building and instead of going straight for my room to be a hermit for yet another night, I take a different route to explore the campus a little more.

Despite what's been crammed in here, there really isn't too much to the freshman campus; there are the three main buildings filled with classes, another building for the cafeteria, lounge, and "rec" facilities. There's a lot to do inside the buildings, but it doesn't look like much to the naked eye. It reminds me of a miniaturized version of Seven Oaks itself; there is a lot more than what we see above the surface.

I walk along one of the main paths, seeing the Science building up ahead on my left. I take my Ornithology class there, but I've only seen a fraction of the inside. My class is right next to the main building entrance, so I haven't even seen the elaborate research laboratory that's apparently hidden within.

The science building looks a little out of the main circuit of the campus, but I think that's intentional, in case some chemical explosion goes off and kills everyone closest to it. Or I'm overthinking it. Either way, it's nice to know that I'm moderately safe.

I follow the trail along the side of the Language Arts building, the intentionally old looking brick almost comforting to me. I graze my fingers against the nearly windowless wall, reaching over the perfect shrubs lining in the shadows. Tiny shrubs seem to be a common occurrence here at SOU, as they appear to encircle all the buildings.

Just outside the cafeteria, there's a well-maintained garden filled with yellow daffodils and white daises. I don't know if it's a trick of the light, but the flowers seem to look prettier here in Seven Oaks.

The pool, currently only populated by three or four people inside, is massive. Not quite Olympic sized, though not too far off, half used for lanes, half for free swim. The entire wall looking inside at the pool is made of glass. It's both beautiful to look at, seeing the sun reflect against the tame water, but I can't help but wonder if anyone swimming feels like they're on display for everyone to see.

Even with the tempting pool, most of the students are outside. This entire stretch looks symmetrical if you stand in the middle, given the path leading from the cafeteria, with a nice little courtyard dead centre. It's a simple concrete lounge, set with four cornered picnic tables, and a large fountain in the middle, custom made with what looks to be a giant bird statue on top. The bird doesn't look familiar to anything real I've seen, and has a long narrow beak angled to a point. The wings are jagged metal, as if the bird itself is made of electricity, and this is confirmed when I can just read the small plaque from where I'm standing; *Seven Oaks Lightning Birds.*

Never heard of a lightning bird before.

The tables are all filled with students, eating their buffet lunches of the day. I have to say, the cafeteria food is phenomenal. I didn't expect it to be anything special, but I can already tell that if I don't force myself to exercise at least now and then, I'm going to gain some serious weight.

There are two guys seated on the ground by one of the sprinkled trees, playing chess. One of the boys, the one wearing glasses, is scratching his head, observing the black and white board as if his life depends on it, and the other boy couldn't possibly care less. I snoop at the game; Glasses only has a few more moves until checkmate.

Even more students are spread out on the grass, tanning in the sun or lounging in the shade. A few of them have some blankets on them with black, blue, and gold colours. I can't see the exact image depicted, but it's a safe bet to say it's the town's high school mascot. Our school barely had any clothing options, let alone fleece blankets. I narrowly avoid stepping on one while identifying the misshapen owl on the fabric.

My tour of the campus is short lived, and I find myself face to face with the girl's dormitory. I know the boys' is further down to the left, but I've never been inside. I caught a glimpse of their walls, also white, but with a dusty turquoise instead of our pink shade.

I hop up the few steps and enter the girl's building, finding the halls buzzing with people. So far, this is the most populated I've seen these halls. There are a few groups of two or three girls, and even a couple sets of five or six. It's a big chunk of the girls who live on resident, so something must be happening.

"Kim!" a girl yells, and for a second, I think it's Rose from back home. I nearly have a heart attack, and I have to force myself to peer over the beautiful girls to find Carolyn bounding towards me, a phone in one hand, a stack of papers clutched in the other.

Breathe, Kim. Rose isn't here.

"Hey," I say as Carolyn stops dead in front of me.

"I wanted to see you today, see how your first week went!" I shake my head just slightly, shaking away any unwanted thoughts from my mind. I'm not sure how resident advisors are supposed to act, but Carolyn checking up on me is a pleasant surprise. "Any issues?"

"No, it's been good," I confirm. It feels like a mantra at this point, just for a little while until I'm more used to it. I've cried to my mom once since getting here, but other than that hiccup, I'm adjusting.

"Good! Oh, I'm so glad." Carolyn smiles widely and exhales loudly, and that's when it hits me that she's definitely had a drink or two. The sickly scent of beer floods my senses; it's just past 5:00pm, I guess it's as good a time as any. Her orange hair is a little frizzy, a few strands stuck to her pale pink lipstick, like she's definitely been bounding around the halls. "Have you made any friends yet?"

There is Owen, the boy I talked to for five seconds, and Georgina, who smiled at me once. There's also Carolyn, but I'm not sure she's a friend since it's her job to spend time with me.

"Kind of," I respond, hopefully sounding more confident than I actually am.

"Oh, don't worry, you'll make friends soon," Carolyn reassures. The solitude is visible, apparently. "I think people just don't know what to do with you." Carolyn leans against the door and runs her fingers through her hair, tugging at the strays caught on her lips. She stares at the other groups of girls, a wistful look in her eyes. "Most people haven't traveled much. I mean, obviously they've traveled, Europe, Hawaii, stuff like that." *Obviously.* "But they don't really meet new people. In all my years of school, I don't remember meeting anyone new. It was all the same kids. You said you were here for, like, kindergarten, right?" I nod. "Yeah. That's about it." Carolyn sighs deeply, and I'm not sure if she realized that she hasn't made total sense, but I understand what she's saying.

"I–"

"There's a party tonight," Carolyn interrupts, meeting my eyes. "You should come. It's in a few hours, in the smaller gym, in the pool building. You know where it is, I think. The Rec." I know where it is, but I'm surprised there's a party being thrown on school property. "You'll get to know people there. Everyone is pretty friendly. Well, everyone *acts* friendly. Stay away from Rian. High school queen bee, she's a real bitch. But other than her, most people are okay, and just want to have a good time. You'll come, right?"

I bite my lips, considering the possibility, and processing all the exposition that my RA just exploded onto me. Kimberly Clay at a party? Almost unheard of. But there's a first time for everything, and it is easier to talk to people when they are intoxicated. New school, new town, new me. "Yeah, okay," I conclude.

Carolyn's face brightens, and she places her hands on my shoulders, her head held high. "Good. If you feel awkward or anything, just come find me, and I'll introduce you to some people."

"Thanks, Carolyn." I adjust the bag on my shoulder; I didn't need more than half of the things I brought to class with me, and the extra weight is starting to sink in. "Um…what should I wear?"

She steps back and grows pensive, her eyes narrowing. I can feel every part of my outfit being judged.

"The dress is cute. But you'll get too hot with tights and that sweater, wear something lighter." She smiles, proud of herself. I'm not sure if she gets asked for her fashion expertise often, but she seems to enjoy it. "I know you'll have fun. We used to have parties like this in high school, everyone has a good time. I'll see you there, okay?"

Before I can respond, my RA walks down the hallway in a curved line, disappearing around one of the corners.

I make my way back inside my room, avoiding the clusters of women in the halls. Upon shutting my door, the noise disappears in a hush, and all I can hear is the occasional squealing or high-pitched laugh.

I lock my door and scan myself in my full-length mirror, observing my choice for the day. I wiggle out of my tights and boots and check out my legs in the dress that is a little shorter than I hoped for. It could work.

I check my closet and pull out some summer shoes, tossing them by the door, and I grab a light cardigan. I face my room once again; I've done my best with what I have available to me. I couldn't pack all my things, especially since I'm well on my way to becoming a hoarder, but I managed to bring a couple of my favourite candles, favourite books, and even posters to decorate the walls. If anyone came in here, all they would know is that I fancy shows about cooking meth, and that my beloved battles happen among the stars.

I caught a glimpse of another girl's room the other day, the room just across the hall, and it put mine to shame. She had lace curtains, colourful sheets, her own desk chair, even a polka dot carpet, and the one thing that I realize I truly need, a mini fridge. That being said, a microwave would be nice, too. I've been enjoying the cafeteria food, a lot more than I expected, but sometimes I crave the late-night snack without having to change out of pajamas. I don't think I've seen a single student in pajamas around campus.

Seven Oaks

I flop back down on my bed, resting my hands on my belly. I press down, breathing deeply, raising and lowering my stomach. I still have a few hours until the party. I pull out my phone and start to browse around online, gathering intel for items to purchase. Along with the incredible academic program here, each student is also given one hundred dollars a week for any extra things they want to buy. I've never heard of any university doing that, but I guess it's included with the tuition. Meals and board are covered, so anything else is just icing on the cake.

As I'm shopping around online, my phone buzzes in my hand, and a text pops up from my screen.

Hey, Kim. Hope your first week went well! Let me know if you need anything XO Mom

I take a breath. *Hey, ma. It went okay, nothing much to tell. Teachers are all nice. Going to a party tonight...* I delete the last part. *I'll call you over the weekend. Love you <3*

A few seconds later, my mom responds with a few hearts, and I set my phone down. Meeting more people tonight will be very exciting. Right now, I'm the odd one out, but hopefully tonight can fix that. Hopefully I'll be *less* of an outcast, anyway.

Thanks to my faithful friend, Netflix, the time speeds by until the party begins. I debated socializing back in the hallway, but once I felt the smooth touch of my bed, I was hooked. Four grueling episodes of my latest binge obsession fly by, and it's already nearing dark out. Carolyn didn't specify a time for the party, but I think it's safe to say that it has started.

I shut my laptop and hop to my feet, slipping on my white shoes, briefly checking myself out in the mirror, and I head out. The thought to touch up my makeup enters my mind, but not before I've already locked the door out of the room. There's no turning back now.

The hall's atmosphere has drastically changed since I was last out here and is now completely silent. There's not another girl in sight, and I can hear the buzzing of the lights overhead. It's *definitely* safe to say that the party has started.

I skip down the eerie hall, out the door, and into the late evening's warm hug. The humidity here is more than I'm used to, something that I hope to acclimate to quickly; I can't stand the wet, sticky heat.

Even outside, the grounds are relatively vacant. As I approach the gym building, I can hear the growing sound of club music floating through the air. When I get to the main entrance, there are about ten people standing outside, probably to take a break from the warm gym, but I'm guessing it's not much cooler out here, if at all. A few people look up at me and even smile, and I smile back; so far so good.

Stepping inside the door, it feels like I've been transported to a different dimension. Most of the lights are off, except for orange lights lining the ceilings of the halls, reminiscent of the emergency lights we had back in high school. In the gym, I can see rainbow strobes flashing, and it feels like I'm on some club drug trip. The walls are strewn with people, keeping just far enough from the center for me to walk through. I bump shoulders with a few students, but none of them seem to notice. I only recognize one girl, Georgina, who's leaning against a locker, holding her head with both of her hands. Someone is beside her, gently rubbing her shoulder, but I can't see who.

I make my way into the gym, and my hearing nearly disappears. I can feel my ears ringing, but I can't even hear it from the loudness of the music. I turn to my right, finding the speakers set up right next to the door, and I skirt further into the room to hear a bit better. Gradually, I can pick up on pieces of conversations.

"Can you believe that?"

"You look great."

"I *love* this song!"

"I'm gonna get some air."

The usual party tropes.

As I arrive to the back of the gym, I find a few long tables set up with at least twenty drinks, each varying in alcohol content. I spot a classic vodka cooler and attract the attention of the man behind the table.

"Hey, new girl!" I cringe a little. "Welcome to SOU. I'm Damien." He holds his hand out and I take it, but he surprises me when he brings my hand up to his lips. He quickly pecks the back of my hand and holds it tightly. "What can I get for you?"

Thankfully in the darkened gym, Damien can't see my blush, but I think it's written on my face. He does have a nice smile. "Cooler," I manage to get out, focusing on the task at hand.

Damien releases my hand and hovers over the drink table. He points to a raspberry flavoured one, and upon my nod, he crouches down and nearly disappears. I peer over the table and watch him rummage through one of the many coolers hiding beneath the makeshift bar. He pops back up, placing the drink before me.

"One Raspberry Smirnoff," he says coolly.

"How much?" I ask.

Damien pauses for a moment, and then releases a thunderous laugh. "You are *funny*! What's your name, girl?"

"Kim," I reply carefully. "Are they free?"

"Hell, yeah they are!" Damien smiles again, and I watch his eyes make a brief glance down before hopping back up. "You're in Seven Oaks now. You don't gotta pay for no drinks here."

In Vancouver, drinks are about ten dollars at any bar or club, so this is quite abnormal for me. "Who buys them?" I realize I might be prying too much into this, but I am so shocked. Free drinks?! I could get used to this.

"Well," Damien says, leaning on the table. "Money is no object here, honey. Few drinks here and there, doesn't matter." I almost press on, but I settle on snatching up one of the many bottle openers and I open my drink. "Where you from?"

"...Vancouver." Something tells me Damien doesn't want to hear the not-so-fascinating story of my moving adventures.

"No, shit. Went there once, pretty nice. You like it here?" His eyes blaze into mine, nearly burning a hole, an intensity that I'm not accustomed to.

"Increasingly so," I respond, much smoother than I intended. I meant it as an homage to the free drinks, but Damien takes it upon himself to smile wide, now thoroughly checking me out. He is classically handsome, a nice chiseled jaw lined with a 5 o'clock shadow.

"Well, damn. Glad to hear it." He runs his hand over his short black hair and opens his mouth to say something else, but a screech comes up behind me, demanding another beer. A girl a few inches shorter than me appears by my side, smashing her hands on the tables. She reminds me of a miniature hulk.

"Beer!" the girl screams again, leaning towards Damien. He rolls his eyes and leans closer to me again.

"Come back later, aight?" He licks his lips and eyes me up and down, hunching his shoulders towards me.

I take a sip of my drink and nod, grinning a little. I whirl around on my heels, strutting away, feeling confident. Looks like this will be a good night.

I shy away from the dozens of students hitting the dance floor, keeping my distance from the cluster. There are definitely not enough rooms on resident to hold all these kids, but I'm realizing that all of them are local and probably just live at home. I suppose in a small town like Seven Oaks, there's not much in the ways of clubs and bars, and these school dances are probably the closest thing they have.

I take a sip of my drink until a small hand clasps onto my back, thrusting me forward. I save my choke and turn around to find bubbling Carolyn, rhythmically rocking from side to side.

"Hey!" Carolyn squeaks, smiling. "You made it! I'm so glad."

"Yeah, thanks," I yell over the music.

"What do you think?" Carolyn has sobered up a bit, and she's also changed into a mauve sundress. "Is it like parties back home?"

I really wouldn't know. "No, it's better." For all I know, I could be telling the truth. Nothing is free back home, that's for sure.

"Good, I'm so glad!" My RA claps her hands together and then hops a little to the side, two more girls appearing behind her. "Oh, these are my friends, Brit and Marla. Guys, this is Kim."

"Hi," I introduce, smiling.

Marla has a stoic, sharp face, and a pixie cut to match. Her dark hair might even have purple streaks, but that could be the ever-changing light show. Conversely, Brit emits colours and magic, dressed in a yellow skirt and pink lacy top. Her sunny blonde hair looks almost too big and fluffy for her tiny stature. Marla looks stone cold sober, while Brit is swaying in her stance, and barely acknowledges me. The girls mutter a hello, and then Marla calls out, "You wanna come dance with us?"

I turn around to take a look at the crowd, and then face the group of girls again.

"Sure," I admit, clutching my glass bottle tightly. I've only had about a third of my cooler, so I still have a lot to go.

"Finish your drink first," Carolyn says, and I bring it to my lips to chug it, but Brit soon stumbles towards the refreshments table.

"I'm gonna get another drink," Brit whines.

"Me too," Marla agrees, trailing after her, moving flawlessly in her snug plum dress.

Carolyn and I are left alone, and she quickly pipes up, "So, what *were* parties like in Vancouver? How's the club scene?"

Being eighteen, there isn't much of a club scene to talk about. I didn't bother wasting time on a fake ID, nor trying to sneak in. For the most part, I threw and attended smaller house parties. That's the extent of my knowledge…but Carolyn doesn't know that.

"Kinda boring," I say, thinking back to what I've heard said about the clubs downtown. "Not my thing. More had house parties."

"Oh, that's awesome. House parties are the best, or just chill parties like this."

I scan the room, and I have to say, I don't really see how this is chill. But I do like it. "Yeah, this is pretty cool. Everyone seems really nice so far."

"Good! I mean, we better be, we have to welcome our newest addition. Literally, our only new addition. You met Damien, the drink guy?" I nod. "Yeah. He's cute, good to have fun with." I see the implied wink in my direction. "And his uncle owns the biggest liquor store in town."

That makes more sense. "Does he just give everyone all this booze?" I take another sip of the fizzy drink, starting to feel a little more relaxed. I really don't drink very often.

"Oh, no. The parents contribute a bit, want their kids to have fun." *Is this real?*

"Is the age eighteen or nineteen here?" I press.

Carolyn pauses for a moment, and I think it's because she's confused by my question, until she responds with, "I don't know, honestly. Eighteen, I think. But I don't know, it's university, everyone wants their kids to have fun."

I take a big gulp of my drink; I don't know whether I'm impressed or just confused. As long as I get free drinks, I'm not complaining.

Marla and Brit appear again, and Brit clutches my arm in her slender hands.

"Come on, let's go dance!" she says, tugging me along.

I down the rest of my bottle, and before my lips have even left the rim, Carolyn grabs it from my hand and tosses it into a recycling bin nearby. I couldn't have thrown the shot sober, so Carolyn must be a very functional drunk.

The three girls drag me on the dance floor, and we fight through the crowds until we're lost somewhere in the centre. I don't even know what direction we came in from. I don't know if it's the flattering lights, or if it's something in these drinks, but everyone looks good. All the guys are looking fine, and the girls are flawless. It's intimidating. Apparently everyone in this town is naturally beautiful, and I did not get the memo.

Carolyn takes my hands and starts tugging my arms back and forth, hopping around madly. I can't help but laugh.

It doesn't take long for the loud music to feel completely natural. My ears stop hurting, and my heart stops pounding, and it just starts to become really fun. I recognize most of the songs, and the four of us scream along. I dance with all three girls for a little bit, Carolyn the most, and I watch Marla and Brit dance. Marla is even a few inches taller than me, Brit a few shorter, so it's entertaining to watch Brit try to keep up, especially given her state. She's having fun though, and so am I.

I'm not sure how long the girls and I dance for, but at some point, all the sweaty bodies are just too much to bear.

"I'm gonna get another drink," I yell over the music.

"What?" Carolyn replies, swinging her head around.

"Drink!"

Carolyn nods and waves her hands at me, signaling for me to go. Brit and Marla are off in their own world, holding hands, screaming along to the song.

I fight my way back through the crowd and make my way to the outer circle. Once I'm free of all the clumped students, I take a huge breath, the air feeling ten times colder just mere feet from where I was. I can just see the top of Marla's head in the crowd, and upon further examination, I can see Brit's head really close to Marla's; their height difference is adorable.

I stumble into the cool air, actually sending chills down my spine, and I hold my arms.

"Hey, Kim!" a voice calls. I jerk to my right, shocked to be called by my name, and find Owen standing near the wall entrance, hovering with a few friends.

"Hi," I chuckle back, approaching. There are two guys with him, whose names I don't know, but one of them has a varsity jacket with a lightning bird on it, presumably for SOU.

There's a girl hiding behind Owen, glancing up at him, and I immediately get the girlfriend vibes.

"Guys, this is Kim" Owen says, capturing the attention of his friends.

"Hey," Varsity Jacket says. The other guy just gives me a nod.

"That's Jay and Cameron," Owen supplies helpfully. The boys don't look very interested in me, instead they're scoping out a small group of girls closer to the refreshments stand. Even from here, one of the girls looks intimidating. Her eyebrows are precariously done in a slightly terrifying manner, and her lips are set in a snark-filled scowl.

"I'm Leslie," Owen's potential girlfriend says, extending her arm past Owen to shake my hand.

"Hey, I'm Kim," I confirm.

Leslie looks up at Owen, and steps a little closer to him, crossing her arms over her chest. She kind of reminds me of me, in the sense that she is not used to parties. She must be boiling, wearing black from head to toe, most of her skin completely covered.

I catch Jay and Cameron's bottles in their hands, and I pipe up, "I'm gonna grab a drink, anyone want anything?"

That catches their attention. "Guiness," Cameron says, making eye contact. "Thanks. Kim, right?"

I nod.

"I'm good," Jay says, but offers a nice smile in return.

"No, thanks," Leslie pipes up.

"Maybe some water," Owen says. "I can come with you, if you want."

"No, that's okay," I say, reminding myself of Damien. I had almost forgotten about him. "I'll be right back."

"Thanks," Owen mumbles, his voice fading as I walk away.

I march over to the makeshift tables, my heart beating a little faster. The warm feeling inside me has grown; liquid courage. There are two guys circling the refreshments, but they leave just before I arrive. Damien smiles widely upon seeing me.

"Welcome back," he says smoothly. "Another one?"

I nod, planning my moves carefully. I'm very new at this, but when in Seven Oaks...

As he's searching through the coolers, I move to the other side of the bar, at the gap between the tables and the wall. He hops to his feet, holding the bottle, and comes over to me.

"You move quick," he says, holding my drink out.

"Thanks." I grab my drink and graze his hand with one finger. I have no idea if this is working or not, or what this even is. I keep eye contact with him, grinning a little. His eyes briefly skip to my lips, and he takes a step towards me. He places one hand on my hip and I instinctively step closer.

Before I know it, we're making out.

His tongue slips in and out of my mouth, his hands snake around my waist and back, and his breaths are soft and short. Kissing an attractive stranger in high school didn't really happen to me, so I'm enjoying this for all its worth, despite the excessive tongue.

I'm sure Damien can feel it and not saying anything out of politeness, but I'm smiling while we kiss. In its so far brief glory, this town makes me feel freer than I ever did in Vancouver, like I'm breaking out of my shell. I have to keep reminding myself that nobody here knows my past, only me; I'm the only one who decides who I am going to be, and I will not let anyone make that decision for me.

"Um, excuse me," a piercing voice interrupts.

Damien and I simultaneously pull away, still in each other's arms, and we find a very impatient girl standing at the front of the makeshift bar. She has her arms crossed beneath her chest, and her distinct eyebrow and lip combination reminds me that she's the threatening girl from before.

"Pretty sure you're supposed to be getting everyone drinks," the girl adds, rolling her eyes. I can't help but stare at her eyebrows; I normally don't notice these things, but they are a dark, unnatural colour, not suiting her dyed platinum hair very well. Even in the forgiving light, she's clashing. "Wine spritzer."

"Pretty sure you can bend down and get your own fucking drink, Rian," Damien shoots back.

Rian? It takes a moment for my mind to click, and then I remember the infamous Rian that Carolyn mentioned before.

Rian rolls her eyes and shifts her weight from one foot to the next. I get a weird feeling in my stomach, the same feeling I got from previous friends who turned out to be not-so-nice, and a shudder rolls down my spine. It's unsettling.

"I am *not* bending over just so you can look down my shirt." Rian places a hand against her chest, tugging her neckline…lower?

Damien laughs, breaking away from me, and searches through the coolers. He pulls out a delicate looking bottle and hands it to her. "Trust me, Rian. Nobody wants that."

Rian stamps her foot on the ground and then quickly glances to me. She scans my body up and down before one last dramatic eye roll, and then whirls away on her heels. My confidence a little shaken, I return to where Rian was once standing, still holding my drink in hand.

"Um…" I say, confronted with an annoyed looking Damien. "So, that's Rian?"

"Oh, you've heard of her?" he snaps, shaking his head. "Bad things, I hope."

"That seems to be the general consensus..." My voice trails off, but I quickly flick the lid off of my bottle and take a swig. "Is she always like that?"

"Oh, no. Sometimes she's worse." Damien pulls a drink out of the cooler and hits it firmly against the table, popping off the lid in one smooth motion. He must have had lots of practice; his execution is perfect.

"Great." *Flashbacks to the mean girls I knew. Rose, Toni, here's looking at you.* I get the sense that Damien is pretty much done for the night, and the tension is currently too much to bear, so I add, nearly forgetting, "sorry, could I also get a Guinness and water?"

Damien nods, disappearing for a moment before producing the bottle and can.

"Thanks. Uh, it was nice meeting you." I hold the can up to him.

He chuckles a little, swallows his mouthful of beer, and gives me a soft smile. "Nice to meet you too, Kim."

I turn back away from the table, chugging a good portion of my drink. I've never made out with a stranger before, but there's something nice about the lack of permanence there. Or I'm just overthinking it. *Whatever.*

I make my way back to the group and hand Cameron his Guinness, stretching my arm out towards him. I'm not sure if it's the alcohol or the kiss giving me such a buzz, but I'm loving it.

"Here," I mumble, releasing the cool can to him, and I hand Owen the wet bottle. I brush my hair back from my face and sip at my drink. I'm hot and sweaty, but it's only really noticeable when I stand still. When I was dancing, I was too busy to care.

"Thanks," Cameron says, laughing a little. Unlike before, the group's eyes are now all on me, Jay and Cameron smirking. "Saw you met Rian. And Damien."

My eyes widen, and I take a sip of my cooler, nodding. I don't like the whimsy in his voice. "Uh, yeah."

"Your lipstick is smudged," Leslie quips, placing one hand on her tiny hip. I quickly wipe beneath my lips, clearing off the natural pink, and I wipe it on my skirt.

"Thanks," I say cautiously, but I'm pretty sure she wasn't telling me to be nice. Her entire aura is currently judgemental, from her arched brow to her taut fingers, slender eyes and sucked cheeks.

"Rian is so hot," Cameron says, ogling after her. She's back with her group of girls, keeping the same stern expression. Owen clears his throat and glances down at Leslie, scratching behind his head, capturing Leslie's attention. Her eyes are filled with affection; it's sweet.

"She's really not," Jay laughs. "You must be higher than I thought."

"So, Kim," Owen intervenes, changing the subject. He holds his already half empty bottle up to me. "How was your first week here?"

"That's right, this is all new for you," Cameron says, and I can now spot his massive pupils and red eyes. "Where are you from?"

"Vancouver." I've said the word so many times that it doesn't even sound like a word anymore. It just feels like gibberish leaving my lips. "And it's been okay. Classes are easy enough."

"What's your major?" Cameron asks, and he has managed to produce a bag of chips out of nowhere. Munchies, no less.

"English. What's yours?"

"Chemistry. It's awful."

"Do you learn how to cook meth?" I joke, and it lands so completely flat. All four people stare at me with an odd look in their eye, but thankfully Owen cracks a smile.

"Mr. White only teaches high school," Owen retorts quickly, and I end up smiling again. I'm really starting to like him; he's actually amused by my painful references.

Leslie clutches quickly onto Owen's arm, and pulls him down closer to her lips. As she whispers something in his ear, another girl comes trotting into the group, gripping my own arm.

"Kim!" Carolyn cheers happily. "Come dance with me, don't let me be a third wheel." She scans around the room, checking everyone's faces, and settles on Jay. "Oh, hey, Jay! How's RA life for you?"

Even in the dimmed lights, I still catch the slightest blush, and Jay starts swaying a little. Carolyn *is* beautiful. "Pretty easy. Don't have anyone new to show around, unlike you." He lifts his can to me and smiles.

"Yeah, but Kim is great," Carolyn says. I know she probably doesn't mean it, but it still warms my heart to hear. "It's nice to meet someone new for a change."

Jay stands there awkwardly, and before Carolyn can press me to go dance, I generally offer, "do you guys wanna come dance with us?"

"Sure," Jay answers immediately and nudges Cam towards us. He could not have hopped on this opportunity any faster. "I'm down."

"Why not?" Cameron throws his hands into the air, smiling. "Time to dance!"

"I'm okay," Leslie says, and Owen glances down at her. She smiles back up at him, and I get the nagging feeling that something is hidden behind those big brown eyes. "You can go dance."

Owen quickly makes eye contact with me and then meets back with Leslie again. He opens his mouth, about to say something, when Carolyn interrupts.

"Whatever, we'll be dancing!" Carolyn tightens her grip on my arm and starts to drag me back towards the dance floor, the two boys in tow. I offer the remaining couple a smile and start to down my drink once more. It does not sit well.

Carolyn manages to pry open the tight collection of students grinding away, and finds us back to our spot with Marla and Brit. The girls pry apart when we arrive again, Marla smiling widely. "Looks like you found yourselves some partners."

Jay is gawking at Carolyn while she begins dancing wildly to the music. He timidly approaches her from behind, beginning to hop to the music, and when Carolyn notices him, she turns around and grabs his hands. Everyone can see his blush now. Everyone except Carolyn, apparently.

The next blur of music flies by in a flurry of sweat and exhaustion. After each song, it feels like my legs are going to collapse and turn to liquid; I have not been built for these parties, not like the students here. I feel like an old lady. After a while, Carolyn and Jay end up dancing together for real, their hips aligned, arms tangled around one another. Marla and Brit spend the evening swaying and whispering nothings to each other, and Cam bobs his head and continues to eat his chips. He occasionally offers me some, and I take all that he offers, my stomach reminding me that I've forgotten to eat dinner.

I don't know how many songs go by before I decide to call it quits. I pull phone out of my purse pocket, checking the time; it's barely after midnight and I'm wiped.

"I think I'm gonna head back to the room!" I yell over the music, and Carolyn looks up at me with such shock and dismay that I'm convinced I said something horribly offensive to her.

"What?! Already?!"

"I'm getting tired." I'm hoping I don't sound as pathetic as I think I do, but I'm inclined to believe it's even more.

"Me too, I want to sleep," Cam joins in. At one point, I honestly thought he fell asleep while trying to dance. He's moving like a zombie.

"You look like shit, man," Jay says, leaning closer to Cameron. "You should sleep it off."

Cameron whimpers, and I decide to use this to my advantage. "I'll take Cameron back to his room and make sure he's okay."

All four of my newfound companions give me the weirdest look. Once again, I've said something out of place.

"You sure?" Jay asks, hopefulness and skepticism in his eyes.

"Yeah. I mean, as long as he can show me where his room is." My eyes tip to Cameron, and he nods, smiling, his ice blue eyes drifting shut.

"Yes. Thank you."

I may be a little tipsy, but I can still function better than Cameron. This may be a small town where everyone knows everyone, but Vancouver is not. Ensuring safety back home is the bare minimum someone can do.

"Okay, let's go." I turn back to Carolyn, smiling. "Thank you so much for this. It was really fun."

Carolyn breaks away from Jay, a look of dismay in his eyes, and she plants both her hands on my shoulders, just as earlier. "I'm glad. You fit right in, Kim."

I can't help but smile at that. The new girl status is slowly but surely disappearing, and soon I'll be one of the locals again. It's exciting. I push away the countering feelings and wrap my arms around Carolyn, and she returns the hug. I hear her giggle and squeeze me tightly, much tighter than I expected from someone so refined.

I say my goodbyes to the two other girls, who resume kissing immediately after Cameron and I start our fight through the crowd, and Carolyn goes back to dancing with Jay. I slip my hand into Cameron's and guide him until we're outside of the main crowds. I don't see Owen and Leslie anywhere.

"I'm so tired," Cameron says, drooping his head from side to side.

"Don't worry, you'll be able to sleep soon," I comfort, moving my hand further up his arm to link arms with him. Not being the big drinker myself, I was usually the one looking out for people, making sure they got home safely. This ain't my first rodeo. "Did you just smoke pot?"

"Edible." I lean closer to Cameron, struggling to hear him over the teen chatter, and the unfortunate soul currently throwing up into a trash can. I move Cam and I along faster, trying my best to ignore the smell. "But it's been a while. I think I just need to sleep."

"Okay." I rub his arm gently. "Which room number is yours?"

"It's number one! My last name is Abbey." It takes me a moment to connect the dots, but it also makes sense why my room is only number five.

"Cool. Did you have fun tonight?" I ask, guiding him gently down the few steps outside. He reaches for the handrail and misses, and he ends up putting his hand into his pocket.

"Oh, yeah. These parties are always good."

"Did you go to lots of parties back in high school?"

Cameron, whose eyes are almost completely shut now, allowing me to fully guide him back to the room, bobs his head once more, his sandy hair bouncing along with it. "Sometimes. There was always at least one party a week, that's a bit too much for me."

"Fair enough," I mumble, and turn around behind me. I take one last look at the building, seeing less people loitering outside now. There's only four of them, all huddled around the hero who brought a lighter.

"They are fun, though. Did you have fun?" Cameron's eyes suddenly pop open, and he stares deeply into mine. "This is your first party!"

"It is!" He doesn't have to know that it's my first party like this ever, as opposed to first party here in Seven Oaks. "And I did have fun."

"It's weird that you're a stranger," Cam continues, and tugs at my hand. We slow our pace and walk leisurely through the courtyard. The leaves rustle in the wind, some strays falling from the dying trees. "I don't think we've ever had anyone new come to our school, but you seem really nice."

"Well, thanks." My heart swells. "I think you're nice, too."

"What the fuck is this?" Cameron stops in front of the lightning bird statue, arms wide open. "This is what won?"

I pause for a moment until I decipher that he said *won*, not *one*. "Won?" I mimic back.

Cameron crosses his arms over his chest and stares at the dramatic bird. "Looks weirdly familiar. Like a fucking..." I watch the gears turn inside his head and he growls, unable to find the words.

"Pokémon," I supply, and Cameron suddenly slaps his hands down onto his thighs, and points both index fingers at me.

"Yes! I voted for a frog or some shit, I don't know."

"Voted?" Cam is losing me here.

He laughs and turns to me, rolling his eyes. "Last year, we were elected to come up with SOU's mascot. We all submitted shit, I guess the lighting bird won." His voice suddenly drops, and he steps closer to me. "But there's a mysterious story behind it. Do you want to listen?"

I shrug, nodding. I keep expecting the sharp odour of weed on him, but that's the beauty of an edible.

Cameron clears his throat and closes his eyes, breathing in the crisp night's air. "Apparently, back in the day, there were birds that controlled storms, and one of them was a lightning bird, so now we have fucking Zapdos as our school mascot."

I chuckle when I realize that Cameron has finished telling me his story. Despite his poor depiction, I think I can piece it together. Old town urban legend turns into high school mascot. Or, in this case, a fucking Zapdos.

"I actually kind of like it," I admit, now that the similarities between Pokémon have been confirmed.

"Oh, it's dope," Cameron says, chuckling. "I just thought a giant frog would be great. Or a toad. Whatever the fuck is the difference." I'm about to explain the difference, but it will not do any good. I will teach him amphibian facts another day. "Just picture it, this huge frog, sitting, satisfied look on his face, always watching over the campus."

"Wouldn't be unsettling at all," I joke.

Cameron stares at the lightning bird again, and then suddenly whips his head to me. "What?"

I grin and extend my arm out to him until he takes my hand. I am glad that someone told me about the school mascot, saves me the trouble of asking. I'll have to look into that. "Let's get you to bed."

Cam skips along beside me, swaying back at forth, head hung down. "Sorry you had to meet me like this."

"Don't be, it's okay. Trust me, everyone has had nights much worse than this." *I know I have.*

We arrive at the boy's dorms just as a bright smile plasters onto Cameron's lips. "Thank you."

I guide him up the few steps and we pull open the door, entering the building. Both of us squint from the bright lights overhead and make our way to door number one. Cameron pulls out his key and hands it to me. He's about to explain, but upon realizing I need no explanation on how to put a key into a lock, he closes his mouth.

I unlock his door and hold it open for him, encouraging him inside. He moves the fastest I've seen him all night and collapses onto his bed. I keep the door open a crack behind me, and approach his slowly breathing body, crouching near his head.

"Hey, Cameron?"

"Mm." His eyes are already closed.

"You *just* had some pot, right? Nothing else?" I have to ask for my own sense of responsibility.

He groans and rolls onto his back, covering his eyes with his forearm. "Not even a drop of liquor."

"Okay," I confirm, accessing my limited knowledge of pot. He'll be okay. "Okay. I'm gonna go, okay? Can you lock the door behind me after I go?"

"I don't have to, they lock automatically."

I pause for a moment, and it suddenly makes a lot more sense why every time I've locked my door after leaving my room, I've earned weird stares. I'm an idiot.

"Right," I save, not that it really matters. "Have a good night, Cameron."

"You too, Kimbee."

I chuckle and stand back up to my feet, briefly checking his room before leaving and shutting the door behind me. I test the theory of the doors locking automatically and confirm that I'm just plain stupid; have I spent the past week unlocking and locking my door before leaving? I think I have.

I skip out of the deserted boy's dorm, entering the fresh outdoor air again. It fills my lungs with the sickly scent of alcohol mixed with magnificent trees, and I start to head to the girl's dorm. I come across the first path leading to the closer entrance of the building, but upon seeing how dimly lit it is, I think better of it. The two lamps that are supposed to be illuminating the sidewalk are burnt out, so I opt to use the entrance where I'm not terrified.

I just about make it to the turn of the path, almost at the door, when I hear a rustling in the bushes. All the buildings have shrubs along the sides, no exceptions here, except that there are some leaves crunching.

My stomach drops, and my heart beats a little faster. My mind flashes back to possible conclusion of a cougar, something Carolyn mentioned on my first day here.

The cougar moans, and I realize that it sounds more human than anything.

I pull out my phone and turn on the flashlight, hands quivering. I step onto the moist grass, almost slipping from all the condensation, and shine my light around the area.

"Hello?" I call quietly.

I almost have a heart attack when my light shines on something moving. I take a moment to calm down and remember my surroundings, and my eyes focus on the breathing of the creature. The red and black animal.

The...*plaid*.

I hold a hand to my mouth, finding my fellow classmate, Georgina, lying in the bushes, flat on her back. She has something around her mouth, foaming and yellow, and her body looks like it's going into shock.

"Georgina?" I say, stepping around her. I crouch down and touch her arm gently; even through her flannel, I can feel her frozen skin. I kneel down, pulling Georgina onto her side, placing her head on my lap. I don't know what to do, whether to call an ambulance, or…

Georgina suddenly vomits violently onto the grass before her, and the second I catch a whiff of metal, I dial 911. Despite the unhelpful streetlamps, I can still see the bright red blood.

My breathing speeds up, tears already warming my eyes.

"Do you need police, fire, or ambulance?" A woman quickly says into my ear. It didn't fully register that I had actually called for help.

My mind is stumped, and I don't understand the question for a minute. I have never called 911 before, and I expected the "911, what's your emergency?"

"Ambulance," I reply after only a few seconds hesitation. "I'm at Seven Oaks University, there's a girl here who needs help, she's throwing up blood, and something is wrong." My voice is shaking, and Georgina vomits again, wailing out.

"Do you know why she's throwing up?" the woman asks, her voice calm and even.

"No! I, I...I don't. I just found her, she's in some bushes." I search the area for anything else, but all I see is the narrow patch of grass and foliage in our midst.

"Where exactly are you right now?"

"I'm with her," I respond, growing angry. "On campus, in front of the girl's dorm. Can you send someone, please?"

"Please..." Georgina whimpers, and tears continue to sting my eyes. My vision grows blurry, but I refuse to let any tears fall.

"Which campus?" the woman presses.

"Seven Oaks University!" My grip tightens on my phone.

"Which year?"

I'm about to yell at her, but I regain my calm. Yelling at this woman is not going to help Georgina, it's not going to help anyone. "First year."

"The freshman campus."

"First year, yes," I growl through gritted teeth. "Can you please send someone?!"

"Responders are on their way. They will be there soon. Is she still breathing?"

"Yes," I say, relief flooding through my entire body. They can't come fast enough. I've never dealt with a situation like this before; I've dealt with drunk or high peers, sure, but not an emergency. Not like this. "How soon will they be here?"

"Just a few minutes. What's your name?"

"I...Kim."

"Kim, I need you to stay calm," the lady says. "Can you do that for me?"

I take a deep breath, brushing some stray hair from Georgina's eyes. "Yes."

I don't know how long it takes. I just sit there, breathing, straining to hear my classmate's struggling breaths. She occasionally winces, and her eyes sometimes shoot open, but they close just as quickly. I keep stroking Georgina's golden hair, and every time she shakes too violently in my arms, I have to bite my lips together to keep the tears from falling.

The lady on the phone takes my information, my name, number, and by habit, I give my Vancouver address when she asks. She doesn't question me, though; she just adds it all to the roster of this developing file.

My legs are cramping by the time I see the red flashing lights. I can just see the ambulance mounting the curb by the main stairs, and several figures trot up along the stairs.

"Here!" I start screaming, waving aggressively towards the responders. My voice is hoarse, panicked. "Over here!"

The paramedics rush over, one of them pushing along a gurney, the other two trotting ahead.

"We got it from here," the only male paramedic says, stepping beside me. "We got it."

I take that as my cue to go, and I gently slide out from Georgina's weight, leaving her in the capable hands of the people here to help. One of the women sets up the board, while the other approaches my classmate's head.

"Can you hear me? Can you tell me your name?" the paramedic asks, shining a tiny light into Georgina's closed eyes.

"It's Georgina," I say, unsure if I'm being helpful or not.

"Do you know her last name?" the man asks, not making eye contact.

"...no."

Blue and red flashing lights catch my eye, and I see a few cop cars enter the parking lot from afar. Before I know it, the area is stormed with troopers and is blocked off by yellow police tape.

Georgina is lifted onto the gurney, still groaning, and one of her arms falls off the side.

"Watch her," one of the women says, tugging on one end of the stretcher. One of the wheels is loose, wiggling in every direction, causing me a bit of unease. "Make sure she doesn't vomit."

"Got it," the man replies, walking backwards carefully towards the ambulance. The third paramedic trails next to them, wrapping a tight plastic cuff around Georgina's arm. I can see her lips moving, but I can't hear anything that she's saying.

"Are you the one who found her?" a police officer asks, appearing out of nowhere. I jump from his presence, his tall and looming figure.

"Uh," I mutter, still seeing traces of bright flannel. I can't focus on anything but Georgina. I try to think about the three paramedics, and even though I just saw them, just *spoke* to them, I couldn't put a face to a single one of them. *Is this shock?* "Yeah."

The officer takes out a notepad and flips it a few pages, then draws up a pen. He doesn't even look fazed, as if he sees this all the time. "And your name."

"Kim." He glances at me, impatience filling his eyes, and I correct myself, "Kimberly Clay."

"Kimberly Clay." The cop takes an exhausted breath and flexes his broad shoulders. "My name is Officer Treehorn, I'm just going to ask you to tell me what happened, okay?"

I nod, still staring off at the ambulance. I just start to notice the hustle and bustle forming around me, the students attracted by the shiny lights, coming to investigate the scene. There are about fifteen or twenty kids hovering about, pointing, gawking, obviously hiding bottles, joints, and who knows what else behind their backs.

"I was coming back from the party in the gym," I begin, wanting nothing more than to return to my room. My body is sweating but feels frozen, and my mind feels all jumbled. I've never seen anything like this before. "And I was walking by and heard something in the bushes. And I found Georgina."

"Was she at the party?" Officer Treehorn asks.

"..." I pause for a moment. "Yeah, I remember seeing her. But that was hours ago."

"Around what time did you last see her, and what time did you find her in the bushes?"

I meet eyes with the officer, feeling intimidated. His beard is long and scruffy, his eyes gruff, his lips stiff. He looks like a teacher I was once afraid of in elementary school.

"I saw her around 8:30, I think. Found her here at… 12:30."

"What happened after you found her?"

"I sat with her," I say, gazing towards the bushes. I don't know if the police around going to clean it up or not, but I guess that's something for the school to deal with. "I turned her over, and she threw up."

"How many times?"

"Just once, I think." The scent of metal enters my nose again, and my entire body shivers. I get queasy at the thought of it. "Is she going to be okay?"

"Oh, yeah," Officer Treehorn replies so casually that it's a little shocking. It's as if he meant to comfort me before, but thought I already knew. "She'll be fine." He closes his notebook and slips it back into his pocket, smiling nicely. "Thank you, Kimberly."

The two of us stand there, him much more relaxed than me, with a look in his eye that suggests he's waiting for me to do something.
"Is that it?" I ask, dumbfounded. I thought I was doing a relatively good job at being calm, but this guy is on a whole other level.
The policeman nods, crossing his thick arms. "Yep, that's all. You can go back to your room."
I laugh out of pure surprise and take a deep breath. *How is that it?!* "I don't..." I chuckle again, shaking my head. "How..."
"You're new to Seven Oaks, right?" the officer asks, something knowing behind his smirk.
Man, literally everyone knows that I'm new. Not that this should have anything to do with that. "Uh, yeah. Why?"
"Well, Kimberly, this isn't exactly uncommon here. Kids like to party here, especially now that most of them can legally drink. We see this every month or so."
"Every month?" My nerves start to calm down; everyone around me is so calm, and they know the situation a lot better than I do, so that must be a good sign. Even so...
I peek at the students around the yellow tape, the number doubling in size. Now that I'm really taking a look at their faces, none of them even look bothered. I even hear two girls giggling at something.
"Oh, yeah. She just had a bit too much, see it all the time." Some garbled mess of words comes through on the officer's radio, and he steps away, muttering the word, "copy." He turns back to me, standing up straight. "You should get some sleep, Kimberly. Don't worry, your friend will be fine. It's good that you were there for her."

Before I can even respond, Officer Treehorn disappears back towards the parking lot, dragging along one of the other cops with him.

I face the scene once more, still disturbed that this is no big deal. This kind of thing happens frequently back home, sure, but that's spread out over hundreds of thousands of people. Seven Oaks can't possibly have more than ten thousand residents, and that's being generous. It's no surprise that this happens within the same crowds.

Regardless, I am on edge.

I make the executive decision to return to my room as quickly as possible, and I break my exit from the scene, ducking below the police tape perimeter. I quickly skip inside the dorm building, shutting the door behind me, shutting out the speculating and intoxicated students. There are thankfully only two girls in the hallway, lounging outside one girl's door at the opposite end of the hall.

"I wonder who it was," one of the girls says, reaffirming that this *is* normal. It may not feel normal for me, but in this school, in my new home, it is ordinary.

"I don't know, but I saw that new girl there," the other girl responds, oblivious to the fact that I'm within earshot.

I tiptoe to my room, trying not to attract any attention, and I silently sneak inside. I close the door, hearing the door lock behind me, and I flop onto my bed. My room is partially illuminated by the police lights in the distance, and I can hear voices outside, mumbling about the situation at hand. It's nothing more than a soft hum, mutters that disappear with my room's heating unit.

I take a deep breath, hands still shaking.

My body becomes glued to my bed, and I wriggle beneath the covers, shimmying out of my clothes. My skin is freezing, and I tug the blankets up to my neck, snatching my little brown bear into my arms. He's warm against my chest, and it calms me down to have something so familiar with me.

I don't think I've ever felt this way before; I think I must be in shock, but my body is urging me to slip off to sleep.

Before I can even begin to realize that I'm falling asleep, I'm transported into a dreamscape reality of what just happened. It plays over and over in my head, like an old movie that I've seen a thousand times but still don't quite understand.

This is normal? This *is the new normal?*

The last thing I see before finally drifting away are those eerie red and blue lights.

Chapter 3

My first experience on a public bus in Seven Oaks is vastly different than I expected. There are only a few students riding the bus, all from senior campuses, and the aisles are large and comfortable. Unlike Vancouver, I don't get the feeling that I'm an anchovy being shoved into a tin filled with other anchovies. I can actually breathe.

Everything in general seems to be nicer in Seven Oaks, even the public buses.

Well, maybe not everything.

I check my phone for the third time, making sure that I'm heading in the right direction; the hospital. I don't know why, but I feel like I owe it to Georgina to check up on her. I think part of it is also for me, too. I keep saying that I am technically from Seven Oaks, but I clearly don't know a single thing about it if kids overdosing is the norm. I have a lot to learn.

The bus bumps in a pothole and I nearly jump out of my seat, clutching tightly onto my phone. The views from the bus are amazing, and now that I am not as tired as my first trek to SOU, I can further appreciate the trees and all the beautiful shades of green that will soon be fading into yellow, orange, and red. It'll be marvelous in the fall.

Contrary to Google Maps, the ride to the hospital takes just a little under half an hour. It helps that there was only a total of eight or so cars on the road around us, so traffic was minimal. The hospital is right on the cusp of town, the last building before Seven Oaks turns to forested mountain.

I hop off the bus at the hospital stop, conveniently located only about fifty feet from the emergency room doors. I dart through the parking lot, checking carefully for any cars swerving around. There are a few cars sprinkled in the paid stalls, but for the most part, the hospital is fairly empty today.

I glance back behind me, seeing stretches of shops, and eventually, the ocean. I only catch glimpses of sand and rocky ruins before it turns to a vibrant turquoise water, which stretchers much farther than I can see. I've lived on both sides of the Canadian region now and it feels basically the same; it's less windy than I expected though, being this close to the sea.

Before entering the hospital sliding doors, I catch a whiff of something delicious. I search around, finding a local bakery plopped just next to the hospital. From here, I can only imagine how delicious those baked goods inside must be. My stomach growls, and I recall that I have yet to eat today, but I silence the grumbles and head inside.

I approach the front desk, located very close to the door, and glance at the vacant waiting room. The hospital is smaller than I expected, and I'm shocked by the lack of patients.

"Can I help you?" an older lady peers from behind the counter. She has one hand on a phone, pressing it to her shoulder, the other hand holding a pen. Despite her harsh demeanor and sharp glasses, her voice is soft and soothing.

"I'm here to visit someone," I reply, holding my hands together. "Georgina?" I can't remember her last name for the life of me.

Luckily, the receptionist nods along, waving her hand to her left. "Room 309." She holds the phone back to her ear and resumes the conversation.

"Thanks," I reply, following her vague directions.

There are two elevators with a directory in the middle, and upon confirming that stable patients are on the third floor, I call for the elevator. Both sets of doors open before me, and I opt for the one on the left. I hop inside, hitting the third-floor button, the highest floor, and I wait. There's no music in the elevator, not even the classically obnoxious muzak, but the ride is over quickly enough.

The third floor is a little more lively than the emergency room entrance, with two patients roaming the halls, both elderly with IV drips in tow, and two women, both gazing over a particular chart. Both ladies are donned in scrubs, with the younger of the two taking notes in a college-rule notebook; looks like a doctor in training.

I count the rooms as I slip through the occupants and staff, until I find 309. The door is open just a crack, and I take it upon myself to knock.

"Come in," Georgina's voice calls. I'm startled by how raspy she sounds, but I realize that I have never actually heard her speak.

I peek my head inside, checking the room for other visitors. I expected her parents at the very least, but nobody else is here. Georgina looks so small in her long, white bed, nestled under the single sheet. The room is surprisingly large, not to mention private, with sunlight beaming in from outside. Thinking it over, I'm not sure if this hospital would even have shared rooms.

"Hi," I say, entering. I steady the door to how it was and approach Georgina's bed. On her bedside table she has a set of flowers, along with a deck of cards and a crib board. Hospitals do tend to get pretty boring.

"Oh, hi," she says. Her mouth moves slowly, like her words are thick. Her blonde hair is gracing her shoulders beautifully, her face dead pale with rosy cheeks. "Kim, right?"

"Yeah." I take a step closer and adjust my glasses on the bridge of my nose, chuckling to myself. "Sorry, I know this is kind of weird. I just wanted to make sure you were okay."

She smiles gently, gazing out the window. Along with her spacious room, she has a personal bathroom, two seats and a sofa, and a TV mounted to the wall that looks like she can move to be in front of her bed, too. *Fancy.*

"I thought you were my parents," Georgina confesses.

"I can go, if you want." My heart races a little faster; I may have crossed a line, just showing up unannounced.

"No, no. I just didn't expect you. They're just out grabbing me clothes and food." It's only then that I notice her hospital gown. "You can sit down." Georgina raises one arm, pointing to a rolling chair near the foot of her bed. I latch onto it and pull it closer to her, taking a seat. The fabric releases a breath of air when I sit down, still deflating while I settle in.

"How are you feeling?" I ask, unsure of where to begin.

"Tired, mostly." She laughs a little, and some colour flushes in her lips. "Stupid."

"Why?"

She meets my eyes, her own bloodshot. "It's pretty embarrassing. My parents were really worried, but it was literally just me being stupid."

I brush some hair behind my ear, plucking out the most delicate way to ask, "can I ask something?"

She grins softly. "Yeah, I was high." Her smile disappears swiftly. "But it was different. I smoke pot, but this time felt...weird."

"How so?" My natural curiosity shines through. Never being high, I don't know how it's supposed to feel.

"I hardly remember anything. I remember nothing, at one point." She sighs and sits up straighter in her bed, holding her hands in front of her. "Like, near the beginning, I remember music playing. But then it just all goes black, and there's nothing. I could still feel some lights, though, but I couldn't really see them. Like, the strobe lights in the gym. I don't remember coming here, the ambulance, you, any of it. It's just a blank."

My hands clutch my knees, gripping tightly through my tights. "Do you think you were drugged?"

Georgina quickly makes eye contact, and her mouth drops open. She has a sad look on her face, like she's ashamed. "I think that weed was definitely laced with something. Something I've never had."

"Do you think someone drugged you?" I ask bluntly, clarifying my previous question. All of my years watching crime shows have made me suspicious, not to mention past experiences.

"I don't think so," she says, her eyes looking a little scared. "I don't know why anyone would." My body freezes. "They checked me when I got here, nobody hurt me or anything."

"Are they running tests now?" I pry. I am not accustomed to the town life where everyone knows their neighbours, and where bad things seldom happen. It sends a chill down my spine to hear her say that, *I don't know why anyone would.* I've never felt so safe to have that mentality, that disbelief of the worst in people.

She laughs out loud, so abruptly that I get goosebumps in the chilled room. "They tested last night, just positive for THC." The words roll so easily off her tongue.

"When I was talking to the cop last night, he kind of made it seem like..." My voice trails off; I don't want her to think I'm insulting her.

"It's a regular thing?" she supplies. I nod, the two of us cracking a smile. "He's not wrong. There's not really much else to do here. But I'm fine now, just tired." A load is lifted off my shoulders when she says that. I can stop worrying now. At least, I can stop worrying as much about her. "Can I ask you something?"

My fingers wrap around my seat, tightening, and I nod, inching closer. "Yeah?"

"Why are you here?" I must say, I appreciate her bluntness, but it takes me off-guard. She speaks much more aggressively than she actually is. "I mean, you barely know me."

"Um..." It never occurred to me, the "why" part of it all. It just seemed like the right thing to do. "To make sure you're okay?" We both share a laugh and I try to reiterate, but I come up blank. I'm not the best at explaining myself, so I usually just don't; I do things because, "It just...made sense to me."

Georgina's face glows in the harsh light and she smiles. It seems she's accepted my weak explanation. "Well...thank you. The paramedics said you really took care of me until they got there, which not a lot of people would have done. So, thank you."

Our eyes meet and I find myself feeling blissful. I'm really glad she's okay. "You're welcome," I reply, not entirely comfortable accepting gratitude for just not being a shitty person.

Before either of us can say another word, the door opens again, and I turn around to find an older couple shuffling inside, holding a black duffel bag, and a paper bag from the bakery across the street. I can smell the fresh sandwiches inside, my stomach flaring up again. I don't have to look twice; Georgina is a perfect blend of both her parents.

"Oh, hello," Georgina's mom says, eyeing me carefully. I jump to my feet. Her mom looks like she's being crying, her eyes almost as pink as her daughter's, and her dad looks like he's just seen a ghost. He's even paler than Georgina.

"Hi," I say, and then turn back to my classmate. "Sorry, I'll get going. I'm really glad you're okay."

"Thanks, Kim," Georgina replies. She turns to her parents, who have now switched places with me. They are both impeccably dressed, as if they stepped right out of a Kennedy party. Classic, timeless, expensive. Georgina has her dad's eyes and nose, her mom's ears and chin, and both parents' bright hair. "You guys, this is Kim. She's the one who helped me last night."

All at once, Georgina's mom shoves the paper bag into her husband's hands and tackles me into a hug. She's petite and frail, but she nearly knocks the wind out of me, and her elbows dig tightly into my sides.

"Oh, thank you so much," her gentle voice wails, squeezing my pinned arms. "Thank you for keeping her safe."

"Oh, my god, Mom." Georgina rolls her eyes and nudges her dad. "Can you make her stop? I'm fine."

Her father reluctantly pulls her mother from the one-sided hug, and I can't help but see the desperation pouring from their eyes. I even start to well up; I don't do well when other people cry. Or at life in general.

"I'm just glad she's okay," I say, offering little sympathy. Georgina's mother nods, biting her thin lips, and returns to her daughter's side. I feel painfully out of place in the room.

"I'll see you at school," Georgina offers me a way out, sensing my own discomfort. Her parents exchange a worried glance before approaching her bed.

I smile sweetly, and I fully shut the door behind me once I've left. It's always felt weird to me, the illusion shattered of this person existing without their parents. It's fascinating to meet and see what someone grew up with.

I re-enter the third floor hall, still with the same four occupants, but this time the doctors are examining one of the patient's IV drip. The younger doctor is still taking notes, hard at work. I retrace my steps back down to the Emergency Room lobby, just as eerie and silent as before, and disturbing machinery sounds echo in the background. I didn't notice those sounds when I first came in.

When I get outside, I'm once again hit with the sweet bakery sensation, but this time, mixed with a little salt. The ocean air is starting to flow further into the city, reeking of wet sand and life. It's a comforting smell, remembering all my time spent on rocky beaches and cliffed shores. It reminds me of home.

Technically, this *is* home.

I start towards the bus stop, but just as I reach it, I change my mind. My stomach churns in knots, and I press one hand against it; I have recently come into some "allowance," so groceries might not be the worst thing.

I walk down the sidewalk towards the vague memory of where a grocery store is. I remember the inside of the store more strongly than the outside, but I recall a store somewhere along this strip.

This stretch of road, the main road appropriately named "Main Street," is the straight shot through town. It starts in the mountains, around the campuses, and leads directly through the hustle and bustle of the miniature city, all the way to an access ramp for Highway 1. Main Street has all the standards to it; gas stations, grocery stores, a convenience store here and there, and even a small strip mall further down. The hospital is closest to the mountains, and the police station is dead in the centre of the city. There must be a fire station, but I can't remember where it is. I'm surprised how much of this information I've retained, but I did spend almost six years straight walking to the beach, enjoying a stroll with my mom or dad, or both. It's funny how old memories shine through.

There's one narrow parallel road down from Main Street, holding restaurants, cafes, ice cream parlors, and basically anything else related to summer, suited for its placement right along the beach. Again, spot-on naming with "Beach Lane." As I walk further, I can see a giant wooden surf board hung above a shack, probably a rental place.

Behind Main Street is Livingstone Lane, where the shops and residentials start to become one. Half of the time, you can't tell if something is simply a house, or is open to local shoppers.

Passing the hospital, a gas station, and a cute diner, the grocery store pops up next. The entire stretch of Main Street is only about five blocks long but has managed to fit a lot into those blocks. I'm surprised how much goes on in little Seven Oaks while still guarding the small-town magic.

A large Frugal Foods sign appears, previously blocked by the diner, and I get a chill down my spine. I remember coming here once with my parents and throwing a fit because they wouldn't buy me something. I think that was near the end of my first Seven Oaks journey, when I was five. I remember it because my dad left shortly after that, and I thought it was because I screamed at him that one time.

Though the sign looks the same, then entire building has changed. It still retains the charm, but has been rebuilt with fake brick, similar to the university campuses. There is a grungy vibe radiating from inside, possibly from the outer graffiti. Even the graffiti here looks professional and clean, a large masterpiece spelling out the word "owls 2014" in black, white, and gold lettering. Looks like a grad prank.

The automatic glass doors of Frugal Foods slide open as I approach, leading into a magnificent display of fruit. Someone created a beautiful and colourful pyramid of eight or nine different fruits, all meticulously stacked to look the utmost appealing; my stomach growls again, and I recognize my mistake of shopping hungry, but I am not going to make an entire separate trip here on another day. I first reach for one of the green baskets by the entrance but change my mind to a cart. Unlike any other shop I've ever seen, they have three sizes of carts; smaller than average, normal sized, and a massive one that nearly doubles the smallest. I opt for the smallest of the three and make my way around the unfamiliar store. I'm about to grab a few pieces of the tempting fruit, but I remember that the fruit in the cafeteria is always free. No sense in wasting what little money I have.

I bypass the entire fruit, vegetable, and meat section, now starting with the baked goods. Through my shopping spree, I grab the non-perishables I crave, hoping that they won't be too heavy to transit with back to campus. Granola bars and crackers are the healthiest of my items, with the unhealthiest being chips, chocolate, and brownies. I try my best to limit myself, and I have to keep reminding myself that

I don't have a fridge, and I don't have a microwave. My options are limited to snacks until I can stock up on cold foods.

I skip out of the line and use the anti-social self-checkout, getting three bags total of snacks. The plastic bags are sturdier than I'm used to, and thankfully are more opaque than I had imagined. No one can judge my horrible food decisions now.

I really should not be shopping while I'm so hungry.

After the shopping trip, I wait conveniently at the bus stop near the grocery store, a short two blocks past the hospital. There's only one bus that comes into town, I've learned from Google, and that's the 136. It starts and ends at the school campuses, and goes to the end of Main Street. It's almost like a sightseeing tour, where you manage to see every part of the city.

The bus arrives just in time to sooth my slowly chilling hands. The wind has picked up, rushing the sea in further, cooling my body to the bones. The bus thankfully blasts heat, despite the fact that it is technically still summer.

By the time I get back to campus, it's already five o'clock. I don't know where the time has gone, but it's gone too fast. I guess I should be eating dinner now, my first meal of the day.

I step off the bus alone to the empty outdoor stairwell. There are usually at least a few people hanging around, but I can't find any. I trudge up the stairs, clutching the weighing plastic bags. I don't know what it is, but anytime I walk up stairs carrying anything at all, my breath escapes me at an alarming rate.

I walk through the nearly deserted campus, just about to reach my room, when I see Owen and Jay. I make a slight detour towards them, even though they're both unknowingly walking towards me. They don't see me until I'm right in front of them, blocking their path.

"Hey," I pant, forgetting that I am slightly winded.

Owen smiles bright and sticks his hands in his olive field jacket pockets. "Oh, hey, Kim. How's it going?"

"Good." I turn to Jay, grinning a little. I don't think anything happened with him and Carolyn, but I want it to, and my gaze is all too telling. Jay blushes but offers a smile before his eyes drop to the ground.

"Get some groceries?" Owen presses.

I look at the bags in my hands, seeing the top of a chip bag, and my stomach rumbles again. "Yeah, just going to drop them off, then getting dinner."

Owen lights up. "Oh, do you want some company? I'm actually pretty hungry."

"Sure, that'd be great!" I try to hide my pride; *I'm making friends!*

I look at Jay again, and he glances at Owen. He has a weird look in his eye; something unspoken is happening, apparently. I've never claimed to understand boys, nor girls for that matter, and I'm not about to try.

"I'm not hungry at all, so why don't I catch up with you later?" Jay pipes up.

Owen nods and makes eye contact with me again.

"Okay," I say, confused by the stiff interaction that just happened. "I'm gonna go put these in my room, and then I'll meet you in the caf?"

Owen nods and I skirt past the two boys, using the closer entrance to me. I haven't eaten with anyone here, so it'll be nice to have some company. I usually try to scarf down my meal, because I don't like the feeling of eating alone, but now I can take my sweet time. I slip into the girls' dormitory and ignore the giggling hovering girls in the hall. I think one of them might have been Rian, but I snuck by her so quick that neither of us noticed. I do not like the vibes I get from her.

I unlock my door, dump my bags just inside, and close up behind me. Before I leave, I heard a small creak, and I notice my door is slightly ajar. I tug on the doorknob, ensuring it's closed; I'll have to be more careful with that.

I rush to the cafeteria, kicking myself for not even caring to glance at myself to see if I looked somewhat acceptable, but I quickly move on; I'm just hungry at this point. I see Owen waiting for me just outside the entrance, and I slow down, sauntering over. I'm already sweaty from rushing around, I should probably calm down.

"Hey," I chime again, and Owen's head flashes up.

"Hey." He holds his arms out towards the open door. "After you."

"Thanks," I chuckle, striding inside.

Despite being a university, the cafeteria isn't much bigger than the one in my old high school. It has twelve tables total, in sets of two lining the opposing walls of the room. The buffet area, however, is massive. I can't see into the stretches of the kitchen, but judging by the constant selection, it must reach pretty far back. I've never seen less than five people cooking throughout the day.

Owen and I grab our trays, a plate on top, and make our way through the circuit. Tonight, it looks like the main course is different types of pasta, four varieties total. It's like a cruise ship buffet, or some all-inclusive resort. I pile my plate with pasta and salad, grab a cookie to snack on afterwards, and snatch one of the complimentary bottles of orange juice. I get a little embarrassed when I see that Owen has taken less food than I have, but I get over it quick; he's probably had at least one meal today.

I'm surprised the cafeteria isn't more regulated, considering people could potentially just walk onto campus and get a free meal, but I recall that, as I've heard a thousand times, everybody knows one another. Anyone who doesn't attend SOU would stick out like a sore thumb.

Case in point.

Despite the buffet area being relatively untouched, there are about twenty kids hanging around on the benches, chatting over the large tables. There are a few boys straggling in the courtyard, but mostly everyone is inside to avoid the somehow cold and sweat-inducing weather. Owen and I find one of the vacant tables inside and take a seat.

"So, how was your day?" I ask, immediately devouring into my creamy pasta.

"Oh, uh, it was good," Owen replies, and I glance to see him picking at his food. He's taken less than half of what I have; I don't think he's actually hungry, but if he's not, I'm not sure why he offered to come with me. "How was yours?"

"It was okay. I went to visit Georgina today."

Owen's eyes widen. "Really?"

I laugh, swallowing a mouthful of noodles. "I know, it's a little weird. I don't really know her, but since I found her…" I sigh, closing my eyes. "I've never seen anything like that. Is it really that common here?"

Owen bobs his head from side to side, popping a few noodles into his mouth. He chews slowly, too slowly. "I mean, not every day. But every so often, someone goes a bit too far."

I lean in closer, trying my best not to sound insulting. "Isn't that weird?"

"Yeah." Owen laughs, baring his pearly whites. Beneath his jacket, he's wearing a black and white raglan with an owl on it, the same owl I've seen before, and I'm certain it must have been their high school mascot.

I chuckle along with him, but I'm skeptical. It's like people don't realize how serious this is. "I'm just glad she's okay."

"Yeah, that's nice you went to visit. How are you doing, though?" I stare blankly into his mossy eyes until he reiterates. "I mean, how do you like it here?"

"Oh, yeah, I like it." I've always been quick to adjust, so moving here isn't as big of a deal as I thought it would be. "It's more humid here."

"Really? I never thought of that…"

"I think you'd have to go away and then come back to notice." Dry heat is much more bearable than the sticky sweaty heat. "Not very many mountains, either, I'm used to seeing mountains everywhere." I've driven through the Rockies a few times, and I will never get sick of those views.

"Wow, that sounds cool." I never thought about how I'd miss the mountains, but I do. I miss seeing the white peaks and snowy scapes; it was a comfort. It's weird to miss things that I had taken advantage of, like I didn't even notice they were there until they weren't. "I've never been anywhere else, so I wouldn't know."

"Have you wanted to travel?" I pry open my juice bottle and scan around the room; I don't recognize anyone until my eyes fall onto someone slightly familiar. He looks posh and proper, but he's brooding. His clothes look like they cost more than my entire wardrobe combined, though he's surrounded by boys in varsity jackets, and his expression is tough and solid. It looks out of place on his face, like he's trying to force it. Almost as if he senses me looking at him, he looks up and makes eye contact with me. I face Owen again, embarrassed by how much time I spent looking at the near stranger.

"One day. After university. You?"

Seven Oaks 73

"Uh..." the unease from the other boy made me lose focus. It takes me a moment to remember what we were talking about. "Yeah. I've traveled a bit, but I want to go to more places." Before I have to expand more on the countries I've been to, I shovel some more food into my mouth, and make a hesitant sound. I hold my hand up, telling him to wait until I've finished the enormous glob of pasta in my mouth. "But it's nice here, most of the people are pretty friendly." *And the people who aren't don't try to pretend that they are. It may not be ideal, but it's better than pretty lies...* For some reason, Leslie pops into my mind. "By the way, your girlfriend seems nice. How did you two meet?"

Owen, taking a sip of his own bottle of lemonade, chokes on the yellow drink and nearly spits it out. He quickly wipes off his chin and meets my eyes. "What?" he sputters.

"Um, Leslie." I start on my neglected salad; I haven't had salad in a while.

"Oh, Les?" I can't begin to describe the disbelief in his voice. Apparently, I was wrong. "Not my girlfriend. Don't have a girlfriend." His cheeks flush for a moment and mine match; *whoops.*

"Oh, sorry, just seemed like you were dating."

"No, she's just a friend." I'm taken aback by how quickly he answers.

I look up to see the serious tone in Owen's eyes. His eyebrows are slightly raised, almost in a challenging way, and he's dropped his fork to his plate. Boys can get so weird sometimes.

"Okay," I mutter, confused. "Well, did you have fun last night?"

His shoulders relax, and he sits up a bit straighter, swiping his fork back up. "Yeah, it was fun. Too tired to go tonight, though."

"Tonight?"

"Yeah, there's another one tonight."

The thought briefly enters my mind to go, but it quickly leaves. I should start and finish my writing assignment about this school, though I'm not sure what to include yet. And two parties in a row? Unthinkable.

"Lots of parties, hey," I poke fun, finishing the last of my salad. My focus returns to the pasta, and I try one of the marinara sauces I'd slipped onto my plate. I really should try to eat throughout the day, so I'm not devouring everything in sight at 5:30pm.

"Every weekend," he says. "Just like high school."

"Intense." My weekends throughout high school were spent either by myself at home, or going to see a movie, or the very occasional hangout with supposed friends. The party life will be an adjustment, but one I'm looking forward to. It *was* a fun party up until the end.

"Are you done?" Owen asks, noticing my empty plate. My stomach feels like it swallowed a metal ball, sinking inside me. I grab the cookie wrapped in plastic wrap to really seal the deal of fullness; I can't say no to a cookie that smells this good.

"Yeah, thanks..." Before I know it, Owen is up on his feet, snatching up my tray from me. It doesn't look like he ate anything more than a bite or two, but either way, I'm glad that he came with me. I unwrap my cookie, deciding to scarf it down before I get too full, while my new friend returns our trays to the Dirty Dishes Drop-off. There's a small station where we stack our trays and plates along with other dirty ones, and soon they disappear to be washed and used again. The system here is surprisingly smooth, and extremely charmed.

Owen skirts back, and I've almost finished my baked snack by the time he gets back. He smiles, about to sit down, but I start to stand up.

"I should get back to my room, I have a paper to work on," I confess, contorting out of the awkward benches. "But thanks for coming to eat with me." I smile brightly, shoving the last bite of cookie goodness into my mouth.

"Oh, yeah, for sure. Anytime."

I stand before Owen, really noticing the height he holds over me. I'm not short, but Owen still towers over me. I chuckle a little and then guide us out the front doors, back into the courtyard.

There are still the strays outside, another group of guys wearing letterman jackets, with slightly different patches than the others inside, are standing in the concrete square. I recognize one of them as Damien, and I have to say, he looks a bit different in the light. He glances over and smiles at me, and I smile back; and that's that.

I can't help but enjoy the lack of permanence that this school seems to thrive on. Always onto the next thing, it's what I've been needing for a long time. It's already so easy to get caught up in that.

Owen and I arrive back at the girl's dorm, and I face him, mindlessly grabbing his hand before he can walk away.

"Hey, wait," I say. Owen looks down, seeing my hand, and I release quickly. I don't want to weird him out; my friend skills aren't exactly the best. "I just wanted to thank you."

He shifts uncomfortably, once again putting his hands into his pockets. "For what?"

"For being my friend," I add. I can feel my face heating up at how childish I could sound, but I'm not about to dump years of emotional problems on someone I've just met. "It's been pretty weird, coming here and not knowing anyone." I didn't know what to expect in Seven Oaks, but it wasn't this. I expected to continue being just another face in the crowd, not the shiny new girl. "Especially when everyone knows everyone else. So…thank you."

Owen's eyes are wide, expressive as usual, and he chuckles, shaking his head. I can almost see the gears turning inside his head, choosing his words carefully. I'm worried that I've said something so weird that he wants to cut me out, until he says, "I can't resist a good TV reference."

I break a wide smile and take a chance, lunging into his arms. I hug him tightly, and at first, he doesn't hug me back. After a few awkward seconds, he finally does, his arms firmly around my smaller body. He's a good hugger. I step back, smiling. "I'll talk to you later, okay?"

He avoids looking me in the eye, staring down near our shoes, but he still nods. "Yeah, for sure. I'll see you later, Kim."

After one final parting shot, I head into the girls building. Owen and I shared a meal together, meaning that we are officially friends now. I know there's no real rulebook, but it seems like a good indicator. That, and he didn't seem too disturbed by my unprompted hug, so I consider this a success.

On my short walk back to my room, I think of my other friends back in Vancouver. I suppose I talked to a few people here and there, but we weren't exactly friends. It was only during class that we spoke. The only best friends I had were Toni and Rose, and…they were *not* good friends.

It's weird how you can finish such a substantial part of your life with one group, and then start the next chapter with a completely new set of people. I know that back home, I thought high school would never end, and I never thought I'd be able to escape.

Look at me now.

I think about Owen; I like Owen, he seems really nice. And I like Carolyn, and Marla, and Brit. I could get used to Seven Oaks.

I settle into my room, accidentally kicking the bags of snacks I had hastily thrown in here before. I pick them up and put them onto my bed, looking for somewhere to keep the goods, but I really don't have many shelves, other than a bookshelf.

A bookshelf is better than the floor.

After tidying my snacks, I sit down on my comfortable desk chair. I had only sat in it once before, but it's a lot more comfortable than I remember. I crack my back with the curved seat, almost sinking into the proper posture this chair offers.

"Okay," I begin, opening my laptop. I plug it in while it loads up and open an empty writing document. "Okay." I write my name and the unofficial title, *What I think of Seven Oaks University.*

I open my curtains and gaze out the window to search for inspiration, watching the occasional student go by. After several minutes of distracted people-watching, I close the curtains and focus back on the blank page before me.

The first thing I noticed about Seven Oaks University is its classic architecture style; despite the ever-changing world around us, it is a comforting homage to our hardworking ancestors that some things really never change.

I stare at my words, already beginning to hate them, but I press on.

Seven Oaks is a beautiful town surrounded by magnificent trees, on the cusp of the Atlantic Ocean, opening up to the world beyond. My family, so I'm told, is one of the founding families from hundreds of years ago, and I feel a special connection to the land here. It only seemed fitting to me that I return here once more, and experience this beautiful, no, *enchanting area as an adult.*

Mr. Ace said he wanted our opinions, and this may not be my complete and honest opinion, but it makes for a good story. I'm sure it's someone's opinion.

I eventually crack open a bag of chips, two pages into my article, more describing the school than anything else. I mention the friendly students and new friends, but I'm really not sure what else to say; it's a university, and I've been here for a week. I'm not about to delve into my past and turn this into some self-discovery journal entry, though I don't doubt that I would earn brownie points for that.

Hours fly by, snacks demolished, and I lean back in my chair, reading over my draft that I've written. I close my laptop, deciding that I'll edit it, and probably change all of it, tomorrow. I stretch my arms behind my head and drift my eyes shut. I could go to sleep right about now.

The sound of my door clicking open and violently shutting gives me a heart attack. I whirl around in my chair, my hand subconsciously reaching in the direction of my hidden bat, now nestled under my bed. The bat peeks out from under my bed, sending chills up my spine; the door slamming must have made it roll.

Standing before me, now inside my room, is a girl, long honey hair, both hands pressed against the door. I stare at the back of her, wondering what exactly is going on. *I thought these doors locked automatically?!*

"Thank god," I hear her mutter, and she drops her head down, taking a deep breath.

I freeze up, tensing, and we bask in a few seconds of silence before I quip, "Um, hi."

The girl whips around, now holding her back to the door, eyes huge. Her deer-in-headlights expression quickly fades, and she starts to laugh the tension away. "Shit, you scared me."

"Same," I admit, clutching my arm rests. My wobbling bat catches my eye, but I quickly return to the girl's gaze. "Uh—"

"Sorry, sorry, I know." The girl takes a few steps inside, crossing her arms over her revealed chest. It's already dark outside, so I can imagine she's pretty cold. She sets down on the arm rest of my sofa, and crosses one leg over the other. "Random girl barging into your room."

"How *did* you get in? I thought they locked automatically."

The girl tilts her head to the side, and then looks back at my door. "Yeah, they do, but your door wasn't closed." *Seriously?!* "You have to really slam it to get it closed."

"Oh." Well, it's a good thing that nobody else came in while I carelessly left my door open. But, back to the task at hand. "Um, who are you?"

"Oh, I'm sorry!" The girl giggles and hops to her feet again, stretching her arm towards me. "I'm Holly. I live on the second floor."

"I'm Kim." I shake her hand, getting slightly lost in her beautiful sage eyes. I feel like I've heard her name before, but I don't remember where. Holly settles back down in her original spot, and I press on, "So, what's up?"

She meets my eyes and laughs, dimples piercing her cheeks. "I know, sorry again. Some guy from the party kept bugging me."

"Are you okay?" I try to calm the urgency in my voice, and my bat is looking very tempting right now. It twitches, rolling a little further out; my eyes must be buggy from staring at my laptop for so long, as if an inanimate object can move on its own.

"Oh, I'm fine. He was walking me back from the party and then wanted to come into my room. When I said no, he got kinda mad, and then I saw your door open, so I ran inside before he could follow me."

"Oh, okay." I push the thought of my bat away from me, ignoring the metal weapon shining so brightly. Holly looks a little shaken up, so I ask, "You sure you're okay?"

She smiles genuinely, beaming pearly whites in my direction. "I am. Thank you. Sorry to bug you, hope you weren't doing anything important."

"No, don't worry." I smooth the fabric of my skirt, resting my hands on my knees. "And just homework."

"Oh, what's your major?" Holly shifts from the side of the couch to the cushions, and swiftly adjusts into a comfortable position. "I don't think I've seen you in any of my classes, but I'm in math courses, mostly. I want to be a math teacher."

"Wow, that's really cool." I always liked math in school. "And I'm in for creative writing, so probably not a lot of crossover there."

"Not so much. Oh, hey, are you the girl who," I think I know where Holly is heading with this, but she takes me by surprise, "helped Georgina last night?" My mind screeches to a halt; I expected her to ask about where I'm from, the usual small talk, not this. "Sorry, when I was coming back, I thought I saw you talking to cops and whatever. That was you, right?"

"Oh, uh, yeah. That was me." My reputation is getting bigger than me.

"Oh, my god." She shakes her head, craning her neck back to stare at the ceiling. Once again, she says something I don't expect. "That's so cool of you. I mean, Seven Oaks is probably the safest place in the world, but it's still nice that you took care of her. Seems like she really needed it."

I'm starting to really like Holly already. Everyone I've met is so shockingly friendly and easy to talk to, and she is no exception. "Well, thanks. I'm just glad she's okay."

"Oh, she's doing okay? Good." She scans around the room, observing the nearly bare walls. "I like your posters. You should get some more."

I laugh; if she had only seen my room back home. "I'm getting my mom to ship me some more. Trying to make it feel more like home."

She points to my newly organized bookshelf. "And I like the convenience store style, all the snacks in a nice display."

"Oh, yeah, that took me a few hours to perfect. It's my dream to live inside a 7-Eleven."

Holly laughs, now kicking off her short boots and laying down on my couch. I've never seen someone so quick to get comfortable with a stranger before. That is, other than me. My mind flashes back to how odd I must have seemed to Owen, hugging him. Somehow, I don't think Holly would mind the random hugs. "Honestly, me too. Unlimited food and Slurpees. My parents live right by the 7-Eleven in town, I miss it so much."

"We literally have unlimited food in the cafeteria," I josh, trying to picture where Holly lives. I only lived two or three blocks from the beach, not too far from our beloved convenient store, so we might have been neighbours at some point. "And it's free."

"Oh, yeah, I guess so. But no Slurpees."

"The things we put up with to attend a private university." I amuse myself at my own joke, but I realize that the students in Seven Oaks might not appreciate my humour about the bourgeoisie.

Holly turns her head to me, rest it on top of her arm, not smiling. She looks pensive. My heart races a little bit, feeling the all too familiar sensation of worry.

"I like you," Holly concludes, now cracking the tiniest smirk. My mind settles. *You're not in Vancouver.* "When I came in here, I was thinking if anyone was here, I'd expect them to kick me out, like, immediately. But you're funny and cool." She sits vertically again, squeezing the bottom cushions of the couch. "We should be friends."

Oh, my god, two friends in one day. Miss Popular, over here! "I think we are."

She opens and shuts her mouth like a fish gulping down food. She hesitates for a moment and then nods. "Yeah. Awesome."

Holly and I end up talking. A lot. She might just be my favourite person here; I move to the couch to sit with her and her scent makes me realize that she has definitely had a few drinks in her. But she's nice; she doesn't ask me where I'm from, or how my adjustment is. She asks me what other TV shows and movies I like, what my favourite book is. I learn that her favourite colour is green, and we are both obsessed with sushi.

"Have you been to The Village yet?" Holly asks, holding her hand out for the bag of goldfish crackers in my hand.

"You mean into town?" I grab another handful of fish and pass her the rapidly emptying bag.

"No, The Village. It's like a five minute walk?" I respond with a blank stare, and she rolls her eyes dramatically. "Carolyn is a great RA, she did not do a good tour. If she didn't show you The Village, she probably forgot the sports square too."

"Sports square?" I sit up quickly; I've seen students wearing letterman jackets, but I had assumed that it was from high school. "What's there?"
"Football field, soccer field...do you play anything?"
"Baseball," I admit, disappointed at not hearing the addition of a baseball diamond. "No team?"
"I don't think there's a team, but there's a batting cage."
"No shit." I pop the last of the goldfish from my hand into my mouth, excited by the prospective batting cages. I was never very good at baseball in school, but I liked it. I wasn't bad at hitting, and not too shabby at catching. Throwing, however, was definitely not my forte. I couldn't throw a solid ball over home base to save my life.
"See, this is what I mean!" Holly exclaims, throwing her hands into the air. Some of the crackers jump just out of the bag, but dive right back in. "Come on, Car. I'll show it to you tomorrow. But anyway, about five minutes from here, there's The Village, which is at the centre of all the campuses. There's a Starbucks, a pizza place, Subway, and, most importantly, the *best* sushi place."
"I had no idea." The Village pops into my head, or my own reimagining of it. The different quick restaurants, the coffee shops, the potential convenient stores. I guess it was pretty stupid of me to do a big shopping trip in town when I might have other places nearby to do it.
"Try the sushi," Holly adds. "We'll go there some time, it's amazing."
"Yes, please," I beg, chuckling. If I could only eat one food for the rest of my life, it would have to be sushi.
Holly and I continue talking well past midnight. It's like talking to an old friend; there's no awkward silences, there's no tension, just complete comfort. It feels nice; it feels

foreign. I don't even realize how much time has gone by until she pulls out her phone and checks the time.

"Shit, it's late," Holly remarks. I search for my own phone, unable to find it, and strain my eyes to read my computer time. It's no use without my glasses.

"What time is it?"

"Past one."

"Oh." *Where did the time go?*

Holly grabs her booties and slips them back onto her feet, and then stands up, giving me the chance to admire her outfit. She has that natural, effortless, fashionable style that I could never seem to quite pull off. She wipes her palms on her faded skinny jeans, and then heads towards the door. I follow suit.

"Thanks again for helping me out," she says with a heavy sigh. "It just freaked me out a bit, I kind of panicked."

Holly is a little shorter than me, but she looks a few years older. She looks a lot more elegant, and actually knows how to apply more than three kinds of makeup. She's really sweet.

"I'm really glad that I'm stupid and didn't know how to close my door," I say, breaking the serious tone.

Holly giggles and opens my door, checking in the hallway. I don't hear a sound, and the evening lights are on. They're dimmer than the normal lights and have a more orange tint to them. It's weird and reminds me of a long flight where they have about eight different light settings for the different times of day, but I like it.

"Have a good night, Kim. I'll talk to you tomorrow."

"You too," I reply, giddy about hearing from her tomorrow, and I watch after her as she struts down the hall to the stairwell. She doesn't turn back, but searches around her before skipping upstairs, just in case. Once I can't see her anymore, I close the door, giving it a hip-check to securely lock it. I hear the small click, something I'm going to have to listen for more often, and nod approvingly to myself. My bat has somehow found its way snuggly back under my bed, and I head into my bathroom to brush my teeth.

I turn off my lights and slink under the covers of my bed, once again reminding myself that I need blackout curtains. I can see all the shapes and shadows of every object in my room scattered along the walls.

I close my eyes.

A week in, and I think I'm doing just fine. I have some potential edits for my article due next week, and my new discovery of the batting cages is an intriguing prospect. I may even have some actual good friendships forming, but let's not get ahead of ourselves. Before coming here, I made myself promise that I would try to make friends, and that I wouldn't let what happened back home affect how I act here. I may not have it all figured out, but this seems like a good place to start.

I'm feeling confident and renewed, which is an odd sensation. It's exhilarating.

I'm feeling like I'm going to take Seven Oaks by storm.

Chapter 4

Georgina isn't in class today. Though she's not in my first class of the day, Ornithology, I heard someone mention her name, caught up in a whisper, and unable to hear what else they were saying. I don't even know who said it. I expected to see her in English Literature in the afternoon, thinking that her name was said because she's back, but there was only an empty seat. If I knew who her close friends were, or if I even had her phone number, I would ask how she's doing.

I hope she's okay; her parents seemed much more worried than she did, so I wouldn't be surprised if she's currently arguing with her mom and dad about whether or not she's okay enough to attend her lectures.

But if this is apparently so normal, why would she be pulled from classes?

At Seven Oaks University, the classes are a bit unconventional. All of my college and university experiences came from TV shows and movies, but this was not what I expected at all. The smaller classrooms, the more intimate assignments, and the fact that it has the home-y feel of a high school course. I was led to believe that university and college

was a place that took your money, and if you failed, you failed. This is not like that at all.
It's like I'm in grade 13.
We weren't assigned any homework last week for English Lit, so Georgina doesn't have to worry about handing anything in; I think that's about to change today. We've spent the entire hour and a bit discussing Shakespeare's language and rhythm, his prose and poise. I was never a huge fan of reading his works, but his stories are pretty spectacular.

Mrs. McKnight checks the clock on the wall behind her, finding our lecture ending in just five short minutes. She turns back to the class, raising a single perfectly sculpted brow, and a wicked smirk spreads across her lips.

"Before we run out of time, let me explain your assignment."

I've noticed that the teachers are very cautious to stick within their lecture time frames, even though there aren't any bells or anything to keep them on lock. Maybe they too don't want to be here a second longer than they have to.

A few groans wave over the students, which only prompts Mrs. McKnight's smile more. My English Lit teacher is more of a traditional woman, and puts effort where effort is requested. She says her door is always open to those who seek help, and that she won't chase anyone down. *That* is what I expected from university, as opposed to the other courses I have, where the teachers seem to hold our hands. I take comfort in knowing that my failures are my own.

Mrs. McKnight strides back around her desk, graciously scanning over her students. She must be around fifty, and she airs regality and elegance. I even wish I could rock some of her business outfits.

"You may choose any work of Shakespeare you like. You will have two weeks to read the play and write me an essay on how Shakespeare's works have inspired the modern day. By this, I mean the media, films, novels, everyday life. Pick an aspect and wow me." Mrs. McKnight sits on the edge of her crisp brown desk, her hands gripping the jutting edge. "No more than three thousand words." The word limit catches my attention; I'll have to be careful. "No less than a thousand." She bites her lips, making a snap decision, and then, defeated, throws her hands up. She knows that we're already gone. "You may go."

The students promptly hop up out of their chairs and gather their supplies together, beginning to leave no more than ten seconds before Mrs. McKnight set us free.

"I'll be sending an e-mail tonight with further criteria, so check your spam folders." The joke falls relatively flat, but Mrs. McKnight doesn't seem to notice. She simply flattens her pencil skirt and takes a seat in her extravagant office chair. It looks more like a black cushioned throne than anything. She throws herself into work on her laptop before any students have even left the room, her tight brown curls framing her face beautifully.

I don't know if she has my e-mail address, but something tells me not to doubt it. I'm sure I'll get the message. This school is so organized that I'd be shocked if they didn't have at least three ways to contact me on file.

I pass by Mrs. McKnight, and she glances up from her desk, offering a curt smile before returning to her work. I can see the reflection of her thin glasses that she's writing something long in a text document.

The moment I step foot into the frequented halls, a piercing squeal fills my ears. I flinch, while a few other students physically hold their hands over their ears. It sounds like microphone feedback.

"Attention students," an echoing voice fills the halls following the painful pitch. I search around the mouldings of the ceilings until I find the source of the noise. *Universities have PA systems?* "I would like to call everyone to the auditorium immediately for a brief information session."

Unlike myself, the other students don't seem very fazed, and they all begin to march towards the exit closest to the auditorium building. *Universities have school assemblies?!*

"Again, I would like to call everyone to the auditorium immediately. Thank you."

I have never heard nor met him, but that must have been the school dean, Mr. Wolfe. My mom said that she went to school with him growing up and knew him about as well as anyone else. He was nice, were her exact words.

I follow my fellow classmates down the hall, filing through the narrow exit. The auditorium, along with the dramatic arts classes, is just a curved path from this particular exit, making it quick and easy to get there. I radar the crowds for any familiar faces, but I come up blank. Looks like I'll be spending another assembly kicking myself for not finding any friends fast enough.

I enter the drama building, and the auditorium is immediately to the right. The doors are propped open and lead into a black and unexpectedly purple room. The stage is huge, and for a second, I forget that I'm in a university, and think of myself in the grand theater of downtown Vancouver. Lack of funding is something that this school will never face. Mr. Wolfe stands on the stage behind a podium, only a speck in the distance from where I am. Students seem to be sitting anywhere, not piling down to the front row, so I trot down a few stairs, slip into an empty row, and take a seat.

The seats and curtains are not a bright red like I had imagined, but a rich plum, making it feel somber. The lights lining the steps and the overhead beams are saving from the otherwise despair. It's refined, albeit a bit Victorian gothic.

I occasionally glance behind me, checking to see if any friends come in, but I don't know anyone well enough to recognize them by the back of their heads, so I pull out my phone to kill the time.

"Take a seat, everyone," Mr. Wolfe says, raising his hands. He's wearing a gray suit that nearly matches his peppered hair, and the skin on his face is sagging in a way that shows every single day of his age. He leans forward, closer to the podium, and repeats, louder, "Everyone, please, take a seat."

I shove my phone back into my pocket and find that four new men have appeared onstage, all donning the same security guard outfits. I haven't seen any security guards around here until now.

"This is so stupid," a girl sneers, stomping down the steps. I glance towards her, recognizing her sharp tone; Rian. She's slowly trudging down the stairs, phone in one hand, coffee in the other, talking to a few other girls. She rolls her eyes, locking them to the floor to watch her step. I have to give her props, I could not pull off the heels that she's wearing. Partially because I couldn't walk in them and I would snap my ankles in two if I tried. "It's not our fault Georgie had too much."

I must have missed the memo, because she apparently knows what this assembly is about. Her statement makes a lot of sense when I consider the security guards; no one was really around to help Georgina, and I'm guessing someone complained, and now we have security guards.

Shit gets done fast here.

Seven Oaks

Rian and her two friends sit one row down from me, but across the barrier of stairs. She takes the aisle seat, stretching out her legs along the steps. A few students jeer at the obstructed path, but nobody does anything more than mutter their grievances.

Mr. Wolfe clears his throat into the microphone hidden by the podium, and the crowd begins to settle down. My principal in high school wasn't very intimidating, and Mr. Wolfe seems even less so. Despite his no-nonsense demeanor and the way his brow has been furrowed since I've entered, he doesn't scare me. He seems to get everyone else to shut up, though. Everyone swiftly takes a seat, and the room falls to a hush.

"Thank you," he says. I think it's his voice, the dead giveaway of his kindness. There's something soft and soothing about it. "I will keep this brief, as I know we would all like to get on with our day."

The students chuckle, and his expression seems to relax. He stands up a bit straighter and places his hands on either side of the wooden stand before him.

"I would like to start by saying that I hope you have all enjoyed your first week here. Obviously, it was not possible for all the students of Seven Oaks to be in attendance today, but I'm sure word of mouth will be enough to spread this news around."

Upon hearing Mr. Wolfe's words, I glance around the room and realize how few students are actually here. There's only about a hundred of us listening to Mr. Wolfe. Now that I think about it, exactly how many students go here?

"Many of us have heard about what happened to Georgina Macintosh." *Macintosh. That's her last name.* The room suddenly feels uneasy, and murmurs arise from every aisle of the auditorium. "As we all know, this has happened before, back at Seven Oaks High." The voices cease, as apparently, we all did know. "We here at Seven Oaks want to create an environment where students can feel as though they can relax and take the edge off when needed, explore and discover new things for themselves."

The sound of a needle hitting the floor could be heard, and for good reason; I'm pretty sure the dean of Seven Oaks University is encouraging drug use. *Is this place even real?*

"Oh, my god," a girl's voice snarls around me, but I'm not sure where it's coming from. It's so piercing that I get shivers down my spine.

"However, safety is our top priority. Mr. Davis has been our school security guard since we opened last week." Mr. Wolfe turns to one of the four security guards, and the one closest to him steps forward, holding a hand up. I'm not sure if he expects an applause or not, but his smile is wiped clean from his face in a matter of seconds. I think I may have seen him around once or twice, but I'm not sure. "Not to mention our security staff monitoring the cameras at all times."

"There are cameras? Well, shit," a man in the row ahead of me quips and a few of his friends laugh, patting him on the shoulder.

"Where are the cameras?" I hear a familiar voice whisper. In the row below me, further to the right, I catch Brit's concerned eyes. She gives me a forced stiff upper lip. Brit has asked the question that I myself thought of as well; where are these alleged cameras?

"With this recent incident involving Ms. Macintosh, and the fact that a student was the only one available to help," Mr. Wolfe continues, and some of the kids search around for this specific student. I force my gaze on Mr. Wolfe, ignoring the stares. I really don't need more attention, "we have increased security. Here is Mr. Bryers."

The man next to Mr. Davis steps forward, hands at his waist, jaw set so straight that it shines like steel. He nods his head down, not taking his eyes off us for one second. He can't be more than forty years old, his hair shaved within an inch of his skull, and he's well over six feet tall. Now, *he* scares me.

"Mr. Bryers is a retired military officer, serving this country for twelve years."

Mr. Bryers slowly scans over the uneasy teenagers, and I almost catch a sense of amusement on his part. *Oh, my god.*

"And our newest recruits happen to be some familiar faces, two of our security from Seven Oaks High, Ronald and Charles Mastiff."

The two remaining men step forward, and the crowd suddenly erupts in a thunderous applause and shouts. I blindly clap along, observing the two men. I first thought that the two of them were partners, but seeing their facial similarities, even from a distance, they look more like brothers. One of them is taller and broader, leaner as well, but the other one has a beaming smile that floats throughout the room like a happy cloud. The shorter of the two steps forward and waves to the students, drawing in more of an uproar. He turns back to the taller but younger brother, who nods along politely.

"Along with these four men, we also have Ms. Dahl and Mr. Peters, who are not here at the moment, but you will see them around," Mr. Wolfe adds.

The four security guards step back into their line, adjusting, and put on a straight face.

"We hope that this brings some peace of mind that you are all extremely safe at this school. We will be trying our hardest to ensure your safety, and should you have any questions, please do not hesitate to approach me, or any of the fine men you see on this stage."

Mr. Wolfe holds his arm out to the security guards, but he is met with silence until he caves in and says, "All right, you are all free to go. Enjoy your day."

There is a brief intermission of clapping before all the clamour starts up again. Opposed to my usual nature, I throw my backpack over my shoulder and attempt to exit the auditorium first. Since my classes are finished for the day, I'm eager to return to my room and do absolutely nothing. I manage to make it out the door quickly, fully intent on making a break for my dorm room, until I hear someone call my name.

"Kim!"

I turn around, just outside the auditorium, only to find a sea of students. I'm about to keep walking until I see Holly's head hopping over the crowd to greet me. I chuckle and step out of line, letting everyone pass until Holly appears before me.

"Hey," I greet. "How's your day going?"

"Boring. I only just got up for this."

I peer down, spotting that she is donning pajama pants and a hoodie, looking ten times more comfortable than I am.

"Night owl, eh?" I joke.

"Not usually. Didn't have time to get dressed before class." Holly glances around her and then steps closer to me, dragging us to the side of the door to avoid the dying crowds. "How's your day going?"

"Nothing too interesting, just classes."

Another familiar face catches my eye, and Owen walks by. Upon seeing me he stops, about to say something, but a friend pushes him along towards a different building. He turns back one last time, offering a polite smile, and I give one back.

"Who are you smiling at?" Holly asks, following where my eyes were. She suddenly turns to me. "Oh, my god, do you have a boyfriend already?" I laugh so loud that Holly jumps back, cracking a smile herself. "Well, that answers that." *It sure does.* "Anyone you think is cute?"

I shrug, and my mind dances back to Damien. It felt like years ago we had our first and last interaction. "I don't know. I kissed this guy at the party on Friday, but that's it." Last time I checked, kissing a guy doesn't mean that you're destined for marriage.

"Who?"

"Damien?"

Holly pauses for a moment until recognition dawns onto her face. "Oh, Damien! Yeah, he's cute."

"Do you have a boyfriend?" I ask bluntly, very obviously changing the subject. Damien isn't a sore subject for me, but I'm more interested in Holly's potential suitors than some random make-out.

"Nope," she admits, crossing her arms over her chest. Her hair is tied up high into a ponytail and looks impeccable. She has the effortlessly beautiful thing down. "Free as a bird. There's this one guy, Landon, but I don't think he's into me." From the look in her eyes, I can tell she's head over heels for this guy. "I really like him, though." Her face scrunches up and she shakes her head, as if to shake out the thought. "You're lucky, being new here. You kind of have your pick."

"Right," I chuckle. Relationships aren't my top priority; hell, they're *not* a priority for me. Surviving my classes, making friends, and somehow navigating this school and town are at the top of my list. Happiness is the ideal priority, whatever that entails.

"Well, I gotta go work on a paper," Holly says. "My one elective, I chose modern history, and it's nothing but papers. Maybe I'll get you to edit them."

I stifle a laugh and Holly leans in for a tight hug.

"Good luck," I offer, and she grins, walking back down the pathway.

Holly and I seemed to have struck up a weird kind of friendship. It started by pure luck, and stupidity on my part, and has turned into this odd connection. It feels like I've known her my whole life.

I readjust my backpack on my shoulders and start down the walkway myself, but a hard body crashes into my shoulder. I nearly lose my footing, stumbling sideways, and I catch myself on one of the cement blocks used for modern decoration along the auditorium pathway.

I look up, finding some douche bag rushing past me. He looks back behind me, a disturbing look in his eye that makes me feel uneasy.

"Seriously?" I growl, holding my hands out. The entire path is empty, except for us, so I'm pretty sure that was on purpose. But why?

The student, obviously my own age, flips his nasty expression back around, his blonde hair shining obnoxiously in the summer haze, and faces forward again. He doesn't even have a bag, so it's not like he's late for class. My hand grips tightly onto the concrete ball, and it almost feels like it's shaking beneath my fingertips, but I know that's just the rage inside me.

"Dick," I mumble, fixing one of my shoes that was dislodged. I kick it back into place, and I suddenly realize that I recognize the jerk that just body checked me. I saw him over the weekend, in the cafeteria with some group of varsity jackets. He's the one that gave me the bad vibes. A shudder rolls down my spine; *who the fuck is that?*

"Oh!" someone squeals, and maybe it's because Mr. Asshole has left me on edge, but I flinch at the sound.

I search around, finding the two sibling security guards peering up at something in the sky. I step out from the undercover area and into the shining sun. I try to look up at what they're seeing, but the sun averts my eyes.

"Do you know what he is?" the shorter one asks. He has one hand held above his eyes, shielding from the beacon of light, the other pointing at the math building. I still don't know which one is Charles, and which one is Ronald.

"I don't," replies the taller one, and I find myself falling in step next to them, also staring at the building. It looks the same from all sides, except this side is only brick walls and windows, no doors. I try to locate someone in the windows, but I come up blank.

"Do you?"

It takes me a moment to realize that the shorter one is talking to me, until I turn to him and see the brothers staring me in the eye. Up close, the similarities are striking. Their noses are identical, their chins almost, and their eyes are the same shade of gray green that feels oddly familiar to me.

"Do I?" I repeat, flustered. I guess I'm the weird one, silently approaching the security guards here.

The shorter one nods, and I briefly glance down to read his nametag; R. Mastiff. That helps.

"Yes," Ronald replies carefully, his eyes rapidly shifting between the two of mine.

"Um..." I blush. "Do I what?"

Ronald doesn't seem annoyed, he instead returns focus to the building, and points again. "Do you know what he is?"

I follow his extended arm very carefully, trying to locate where he's pointing to. I search all the windows, not finding any students inside, nor anything that would fit his criteria. I'm about to admit defeat when I hear a gentle whistling, and my eyes shoot up to the roof.

"Oh," I laugh, spotting a red and black bird. He's perched on the edge of the building, a small shape of vibrant colour on the muted campus. He chirps again, his little beak flexing. "I think he's a scarlet tanager."

"Yes!" Ronald exclaims. He claps his hands together, grinning wildly. "That's right. He should be looking to build his nest in a nearby forest now."

"He's very pretty," I agree, feeling confident that I guessed correctly. Birds are so cool and have become increasingly so since I started taking ornithology.

"See, Charles? *She* knew what the bird was."

Ronald and I look at Charles, and he shrugs dramatically. "I have a lot to learn," he confesses, and then grows a bit more serious. "What's your name?"

"Kimberly." I don't know why I said my full name, but it's too late to turn back now.

"Kimberly," Ronald repeats.

"You didn't go to Seven Oaks High, did you." Charles says it as more of a statement than a question.

"No, I'm from Vancouver." As I speak, I'm starting to slowly disassociate from the winding streets of Vancouver, the aggressive hipsters, the over-priced homes. I still remember it fondly, but I'm shocked by how quickly I've moved on from Vancouver. Maybe it's because I know I'll be going back, that it's not a permanent goodbye. Maybe.

"Is that on the West Coast?" Ronald asks. I nod. "I like the West Coast."

"I'm Charles Mastiff, this is my brother Ronald," Charles says, and Ronald immediately distracts himself with the tanager again. "As Mr. Wolfe said, we worked at the local high school."

"Why did you come here?" I pry, not sure if I'm going too far or not.

Charles doesn't seem to think so. He looks nostalgic, almost. "We love the students. I don't know what it was, but the school felt different with this class gone. We were very glad to be offered the positions here."

"Everyone is very nice," Ronald mutters, eyes still fixated on the bird.

"Yeah, it's nice," I agree, the fluttering red bird catching my eye again. He quickly dives off the roof's edge and begins to flit away, towards one of the endless forests.

Charles carefully steps in between Ronald and me. "We're both lucky to be here, where they'll let us work together." Charles keeps his voice low, ensuring his brother doesn't hear him.

"That's really nice," I say. We glance back at the distracted Ronald, toying with his fingers. "He sure knows his birds, too."

"Oh, I know," Charles chuckles.

It must be nice to have a sibling, someone there for you like that. I know that my mom wanted more kids, but that it was apparently really hard to get pregnant with me. Years ago, I overheard my mom talking to one of her friends about kids. I remember hiding in the hallway, listening to them chatting on our patio, the door wide open on the summer day. I heard Mom confess that before my dad left, she and him were planning on having another kid. The brother or sister that never was.

"Well, we should get back to walking around, eh, Ron?" Charles pats his brother on the shoulder and he nods quickly.

"Indeed," Ron replies, and gives me a smile and nod. "It was nice to meet you, Kimberly." His voice is slow and clear.

"You too," I say. I make eye contact with both men before heading on my way, returning to my room.

I wander through the campus, now enthralled with spotting different birds around, but all I see are crows. I think that one scarlet tanager is the only bird I've seen here that wasn't a crow, robin, or a seagull back in town.

I finally reach the girl's dorm, my fingers grazing the entry door handle when my phone starts vibrating in my pocket. I scramble to get it out, and check to see the number; it's not one of my contacts, but I think the area code is Seven Oaks local.

"Hello?" I frantically answer, hoping I made it before the last ring.

"Hi," a female voice responds. Even *her* tiny greeting sounds hesitant. "Is this Kim?"

"Yeah," I reply, stepping out of the way of the doors. Two other girls enter the building, not giving me a single glance. I lean against the railing lining the steps, clutching the chilled metal with one hand.

"Okay. Well, is this Kimberly..." the woman pauses, and I wait patiently. She sounds slightly familiar, but I can't place it. "Fuck, I don't know your last name."

"Who is this?" I finally ask. She sounds familiar, but I can't quite place it.

"Georgina."

"Oh!" I laugh, finding myself elated to hear her voice. I've heard nothing about her since I saw her on Saturday, and her voice sounds a lot clearer now. She must be doing better. "Hey. Yeah, it's Kim. Um, how'd you get my number?"

"Carolyn." *Does Carolyn just know everything about everyone?* "I hope that's okay."

"Yeah, of course." I push past the strangeness and move onto what's more important. "How are you feeling?"

"Uh...I've been better. That's actually what I wanted to talk to you about." She clears her throat and her end goes silent. I wait a few seconds before questioning.

"Are you okay?"

"I'm actually in the parking lot," Georgina says, and my head shoots up. I can't see much of the parking lot from here, only a couple cars unhidden from the campus' distinct design. "Do you have time to talk?"

"Yeah, totally. I'll head over."

"Okay."

I think about how Georgina lucked out with this good time to contact me, considering I don't have any more classes for the rest of the day, but then I remember that we have almost identical class schedules. Of course she'd know when I was free. Not that I would be totally opposed to skipping class, I know I was more than fine with it in high school.

"Um, so how have you been?" I ask, avoiding the stray students staggering the sidewalk. "Do you feel okay?"

"Physically, yeah. I went home on Sunday, my parents wanted me to stay in the hospital Saturday night." The tone in her voice makes me worry, but I try to put it at ease for now.

I get to the top of the stairs of the parking lot and begin my search. It's incredible that the parking lot is nearly filled, that so many students drive here on their own. I don't know if I'll even own a car before I'm thirty.

"Well, I'm glad you're back home," I console.

"Thanks, me too. Beige truck," Georgina replies.

I spot the only beige truck on the other end of the lot, directly facing me, and I walk towards it. It looks at least twenty years old, but is in relatively good condition considering.

"Okay," I say, and the two of us hang up. I get closer and I can see inside her window more clearly; her blonde hair is straightened, overflowing from her shoulders, and she's dressed in her classic red plaid. I smile and skirt to the passenger side, seeing more signs of wear near the wheels; rust is a bitch. Georgina reaches over and unlocks the door, letting me inside.

"Hey," she says, snatching up a coffee cup in one black manicured hand.

"Hey," I say.

We both sit awkwardly in silence for a moment. The nerves of meeting up one on one with a near stranger hit us harder than expected, but we both end up smiling our way out of it.

"So, what's going on?" I start.

She sighs, resting her arms along her steering wheel. She looks tired. Her eyes look bloodshot, and she has deep purple bags beneath them. Her flannel sleeves are tugged to the tips of her fingers, and she's wearing extremely comfortable looking gray sweatpants.

"I know this is weird, because we don't know each other very well. But…" Georgina turns to me, her expression nearly breaking my heart. "I'm really freaked out. And you were the person that helped me, so I want to trust you."

I rub my hands together, starting to feel sick. All the reassurances that this is normal and okay are clearly not making this okay.

"What's going on?"

Georgina takes a deep breath, her eyes unfocused before her. "I thought I didn't remember anything from that night. Like, I thought it was one big forgotten moment. But I do remember something. A red light."

"What?"

Georgina nods, and I finally notice her quivering hands. "Yeah. And everyone kept telling me it was the ambulance or police lights, or a stop light. But it wasn't like that." She takes a breath, shutting her eyes. "It was small. A small red light. And then this."

Georgina turns to me and rolls up her plaid sleeves, revealing her dainty wrists. I don't see anything wrong until she traces a few lines along her skin. "It's healed more now, but my wrists were bruised, too." Shudders role up my spine.

"What did the doctors say?" I ask, trying to remain calm. The truck suddenly feels colder, and my arms feel bare and frozen. I don't like where this is heading.

"They said they had to restrain me in the ambulance, because I was apparently going crazy." She growls, hiding her ligature marks again. "I don't remember. It just feels like something happened. I know it might sound dumb–"

"It doesn't," I unintentionally snap. She meets my eyes and I take a deep breath. "It doesn't sound dumb at all. You hardly remember anything, that's really scary."

"I'm so worried that something happened." She crosses her arms, digging them into her stomach.

I don't mean to play Devil's advocate, but flashing back to our conversation on Saturday, she seemed fine and eager to be back at school; it's like I'm talking to a different person. "What makes you think something happened?" She meets my eyes and I lean back into the passenger seat. "I'm not doubting you at all. I just meant that on Saturday, you–"

"I know, I know." Her whole body has started to shake now. "I thought it was all fine, but my parents were freaking out, and they got me tested for all this shit. Even like..." Her eyes glance down, and by context, I know what that means.

"And?" I press, terrified of the answer.

"Nothing." *Thank God.* "Everything was negative, except for THC. Maybe it was just really strong, but...I don't know. This all might sound crazy."

Georgina inhales sharply, trembling, and I take one of her hands in mine. "It doesn't." I rub one of her hands gently, feeling her soft skin.

"But it makes no sense. Why would someone drug me? I've known these people all my life, I don't know anyone who would do this." She swiftly piles her free hand onto mine, until all four of our hands are holding one another. As soon as she uses the word "drug," my heart is set into motion. "I thought it was fine at first. But now my parents want to pull me out of school."

"Really?" I ask. I just spent the past four days being told that everything was fine by everyone from new friends to cops, but clearly it is not. "That's...intense."

"Yeah, it is. And makes no sense, I don't live on campus, I live with them."

"It sounds like they're just worried." I really can't say whether or not this is an overreaction. My mind hasn't even fully processed what Georgina is saying to me.

"Yeah." Georgina suddenly pulls her hands away and cradles her face, leaning onto the steering wheel. "It's so stupid. This whole situation is just stupid."

I lean as close to Georgina as I can, stretching over the centre console. I rub her back in circles, searching her distraught expression. I don't know what I would do if I was her, terrified with the thoughts of losing and forgetting time.

"It's fucked up," I correct her, and she smiles a little.

"Do you remember anything from that night? Did I say anything?"

I flash back to that night, thinking of anything of importance to share. The urgency in her eyes is painful to see, but I can't really offer her anything to help. "I don't think you said anything...you threw up, and I just waited with you until an ambulance came."

Georgina cringes, now resting back into her seat. "That's gross, I'm sorry."

"Don't be sorry!" I couldn't care less about that. "I'm just glad you're okay."

She tries to give me some kind of appreciative expression, but her face scrunches up again. "It is really fucked up. I feel really stupid for letting it go that far, but I've been smoking pot for three years. I didn't expect *this* to happen." I'm about to respond, but she adds, "Whatever *this* is. What do you think happened?"

Georgina must recognize my deer-in-headlights look, because her face softens, and her shoulders relax. She's going easy on me.

"I don't know," I admit. "But trust yourself. If you think something's wrong, then you can try to figure it out. And I'll help, in any way I can." I don't know how she'll respond to my response. I know some people back home used to make fun of my "naivety," used to tell me to wake up and live in the real world of "facts."

Don't think about it, Kim.

"I don't even know if something is wrong," Georgina says, and I throw myself back into the present conversation. "I think it's just my parents freaking out that's caused me to freak out so much. I'm just...irrationally scared. They're putting all these ideas into my head, fuck." She holds her head in her hands, resting her forehead on top of the steering wheel. I haven't been through what she has, but I can relate to the feeling of exploding into words to try to make sense of chaos. "Such a shit show."

The centre compartment between us starts to vibrate viciously, and Georgina and I jump back. She rolls her eyes and opens the lid, drawing out her cellphone.

"Hey," she answers her phone. I can't hear any voice on the other end, only what Georgina is saying. "Okay…yeah…okay…I'll be there soon…love you too…bye." She chucks her phone back inside the cubby, slamming the top shut. "Sorry. Just my mom."

"Gotta get home, I guess?" I guess.

"Yeah. But listen, thank you." She turns to me and awkwardly wraps her arms around me in a tight embrace. "Thank you for just listening, and for helping me."

"Of course," I counter. I feel kind of useless, unable to *really* help her. I wish I could do more. "I'm just really glad you're okay."

She pulls away and starts her truck's engine. Before I even have time to get out, she starts driving forward, lurching me backwards.

"You're pretty cool," she says, slowing us down in front of the stairs leading up to campus.

I laugh and pull the old latch on the door, thrusting it open. "Right."

"Hey," she captures my attention again, just after I physically slide out of the high truck. "I don't want to freak you out, I know you're new here. I think it's my anxiety talking, I've never experienced anything like this."

I smile at the small comfort, though I'm extremely skeptical, and I nod graciously. "I'm fine. Just take care of yourself, okay? And I'm here if you need me."

"Thank you," she says glumly, and offers me one last wave before I swing her passenger door shut.

I watch her truck peel away, turning sharply and disappearing behind the grassy knoll lining the school grounds.

"Shit," I mumble, thinking of our conversation. I have to agree with her, that everything she says does add up to an accidental overdose, not to mention the constant barrage of adults and students alike confirming how real and usual it is. But if something doesn't feel right, then there could be a serious problem.

I feel conflicted between trying to believe Georgina's attempts not to worry me, and between what my gut is telling me, and I think what her gut is telling her. Something is amiss, but we don't know what.

It just doesn't feel right.

Walking back to my room, my worries slowly slip away after managing to always find contact with one of the security guards wandering the grounds. This place feels at least ten times safer than the downtown streets back home, so I really can't complain much. But that conversation with Georgina, even with her blowing off her own suspicions...

I enter the dorm room, a few girls lounging in the hallway. It's only when I get to my door, attempting to unlock it, that I recognize one of the girls as Rian.

I have not had any real interactions with Rian. I have only heard what others have said about her, and have felt the immense discomfort of being around her in general. I get major déjà vu when I look at her and see what she says about people.

"I can't believe she thinks she can wear that," Rian says, pursing her thin lips. Her eyebrows look especially sharp today.

"It was a cute dress," one of her friend's counters, and Rian scowls at the girl. I swear, her scowl can be felt from space. It feels like an awful wave of heat, charging right at me, and I'm not even the recipient.

"Not on her," Rian says. She holds her hands out from her hips, extending them. "She just doesn't have the body for it."

A chill runs through my body just looking at Rian, cringing at her words. She reminds me of some girls back home. The snide remarks of Rose, the weaving pettiness of Toni, the unbearable dread I felt every single day for so, so long.

Unfortunately, I'm lost in thought of memories best forgotten for too long, because Rian looks up and narrows her frosted eyes at me. She goes from laughing about some girl daring to wear a nice dress to a death stare at the drop of the hat.

She physically shoves past her friends, nudging in between both of them to step closer to me. She's still one door away, but that is plenty close.

"Is there a problem?" her voice reaches a high pitch, condescending, and I debate scurrying inside.

Instead, I say the first thing that comes to my mind. "I just didn't think you were real."

My words don't make sense to either of us at first, but it seems like she's taking it as a compliment.

"Excuse me?" she prompts, hungry for more. I think my comparison between her and my past friends was too hasty; their actions are similar, but their intents differ wildly. Rose, Toni, they always wanted something. Rides, to feel better than somebody else to calm their ego, attention. But Rian...she's a wild card. From my very few brief exchanges with her, it doesn't seem like she knows what she wants.

"I just..." I sigh, my face going red, but I stay strong. Time to do what I never did. "I didn't think girls like you existed, who just criticize other people for the sake of being mean."

Her pleading eyes disappear, and she scoffs, scanning my body up and down, ensuring that I notice. Her refined hand finds its way to her hip, her fingers lean, and her nails bitten short. "And who are you, some nobody from across the country?"

"Yeah." My mind speaks before I can fully process it. Her eyes flash a hint of panic; my straightforward attitude is sure sparking up some interest.

Rian hesitates for a moment; she can't seem to settle on the right words to say.

As she opens her mouth for the fourth time I say, "Maybe just be a bit nicer to people." I realize how juvenile I sound only after I've spoken, but my message holds true. I quickly unlock my door, ripping the key out. "Have a good night."

Rian's face is burning by the time I slip inside my room and close the door. I press it hard, making sure it's locked this time to keep out unwanted visitors.

Kim, you just made friends. At least wait a little while before you start making enemies.

I lean against the door, feeling safely contained within these walls. Keeping my mouth shut until it's too late was a specialty of mine back home, and I hated it. I don't want to be that person anymore. I'm shocked that I even said that much, my heart pounding in my chest, body quivering, hands and face growing clammy.

I can't hear Rian and her friends, but it's already been established that these rooms are fantastically sound proof. Now that I'm thinking about it, I guess it's more of a necessity than anything, considering how rowdy university students can be.

I take a seat on my bed, my hands gripping the sheets and comforter. I tense and release, and my breathing finally begins to steady.

I'm definitely not in Vancouver anymore. The old Kim wouldn't dare say anything like that, no matter how much she wanted to.

My cellphone starts vibrating in my pocket again, and I scramble to tug it out, worried that it might be Georgina again.

Not even close.

"Hey, mom," I answer, hoping I sound a lot less frazzled than I feel.

"Hey," her gentle voice responds, putting me more at ease. "I don't have much time to talk, but I just wanted to check in and say hi."

I smile, flopping down further onto my bed. Leave it to my mom to make things feel a little bit better. Thoughts of Rian slowly slip away, and I reminisce about the best part of my old life.

"How are you doing?" Mom presses.

"I'm good," I say, hoping that confidence is radiating through my voice. I haven't talked to her in a few days. "I actually have friends now, I think."

"Really?!" The disbelief in her voice makes me roll my eyes, but I really don't blame her. "Well, that's exciting! And quick. It's about time you make some good friends." Mom knows my struggles better than anyone.

"It's nice not eating alone anymore." I ignore how pathetic I sound, and conversely ask my mom, "How are you doing?"

"I also made a new friend," Mom replies, stifling a giggle. "I sent you a picture."

"Okay…" I put my phone on speakerphone, noticing a message from my mom. I connect to the dorm room Wi-Fi and download the attachment. I'm surprised, to say the least. "A cat?"

"His name is Bailey. Isn't he cute?"

I sit up abruptly. "Wait. You got a cat?"

"Yeah, it got a bit lonely without you."

Three more attachments come onto my phone, different pictures of the same gray tabby. He is adorable and has stellar yellow eyes. "I've wanted a cat for years and you get one the second I leave?!"

"Oh, relax. You'll see him when you come back home." My mind sits puzzled for a moment, taking a second to click that my mom thinks home isn't here. It's Vancouver.

"I can't believe you replaced me with a cat." I'm more upset that I don't get to live with a cat, but she doesn't have to know that.

"No, not replaced! Besides, he won't move away for university someday." I have to laugh. Despite raising me on her own, I never felt like I missed out on anything. Sure, the elementary school Father's Day events were a little rough, but my mom did a good job. She taught me that romantic love is not the dire life or death situation it's been caked up to be in romantic comedies. Any kind of love is just as important.

"How old is he?" I ask, drawing my mind back to the topic at hand.

"Almost three, that's what the lady at the shelter said," Mom says. A few more pictures come in of Bailey adjusting nicely into the house. In one of the pictures, he's yawning and stretching on the floor, his back deeply arched. He's precious, and he has a tiny white patch on one of his paws. "But anyway, I gotta go, meeting up with a friend."

"Is it Bailey?" I joke. I wouldn't blame her if it was.

"Ha-ha. No, it's Mel. I'm glad you're making friends, honey. Call me soon, okay?"

"Okay. Say hi to Mel for me." Mel is Mom's oldest friend in the city, they met almost instantly when we moved there. I must get my friend-making skills from mom. That, or everyone is *that* sick of the same old people here in Seven Oaks.

"Will do. Love you."

"Mom?" My words catch up before I can fully process what I'm thinking.

"Yeah? Is something wrong?"

I take a deep breath; I don't really know what to say. "No," I manage. "This town is just...Seven Oaks is weird, Mom."

My mother starts laughing up, and I can hear her nodding through the phone. "It really is. Anything in particular?"

"The...people." My voice is hesitant, as if someone might be listening to me. "And what they consider to be normal."

"...what's going on, Kim?"

I bite my tongue; I can't freak her out. I sit up and wrap my free arm around my legs, forcing a smile onto my lips. "Nothing. Really, just adjusting."

"Are you sure?"

"Yeah. Really."

We both pause, waiting for the other one to crack first. I've always been better at this game than my mom.

"Okay, well, you know that–"

"I know," I interrupt, smiling. "I know, I can talk to you about anything."

"Good." She sounds happy, proud of herself. "I love you, Kim."

"Love you too." I sigh, disappointment tinging at my heart. I miss my mom. "Bye."

"Bye."

The phone clicks and the calls ends, and I have yet another message waiting for me on my phone. I am jealous that my mom has a cat now, but I'm really not surprised. If I could get a cat in my dorm, I would have one in a heartbeat.

To my surprise, the last message isn't from my mom, it's from an unknown number.

Hey it's Carolyn.

I guess it's from Carolyn.

Holly gave me ur number. I forgot to show u the village! if ur free today I can show u it and the batting cages. Holly said u like baseball, so cool!!!!

I respond immediately, asking for a plan for us to meet up. I don't really know a lot about Seven Oaks, and I sure as hell don't know what's currently going on with Georgina, *if* or *what* happened. Everything so far has been, and continues to be, one big question mark.

Even so, despite all this, and I'm not totally sure how to explain it, Seven Oaks is starting to feel like home.

Chapter 5

It has been so long since I've played any form of baseball that I am in rough shape. I didn't realize how long it had been until I held my bat in my hands again, preparing for a swing. It hits me that I hadn't so much as picked up a ball and a bat all summer; I was too busy prepping for university that I completely forgot about baseball.

I wasn't great in high school or anything, not even close to team captain, but I enjoyed the sport, so that stuff didn't really matter. There were a lot of girls who were way faster, and who could consistently catch the ball, and some who could even hit the ball more dependably, but boy, could I hit them far.

I get to the batting cages around 8:00, the skies already darkening around me. Carolyn showed me the cages yesterday on our way to The Village; after profusely apologizing for neglecting to show me another half of the campus, she led me on a tour to the sports centre and the miniature city. The Village was quaint and tidy, and the convenience store and restaurants will definitely come in handy. It's a quarter the size of the campus itself, set up in a giant square with stores lining three edges of it. I found the sushi place Holly had mentioned and it was packed, so I guess the East Coast likes sushi, too. There were different coffee shops, a pita place, pizza, a noodle house, basically every type of food placed in one common area.

Surprisingly, there are even a few clothing stores in The Village. One of them is a sort of exchange store, where students can bring in "lightly worn" clothing and trade them for other articles. Another one looks like a smaller version of Winners, but with a boutique flare to it. I'll be spending way too much money there.

The sports centre, halfway between The Village and the main campus area, is a lot bigger than I thought. I never even realized that between the girl's and boy's dorm, there's a path leading to the area. The path gets swallowed up briefly into a charming forest before revealing the elaborate sports area. There's a massive football field, along with stands lining one side of it, opposite to an equally intimidating soccer field. There's one big concession stand next to the football bleachers, closed right now, but will surely be open during any and all games. Completing a kind of triangle shape are tennis courts, where someone is always playing, whether it's by themselves or with a partner.

Tennis seems to be a big thing here.

Finally, nestled in the corner area, are the batting cages. Despite being built within the past few years, their seclusion makes them look dingy and old. It's extremely well lit, and the fences reach far and wide, leaving a lot of room for hitting homers.

I step inside the deserted cages, unsettled by the creaking gated entrance. There are about eight different cages formed in a quarter circle, all protected along the sides with their own elongated chain-links. I search around one more time, still staggered that nobody else is here, but baseball isn't exactly popular. In high school, we barely had enough members to constitute as a team.

I pull my bat out of my bag and hold it tightly in my hands; shivers crawl up my bare arms, nostalgia flooding over me. The baseball team was filled with great girls, just supportive and kind. I didn't realize I missed them until now.

As disappointing as it is, there's no baseball team here, but from what I've heard of this school, there is potential to make one come springtime. Carolyn has the can-do attitude, so if I recruit her help, I'm sure it's possible.

I kick the end of my bat, loving the echoing sound against my shoes. The sandy dirt looks fresh, almost like no one has ever stepped onto it. I boot my bag towards the edge of my cage, switching my focus to the control panel for the automatic ball thrower. The control box is set just at chest level in each of the eight cages, and with one weak tug, the box flips open to reveal the different settings. I set the balls at a relatively slow speed, thirty miles an hour, and hop to my stance on the plate.

I've never seen a pitching machine like this before, where the balls are automatically loaded into them. It looks like there's a sloped underground area where they all pile up, and the eight machines gather them from beneath the earth. It's very elaborate. The batting cages I used back home could only hold thirty balls at a time before needing to be manually refilled.

I bend my knees, clutching my old friend, waiting for a ball to fly my way. It's about twenty seconds before I actually hear the ball thrower warm up, and it begins to emit a small whirring sound.

"Okay," I mutter, perfecting the placement for my hands.

The first ball comes much faster than I imagined, and I don't even swing.

"Well then."

I adjust my position again, counting the seconds in my head before the next ball comes. Ten seconds go by, and another ball pops out. This time I swing and miss dramatically. I'm severely out of practice.

Another ten seconds, and the third ball fires at me. Swing and a miss.

After an unfortunate amount of swings and misses, I adjust my positioning on the plate, and finally hit one. The satisfying crunch of the ball against the bat makes the hairs on the back of my neck stand up. The ball flies off, disappearing into one of the bright lights above.

The night drags on, hitting one ball after another. I don't know if it's just this machine, but the balls tend to fly in slightly different directions, and don't exactly shoot in a straight line. I almost get hit at one point.

And the end of fifty, I fiddle with the machine and load up another fifty. I miss the first few again, getting into the rhythm, and then the crack of the bat starts to satisfy once again. I haven't seen anybody around, and the only thing I've been hearing is my tight breathing and the delightful smash. It brings a smile to my lips.

Nearing the end of my second set, the machine starts to act really screwy. It starts shooting balls way too high and way too low for me to properly hit. The best I can do is get a few bunts off.

I'm not sure how many more are left, but I'm debating stopping entirely when one ball starts flying directly at me, bearing far more left than it should be. My feet are frozen on the plate, only watching the thirty mile-per-hour death heading straight for me, and all I can do is stare. I clench with my bat, unable to do anything but pray for safety, when all of a sudden, the ball veers to the right. And not just a little bit, a complete 90 degree turn to the right, so close to me that I can feel the air ripping against my skin. The ball crashes into the fence near the entrance, the hit vibrating the entire squared fence.

I lower my bat, shocked by the abrupt change.

"What the hell?" I mumble, placing one hand on my hip, the other still holding my bat. I stare at the ball, now rolling on the sloped ground towards the grotto beneath the diamond. I've never seen a ball change trajectory like that before. How did that even happen? *Did* that even happen?

Before I know it, the ball thrower pitches out one last ball, and I only realize it when it strikes me in the leg.

"Fuck!" I scream, nearly collapsing to the ground. The ball falls flat at my feet and I limp out of the way, checking the settings for the pitching machine. There's a small number that reads "0" and I'm guessing that means that there's no more balls programmed to shoot at me.

I glance back to the mystery ball that snapped away from hitting me, now gone without a trace. I still don't understand what happened there. Maybe my mind was playing tricks on me?

"Shit," I groan, sitting on the ground, my leg throbbing. *I can't even think straight with this pain.* I slide down onto the dirt and check my legs. I managed to forget to bring any kind of athletic pants to Seven Oaks, not that I had many back home, so I thought that if I wore socks long enough to nearly meet my shorts, I'd be okay. I touch my thigh gently, finding that the ball hit the small few inch areas of pure skin, avoiding my socks and shorts entirely. Not that the fabric offers much protection, but this is just the cherry on top.

We're done for the day.

I force myself up to my feet and dust myself off, barely grazing where the ball hit me. There isn't a bruise yet, but there will be.

I tuck my bat back into my bag, not bothering to zip it shut, and I head out of my cage.

"At least I can still hit," I make note to myself, trying to see the positive side of this bulging ache. I have yet to lose those abilities.

I stray back to the concrete pathway, trying to gently press around my hit, wondering how big the bruise is going to be.

About the size of a baseball, I'd imagine.

The sun has managed to completely set in the time I was spending with the pitcher, and there are blaring lights illuminating every inch of the sidewalk. Until the bleachers, that is. It's an odd design choice, the soccer field on one side of the path, the football field the other, and the two sets of bleachers reaching up high into the air; it's like walking through a tunnel. It's weird to have this trapped walkway compared to the openness of the rest of the campus, and it's unsettling to have something so contrastingly dark. There are only lights underneath the seats of the stands, and they don't light the path very well. It gives me chills.

I stop dead in my tracks when I see two figures standing beneath the sketchy bleachers. I panic and hop behind the convenient concession stand, heart racing. I chuckle to myself a little, finding it ridiculous how on edge I am. This is a university campus with people crawling everywhere, of course there would be a few people hanging out by the bleachers; it's probably the most secluded spot around without disappearing into the surrounding forest.

I take a deep breath; the batting cages have me on edge. That's all.

Just breathe.

I nearly emerge from the shadows, until I hear their conversation floating through the air.

"Not yet," a thick voice says. It sounds like an older man, maybe even an adult. *You're an adult too, dumbass.* An *older* adult. It sounds controlled and calm, but very assertive.

"When?" a meeker man asks, his tone nearly disappearing into the soft breeze.

"Soon, hopefully."

My hand slowly reaches for my bat; there is a high chance that I am over reacting, but better to be safe than sorry. I silently slip it out of my duffel, only hearing the sound of air escaping my soft lips. I close my eyes for a brief moment and take a deep breath.

Calm down. Just walk past them.

It takes me a few seconds to find my courage before I triumphantly step back onto the sidewalk. I stand there, holding my bat in one hand, ready to "casually" walk past the two men, but I'm confronted with…nothing.

Nothing?

My stance relaxes, and I chuckle to myself; this Georgina situation is starting to get to me more than I thought.

"Hey," a voice startles from behind.

I immediately throw both my hands onto my bat and swirl around, ready to strike. A terrified Owen takes two steps back, holding up his hands. One of them is holding a plain white plastic bag with some takeaway containers inside, the other is open, palm facing me.

"Oh, shit!" he says, stumbling backwards. He peers over his raised hands, and in one smooth motion, I slide my bat back into my bag.

"Oh," I state blankly. Owen stands up straight, eyes wide. I break out a chuckle to ease the tension. "Sorry."

"Why do you have a bat?" he asks, looking a little too stunned for words.

"Sorry..." I don't know if he can see me blushing in this light. *Great way to keep friends, Kim.* "I was at the batting cages," I point to the diamond behind us, and his eyes follow. "And, um..."

I turn around and search for the figures, but they have vanished without a trace.

"You okay?" Owen's question draws me right back again. Between the weird ball mishap, getting hit in the leg, and the potentially cryptic-sounding conversation, it's been a hell of a night.

"Yeah," I snap too quickly.

He shifts a bit, taking a step closer to me, and drops his tone. "Yeah, it can get a bit creepy at night."

I arch an eyebrow, about to snap again, but I resist. Owen probably thinks I'm just in over my head, walking alone in the dark, and he could be right. He's trying to comfort me. I smile, giving in. "Yeah."

His expression eases, the corners of his lips curling up, and he sighs heavily. "Hey, let me walk you back to your room." He opens his mouth, about to add more, but instead just waits patiently for my response.

"Sure," I blurt out. It's probably better this way than accidentally batting someone else. "Okay. Thanks, Owen."

He nods a single nod and holds his arm out towards the small walkway nestled between the bleachers. I skip ahead of him and he quickly falls into stride next to me, now eyeing me cautiously. Neither of us say anything until we're halfway through the abnormally disturbing walkway.

"So, what were you up to?" I ask. Without a word, he holds up the plastic bag full of food that I had forgotten about. "Oh, right."

"Sushi," he supplies, licking his lips. "It's really good."

"I've heard." We step out of the dim domed area and into bathing light, nearly too bright to bear. "What's the sushi place called?"

"No idea, but it's the only sushi place in The Village. Have you tried it?"

"Not yet. Soon, though, because I love sushi." My stomach growls as soon as I say the word; I might be hungry.

"Definitely recommend it…" Owen's voice trails off and then he clears his throat, leading us through the forest. Unlike the small stretch between the stands, this part is nothing but magical at night. The street lamps are much smaller than the blinding stadium lights, and they emit a gentle orange glow, like I'm walking through some enchanted woods. The smell of fresh trees fills my senses, reminding me of long lost hikes that I used to take when I was younger.

"This is so pretty," I sputter, shocked by the change in scenery. I went from worried about being murdered to living in the middle of a fairy tale. "I haven't walked here at night."

"Me neither," Owen says. His voice matches the charming trees, calm and soothing.

The forest walk is too short, and I'm tempted to take a seat on one of the few benches inside, but I keep trailing along with Owen.

"So, you like baseball?" Owen changes the subject.

I laugh, meeting his eyes, and he utters a forced chuckle. I guess it's not as funny for him, since he's the one who I nearly beat with a metal bat.

"Yeah, I played in high school. Just found out about the batting cages, they're pretty cool."

"Yeah…" He quickly glances me up and down, taking in my outfit, and winces a little. The anxious side of me flares, and I habitually fidget with my shirt, tugging it away from my skin. I'm no stranger to the judgemental glances towards my body in general.

I clear my throat and Owen must notice my sour expression, because he chokes, too loud on our tranquil walk, "Sorry, just looks like you got hurt. You're limping a bit."

"What?" I'm even more surprised than he is. Thinking about the bruise makes it sore again, and I realize that I have been favouring my right leg. "Oh, yeah, I got hit by one of the balls." I shut my eyes and elaborate. Leave it to the teenage mind. "At the batting cages. From the pitcher."

"That must have hurt, are you okay?"

I nod, taken aback that he's showing concern. I still find it odd when anyone who isn't my mom shows concern or care for me. It feels strange. "Oh, yeah, I'm fine." *I've been hit by worse.* "But thanks."

Owen nods, glancing at my limping thigh once more before focusing back on the bending path.

We arrive back into civilization, the campus alive with club music. It is a Friday, so I'd be ridiculous not to expect some kind of party.

"Okay, cool," Owen says abruptly. He's acting a little weird, but I can't quite place why. He keeps toying with his sushi bag, tearing small holes into the plastic with his thumb. Maybe I'm not the only one on edge. "Hey, are you going to the homecoming party?"

My blank stare speaks volume, but I still add, "What?"

"Homecoming," he says, expecting me to know what exactly that is. "Did you ever have any homecoming parties at your school?"

I shake my head. Our school only ever had one dance, and it was fun, but it's not like the parties here. No drugs, no booze, and much more supervision. As pathetic as it sounds, I was friendlier with some of the teachers than my peers. I like to think it's because the school staff was, for the most part, exceedingly excellent. "No, but it's like a beginning of the year thing, right?"

"Yeah, exactly."

Owen and I walk along the side of the girl's dorm, and I realize the music is coming from my building. One of the girls must be blasting her music.

"When is it?" I ask.

"Next weekend. It's actually at the pool, should be a lot of fun."

"Like a pool party?" I wait for Owen to confirm before getting too excited. My course load, despite being five courses, is light and easy to handle; I could swing another party. "That sounds awesome, I'll definitely be there." *And this time, I have a few friends to go with.*

Owen exhales quickly, sounding like he'd been holding his breath for a long time. "Awesome."

The two of us stop near the steps leading into the building, into the entrance closest to my room. I place my hands on my hips, grinning. "Thanks for walking me home."

"Anytime." He laughs and flexes his arms inside his grey knit. "Hey, uh–"

A piercing scream comes from behind me, and I have to resist the urge to pull my bat out again. I whip around, getting real sick of the surprises of tonight, to find a stranger running towards me. She's at least three or four inches shorter than me, and she wraps her arms around my neck, embracing me in a weak hug.

"New girl," she squeaks, and I can smell the Palm Bay on her breath. "We're having a party." I follow the sounds inside, and it looks like the "one girl blasting her music" is actually the entire building.

"Okay," I mumble, craning my head to turn back to Owen.

The girl hanging from me suddenly grows extremely serious, and her voice drops an octave. "No boys allowed."

I face Owen again, ignoring the glaring expression of my new companion.

"I'll be in in a sec," I give in, and the girl squeals again, bounding off back inside. There's one girl left outside smoking, but I can't tell whether it's a cigarette or pot. *Looks like I'm going to a party tonight.* I hold my hands together, facing Owen again. "What were you saying?"

He laughs, rolling his eyes, and he runs his hands through his light hair. "I was just gonna say, if you ever want me to walk you home again…"

A smile unfurls onto my lips, widening across my face. My stomach flutters a bit, grin growing. "Thanks, Owen. You're a really good person."

"Guilty," he jokes. I try to catch his gaze, but I can't seem to make contact. "Looks like you better get inside."

"Apparently." I start towards the door, catching the short girl watching me like a hawk from the entrance. "Thanks again for walking me back. Enjoy your sushi and have a good night."

"You too." He holds a hand up to wave and then heads back towards his building, being careful not to swing his to-go bag too hard. He looks more tense than usual, but I can't blame him; I did potentially try to attack him.

I head into the girl's building, and the surprise party is in full swing. I don't know how it went from completely deserted to popping bottles and pills in just one short hour. The girl who hugged me is now running around the halls, making brief eye contact with everyone she walks by. She smiles madly when she sees me enter and then turns back around, disappearing into the crowd.

Holly, as if waiting for me, appears out of the group of girls to greet me. She's wearing a beautiful green sundress that nearly matches her eyes exactly.

"Hey, Kim." She peers quizzically at my duffel bag, and then scans my peculiar outfit. "Oh! You found the batting cages, eh?"

"I did," I confirm, feeling very underdressed for the occasion.

"Nice. Go throw your bag in your room and then come on out."

"I should get changed..." I reach for my key in the outer pocket of my duffel and slip it into the lock of my door. There's no way in hell I'm not getting changed.

"No, you look great," Holly counters.

I observe myself; I'm covered in dirt, and the circular pink spot on my thigh is more prominent than ever. My ankles are itching from the amount of dust sneaking between the fibres of my socks.

"Don't lie to me," I laugh, shutting the door on her before she can come in.

"I'm gonna go get us some drinks!" Holly yells, and I can only hear her because she's screaming directly into the doorframe. I'm still amazed at how little I can hear from outside my room; the bass from the speakers is thumping, but it's almost a relaxing beat and vibration. I might be able to fall asleep to this.

I strip down and throw my dusty clothes into my makeshift laundry hamper, which happens to be a cardboard box Holly was getting rid of the other day. I'm starting to run out of clothes, so I better load up on my quarters.

I slip into some linen shorts, pull the first top I find from my drawers, and slide into some flip flops. I check myself in the full-length mirror, my eyes falling to my thighs. Let's hope nobody notices the reddening meteor on my leg.

I carefully maneuver back into the hallway, and it is a lot busier than I thought it was. It looks like all the girls who live here must be in attendance, and at least twenty more on top of that.

Searching around, I spot Holly's unmistakeable hair flowing gloriously in the crowd. I head over towards her, finding her stopped by someone. When I get to her, she's holding two drinks in her hands, both of them pink.

"Hey," I accidentally interrupt. Both Holly and another girl, a tall brunette, make eye contact with me.

"Hey!" Holly exclaims, handing one of the clear cups to me. She almost spills some on me, my hasty hands just steadying the cup. "This is Gretchen. Gretchen, this is Kim that I told you about."

"Oh, hey," Gretchen says. She extends her hand to me and I shake it, mesmerized by her maturity. How she carries herself, her stellar posh lips, steady shoulders; she looks like she's already more successful than I'll ever be in my entire life.

"Hi, nice to meet you," I spit out. I wonder what first impression I strike upon people.

"You too." She twitches her lips, and something about her reminds me of Holly. There's something similar about the two of them, but I can't quite place what. Gretchen turns to Holly and says, "I'll catch up with you later, gotta go check on Vic."

"See you later," Holly jeers, giving her hand a tight squeeze.

Gretchen gives me a polite smile before disappearing into nothingness.

"She seems nice," I find myself saying, even though we exchanged no more than ten words.

"She's my cousin," she quips. *That explains it.* Holly sips her drink and then holds it up to me. "This is delicious, by the way."

"What is it?"

"Pink lemonade, vodka, and 7up."

I cautiously bring the tasty drink up to my lips. Georgina's words suddenly echo through my head, along with my own worries, and her fears spread to me. "And you got our drinks?"

Holly laughs, placing her free hand on her hip. "Yes, I did. One of the girls is making pitchers of it constantly, don't worry." I think that Holly and I have very different concerns regarding our drinks.

I hastily take a small sip, and I'm already hooked. It doesn't taste like alcohol, meaning it's a very dangerous concoction. "Wow, that's good."

"Yeah. I've had like four cups."

"Are you drunk?" I ask, stifling a laugh.

Her face suddenly turns very pale and she steps closer to me. "Why? Do I seem like it?"

My smirk grows. "Now you do."

Her jaw drops and then she snarls, scrunching up her face. "Just let me have fun."

I hold my glass up to her. "You got it."

Holly smiles wickedly, and we clink our cups together, chugging the entirety of our drinks. I can feel the fizziness gurgling inside my stomach the second I swallow the danger, but there's no turning back now.

"Let's get number five!" She plucks the plastic cup out of my hand and trots around the corner, where I'm assuming the drinks are being made.

Holly disappears as soon as she reappears, happily clutching two more cups of pink danger. I barely had enough time to people watch, seeing some of the girls passing around some pills and swallowing them in one swift gulp.

Woah.

"Here," Holly shoves my cup at me, barely getting it into my hands before she lets go.

"Thanks. That was fast."

"She makes them fast." She clinks her cup against mine and downs half of it in one sip. I nurse my own, my belly still swelled from chugging it before. I don't usually drink pop nor alcohol, so this is a pretty wild night.

"How was your day?" I ask, only now noticing what music is playing. It seems to be some playlist of famous songs that I remember from middle school, back before it got all petty pop. It's a comforting nostalgia.

"Boring. Classes are boring." Holly follows suit with me, now only casually sipping the remains of her drink. I found out rather quickly that Holly is brilliant when it comes to math; while I see the world made of stories and new ideas, she sees the world in numbers, where everything has a proper answer. I know where I'll be going if I need help with anything logical. "I miss summer."

I fancy going into the technical debate of 'it's still summer for another few days,' but decide against it. "What did you do in the summer?"

Holly pauses for a moment before exploding into a fit of laughter, and then shakes her head. "Well, now that I'm thinking about it, *this*." She continues to giggle and wipes some mascara from her eyes. "Parties. I think I mostly miss the beach. Have you been to the beach here?"

"Not for a long time." My eyes travel over to a group of girls dancing to an old beat, chanting along with the music. I love dancing.

"Well, if you're here next summer, we'll go. It's too cold now, it can sometimes get too windy there. What did you do in the summer?"

I turn to her and realize that our summers weren't that different. The occasional party, the beach, even going on a trip here or there. "Same as you. Beach. Well, not by the ocean, by a lake."

"A lake beach?" The disbelief in her voice shocks me. "That's a thing?"

I nod, chuckling. "Yeah. Less wind, and the water is usually warmer."

"That must have been fun," she mumbles, and finishes off her drink. She squints her eyes and stamps one foot on the ground. "Fuck, my drink is gone. I'm gonna get another." Before she can go back to get another cooler, a new song begins playing and hypes Holly up. "I love this song! Let's dance."

She tosses her cup into a nearby recycle bin, and I do too after I chug my second danger for the night. We mix ourselves up in the closely-knit group of dances, and after only a few seconds, I really begin to feel the vodka weighing heavily on me. My moves become more and more sloppy, my hips swing without rhythm, and my endless screaming along to the music, despite everyone else doing it too, is not my finest moment. The best part is that I don't care at all.

"I love parties with no boys," Holly screams at me.

I don't realize how enjoyable it is until she brings it up, but, "I do, too!" The pressure is so significantly less.

"Are you drunk?" Holly follows up.

"Kind of." I feel warm and tingly, and everything takes that extra second to register.

"Good!" She grabs my hands and draws us closer, swaying to the music.

I try to step closer, but suddenly someone roughly shoves me into her, and I stumble into her arms.

"Oh, hey," Holly jokes.

I laugh, standing up straight again and look behind me to a very apologetic looking Carolyn.

"Sorry, holy shit," she says, holding her hands up. Carolyn turns behind her, identifying who pushed her into us, and a random stumbling drunk appears, mis-stepping her way through the hallway. She manages to make her way to the stairs before collapsing.

"Guess she had too much," another students sneers, giggling away.

I step towards the struggling girl, but she's soon followed by two other girls who help her to her feet and up the stairs. My humble and wholesome Vancouver beginnings did not prepare me for the clear onslaught of parties that I will be attending. I haven't heard of any dispensaries here, unlike the West Coast, so drugs here must be pretty scarce. That doesn't exactly help with the safety aspect of it.

"This place is fucking wild," I finally say, the thought been nagging at me since last Friday's party.

I mean it sincerely, but Carolyn and Holly start laughing hysterically.

"We know how to party!" Carolyn screams, and all the girls surrounding us scream along with her.

"There you are!" a familiar voice calls, and Brit soon appears through the crowd. Marla is close behind her, holding her hand.

"We heard your call from miles away," Marla jokes, and I crack a laugh. She smirks, victorious. Her black hair is coating her shoulders beautifully, matching her impeccable eyeliner.

"I wanted to dance," Carolyn whines, and she latches onto Holly's hands. "Let's dance!"

"Yes!" Holly screams, and the two of them start dancing wildly; Brit hesitates, trying her hardest not to move to the beat, but she's failing miserably.

"I need some air," Marla states, releasing Brit's hand, but not before dramatically twirling her girlfriend towards Carolyn and Holly.

"Yeah?" Brit says, already dancing away. All of her tension has suddenly released. She tugs at her pink crop top, drawing it further down over her stomach, but it rides right back up.

"I could go for some air," I blurt out, partially so Brit feels less guilty, and partially because clean air sounds really good right about now. I make eye contact with Marla. "I mean, if that's okay, obviously."

"Yeah, of course."

"Cool," Brit says as she, Holly, and Carolyn find themselves further into the dancing group of girls; I could definitely get used to having girl's dorm parties.

I follow Marla's lead outside, using the exit back towards my own room. We step outside and the cool night shocks my skin. I immediately cross my arms over my chest, the sweat all over my body turning ice cold.

Marla takes a seat on the stairs, and I trot down them so we're closer to eye level.

"Sorry," she says and begins digging through her purse.

"For what?" I ask, hopping up and down to keep warm.

She finds what she's looking for and briefly flashes me a pack of cigarettes. "You smoke?"

"No."

"Then I'm double sorry." She places the cancer stick in her mouth and pulls out a purple lighter from her bag, the same colour as her tight dress.

"No worries," I chime, searching the darkened campus. I'm not sure if the lights are new, or if I've never noticed them before, but they seem brighter than before. Nothing like the sketchy path between the bleachers. I shudder at the thought of them.

"Cold?" Marla asks. I shrug it off. "It gets weirdly cold at night sometimes, eh? Like, the sun disappears, and all sensible heat does, too." I watch her take a drag from her cigarette. She seems to have this unspoken wisdom, and she carries herself with such grace; it's intimidating.

"Do you get a lot of snow here?" I planned partially for the winter, but my winter coats and boots took up a lot of my suitcase, so my mom said that she would send them later in the year, when I could actually use them.

"Yeah, a solid few months. Did you get snow in…" She flicks some ashes on the ground, crosses one long leg over the other, and meets my eyes. "Where were you from?"

"Vancouver," I respond, mesmerized by the flickering blaze reflected in her eyes. "And sometimes. It usually lasts for a few days before the rain washes it away…it rains a lot."

"Really?" Marla perks up, arching her back regally. "We don't get much rain here. And when it does rain, it's a storm. Lots of thunder and lightning. Try not to wear anything metal."

She chuckles a little, staining her cigarette with her lipstick once again.

"Guess I'll have to hide my metal jacket." I gaze off again; there are no students wandering around, but maybe the guys are having their own party. "Do you know how many people go to school here?"

"Nope." I turn to her, appreciating her blunt response. "I know that about a hundred students live on campus, and the rest of us live at home."

"How's the commute?" I'm honestly surprised and a little proud of myself for keeping the conversation going. Marla and I have quite different personalities; where she always seems to know what to say, I just kind of put words together and hope for the best.

"I carpool with Brit, so it's pretty nice." Her smile turns wistful and she closes her eyes, blowing smoke from her lips. I can see the attraction. "And not very long. You with anyone? Long distance?"

"No," I chuckle, rubbing my bare arms. I liked some guys back in high school, sure, but the unrequited love thing was my teenage destiny. I think part of me liked it better that way. "No, nothing like that."

"I'm sure you'll meet someone here. Everyone gets with everyone."

I whip my head towards her and she merely shrugs one shoulder and takes another drag. How is she managing to be this timelessly classy?

"What *is* this town?" I press, sniffing the mostly fresh air. I'm just on the cusp of Marla's ring of smoke, and through it, I can see two figures pattering towards us.

"Wild," she teases.

"Hey, it's you," one of the shadowy people calls out, and I stand up straighter, setting my arms down. I'm on high alert now. My tension heightens, but if anything, Marla's falls.

I wait patiently until Damien finally looks up from his drunken stagger and smiles widely. "It's been a while."

"It's been a week," I counter, hiding my surprise nicely. A hell of a week, but still just a week. I can smell the bitter beers from here, just as I'm sure he can smell the lemonade. I can still taste it on my lips.

"That's a while," he says, beginning to slur his words. The second figure pops out of nowhere, somehow even more intoxicated than Damien. I don't recognize him.

"Hello, ladies," the second guy says, baring a nasty and toothy grin.

"Oh, hey, Marla," Damien says. "How you doin'?"

"Fine, thanks," Marla says, her voice reaching higher. She discards the long ash built up on her smoke, and then sticks the cigarette back into her mouth. "You?"

"Good. Happy to see this girl here." Damien points back at me.

I don't think he knows my name. "Is that so?" I jest.

He laughs and stands up straighter, now clutching his letterman jacket on either side. "It is so. You know, we should go on another date."

Another? "Another? I don't remember the first one." Marla seems amused by this, and leans in closer, as if that extra inch will help her listen better to the conversation.

"Then we can just make out again," Damien says and licks his posh lips. "Maybe a little more."

His disoriented friend suddenly crouches down to the ground and puts his hands next to his mouth, amplifying his long and awkward "oh!" sound.

I roll my eyes, a little embarrassed. "Yeah, this is actually a girl's party," I find myself saying. I don't care if people know that we kissed, that doesn't matter to me, but my discomfort levels are rising. My shoulders tense and I take a step back; I especially don't like his friend.

"We should go out," Damien then says, as if this can save him, and takes a step towards me. I take a step back.

"No boys allowed," Marla says, enunciating every word carefully. She holds her cigarette between two fingers so effortlessly, just like a model.

As if he just realized that he's bothering us, Damien meets my eyes and holds his hands out towards me, like a man trying to calm a wild animal. "Gotcha," he says so quickly that it sounded like a click of his tongue.

Damien and his friend stagger off together, and in a few seconds, we hear them both laughing madly about nothing, I'm sure. I can't help but feel awkward from that entire exchange.

"You're pretty popular, you know?" Marla says suddenly.

That captures my attention, drawing it straight back from Damien. "What?" Marla nods, reassuringly. "Yeah, right."

"No, really, you are." At first I think that she's mocking me, as her dry humour would indicate, but she continues. "You've made friends really fast, you've apparently made out with Damien…"

"Once," I defend, not liking that I have to even defend whether or not I kissed someone.

"I'm not saying it like that," Marla counters, and my swelled temper calms. "Not at all. I'm just using it as an example. You're pretty popular here, you hang with Carolyn, Brit, now you're besties with Holly, I saw you talking to that other group a week ago, at the last party." Another drag.

"I'm just the new toy," I say, realizing that she might be right. I have made friends very quickly, even though it's felt like a long time. I try not to think too deeply into it; I don't know anyone well yet, and I knew Rose and Toni for years, and that ended horribly. I can't have that happen again.

"Whatever you say." Marla takes one last puff from her cigarette and then crushes the stub into the concrete. She tosses it into the dirt patch nearby, the moist dirt immediately eating it up.

"What do you do for school?" I ask, stepping closer to her again. I still feel gross from Damien's words, so I try to change the subject in hopes of distracting myself.

"Psych." She meets my eyes and smirks mysteriously. I should have guessed. "Gonna be a shrink like my mom. You're in writing?" I nod sheepishly, and Marla suddenly hops to her feet, now towering over me. "Figures."

I'm tempted to ask what Marla means by that, but I decide to let it slide. I give a brief eye roll and chuckle it off, trailing behind her back inside the dorm. She holds the door open for me, and the wave of humidity hits me again; I had forgotten how warm it was in here, a nice change from the freezing outdoors.

Marla and I meet up with our group once again, where Brit and Carolyn are still having a great time. Holly, on the other hand, doesn't look so great.

"Hey," Marla greets and leans into Brit for a quick kiss. "Having fun?"

"More fun now," Brit squeaks, clutching Marla's elegant hands. They start to dance together, swaying to the music, and Carolyn shifts her attention over to me.

"She had a few more drinks," Carolyn says about the red-faced Holly.

"Only two more," Holly says, her voice now strained. She does not look well.

"Are you okay?" I ask, grabbing onto one of Holly's flailing arms.

"Yeah, no, yeah, I'm good." She forces eye contact with me, and when her eyes finally land on mine, she forces a giant smile. "I'm good! Let's keep dancing."

"Are you sure?" I recognize this face from my own drunken misadventures. "We can go back to your room."

"No, I love this song!" she counters. I listen carefully and nostalgia hits again, but I feel like it's already been played tonight. The list must be on repeat. Speaking of, where is the music even coming from?

"She'll be okay," Carolyn says, bumping hips with me. "Nothing will happen under your watch."

Her indicative smile fades and she moves faster to the Gwen Stefani song, joining in with Marla and Brit.

This shit really is bananas.

Holly only lasts a few more songs before her face turns from red to green. Her dancing has slowed to hardly detectable movement, and it's like watching someone try to stay balanced on a tiny boat in the middle of the stormy ocean. I stay close to her, and the first time she dry heaves, I call enough.

"Let's go to your room," I say, now taking her arm gently in my hands.

"Yeah," Holly replies, not even bothering to fight me on this. She leans into me, and I excuse us from the other three girls.

"Feel better, Holly," Carolyn chimes, guilt spreading across her face.

"Have a good night," Brit and Marla each echo, both to Holly and me.

"Thanks, thanks," Holly replies, and we find our way to the nearby stairs. I finally see where the girl who's making drinks is set up, but she's long gone now. All that's left on the packed table are eight or nine empty pitchers, and three unattended full ones that make me nervous to look at.

Each stair takes Holly a solid few seconds to manage. She throws her arm across my shoulders and I help hoist her up to the second floor. Once we reach the first landing, it is foreign territory for me.

"Hey, which room is yours?" I ask, tugging her up the last of the stairs.

"Huh?"

"Your room number?" The second floor looks similar to the first, except for its absolute vacancy. On the left hand side, there's a lack of three or four rooms that's been converted into a common room that Carolyn mentioned to me, I think. The lights are off, but I can see shadows of a few couches.

"Oh." Holly tries to adjust her hair and briefly loses her balance, nearly dragging us both down in the process. "It's…eighteen."

"Okay."

We finally reach the top of the stairs, the music still blasting up on the second floor. It's especially loud right above my head, and when I look up, I see that it's been playing through the announcement speakers all over the building. I don't know who hacked it to work that way, but it's pretty smart.

"It's my lucky number," Holly says, giggling.

"What?"

"Eighteen," she repeats as I see her room nearby. Nice and close. "It's my lucky number."

"That's cool," I play along, her arm weighing down heavily on my slowly aching shoulders. My thigh twinges a little when Holly stumbles into me, but it's the first I've thought of it since I first entered the party. "Why is it your lucky number?"

"Well, it was." She abruptly stands up straight before her door and digs around in her pocket for her key. She pulls it out, and before even attempting to fit it in the door, she hands it to me.

"Why is it not anymore?" I pry, opening her door and letting her in first.

"Because." She takes two steps inside before making a bee-line for the bathroom. Her dorm is identical to mine, except flipped around. Her bathroom and closet are both on the right, her bed and desk on the left.

"Holly?" I trail after her into the bathroom, the door still thrown open, and find her vomiting into her toilet. "Shit."

I crouch down next to her and start to gather her hair. The smell makes me gag, so I swiftly crack the window open above her toilet and keep my head clear of the scent. I bunch her hair behind her and tug an extra elastic from off my wrist to tie down her luscious locks.

"It's okay," I comfort, gently rubbing her back.

I think she tries to say "fuck," but it's hard to tell with all the extra noise. The music is now flowing through the night air and in through the window, but Holly is not in the mood to dance anymore.

Holly flushes the toilet and sits back, scooting until she's leaning against her bathroom sink, black mascara smudges running down her cheeks. I settle in against the small patch of wall, mostly closing the door so I can see her.

"Are you okay?" I ask.

"Yeah," she chokes a little. "I feel a bit better."

"Good." I smile. "Do you have crackers or bread or anything like that? It could help, too."

"I want to talk about it, but I don't want you to judge me," Holly says, and for the first time in a long time, I'm speechless. I don't often find myself without words, but this is one of those times. "So, I'll tell you, but I don't want to talk about it." She holds her hands together, resting on top of her bent knees, curled up neatly against her chest. I wait silently, not sure whether or not to encourage her to speak. "My parents are getting divorced. They called me today. And, I don't know, are your parents divorced?"

I hesitate; I don't usually talk about my parents, or my dad at all, but Holly is opening up to me. I can't find it in me to go fully into it, but the least I can do is reciprocate a little. "Yeah."

She rolls her eyes, slapping her hands against her knees, and more tears stream her cheeks. "Yeah, so it's even more stupid. *You're* not freaking out because they're not together. I don't normally drink like this, I was just upset, and it's embarrassing, and, and..." Holly buries her face in her hands and starts sobbing hysterically.

I crawl by her side and put one arm around her, drawing her close. "We're not talking about it," I reassure, and her head pops up. "But this isn't embarrassing. Everyone drinks too much sometimes, I'm not judging you at all. Drinking doesn't make me think less of you, I don't judge you for it."

She sniffs and wipes her face with the back of her hand, rubbing the dark streaks along her cheeks. "I just wanted to forget about it. As if that could make it normal."

"Yeah, how dare a new university student drink a lot at a party."

She snaps her head up to me, shocked, until she realizes that I'm joking. She chuckles and rests her head on my shoulder. "It just...it sucks."

"Yeah," I comfort, relaxing my head on top of hers. "It does...did you at least have fun tonight?"

"Yeah, I did." Her voice is so fine and sweet, it makes me smile.

"Then, good! That's all that matters. You had a good time, you did what you set out to do."

Holly finally wraps one of her arms around me and nestles closer. I can definitely relate to drinking to forget. Not the best way to handle things, but sometimes one drunken night can help. At the very least, it gives focus in a new direction, away from the original problem.

"You're a good friend," she whispers to me, and a happy warmth fills my eyes.

"So are you."

I can feel her smile against me, and she finally sits up, stretching her legs out in front of her. "I think I should sleep."

I struggle up to my feet, ignoring the tipsy feeling I still have, and I help Holly up to a stand. I lead her to her bed, and she flops down onto the mattress just in time for me to move the sheets out of the way. I drape one sheet over her, thinking she might get too hot with any more, and then begin my room search for something to eat.

Digging through her backpack, I find a box of crackers and I put them near her bed.

"If you feel like eating, eat these," I say, waiting until she opens her eyes to see the crackers before moving onto the next thing. She already has a glass of water on her bedside table, so she's set. "And there's water here, too. Do you need anything else?"

"No," she mutters, already beginning to fall asleep. I can see her fading expression in the faint light of the bathroom. "Thank you for taking care of me."

I pause, feeling extremely vulnerable. I'm not very good at accepting compliments or gratitude of any kind. I never thought I was worth the time. However, I never lost hope in good things to come.

Maybe they're really here this time.

"Anytime," I conclude, smiling to myself.

Holly giggles to herself, shaking her head, and soon falls asleep, her mouth drooped open, breathing heavily. I quietly place her dorm room key next to her glass of water, and then tiptoe over to her bathroom, flicking out the light. She groans lightly as the switch clicks, but is back asleep within a moment.

"Good night," I whisper, carefully maneuvering the contents of her room. My shoe makes contact with her backpack, and I nearly have a heart attack from bumping into something, but I press on. I make it to the hallway, eyes burning from the change of lights, and ensure that the door is shut behind me. I even try to gain access inside again and happily fail.

Skipping down the stairs, it's like everyone took Holly going to bed as a sign to leave themselves. The music has gotten quieter, and there's only a few girls left dangling around, chatting with one another. The floor is dirty, but not as dirty as I expected. A few stains here and there, but the discarded cups have all been centralized near the overflowing trash and recycling bins. The rest of the hall is pretty neat.

"They're totally real," I overhear one girl say to another as I pass by.

"I don't believe it," the other girl says. "Maybe they exist, but visiting Earth?"

"Have you ever heard of NETRAD?"

"What?"

Ah, aliens. Totally real.

I grin at the thought, heading into my dorm room for the night. I'm surprised at my own room after seeing Holly's; I didn't realize how much I had observed in her busy room until I come back to my empty one. Her walls were plastered with different things, and she had her own coloured bedsheets. I really need to fix this room and make it my own.

I think that I haven't fully come to terms with all the freedom I have here. I had freedom back home, sure, but not like this. I can be a whole new person, as I've been so often telling myself. I can be myself, who I want to be.

Like Holly, I flop onto my bed, only burying myself beneath one single sheet. I slip out of my clothes, loving the feeling of the soft cotton against my skin after a busy night. And for the first time in a long time, I'm asleep within seconds, with nothing but lovely thoughts.

Chapter 6

Georgina is finally back at school after missing a week of classes. Our professors have apparently kept her up to date on homework, according to her most recent text, but we haven't had much to deal with anyway. Not to mention that she will probably be excused from most of the work, and rightfully so.

I had Ornithology before this class, where our prof, Mr. Evans, informed us that we will be dissecting our first birds next week. Each of us will get a different species of bird to dissect, and we will have one week to write a report and fill out information on said type of bird, as well as create a presentation for the class. I don't normally like presentations, but I am excited for this project. I was even thinking of asking Ronald to help me with it, since he clearly knows his stuff about birds. It would be a lot more entertaining than just going onto Wikipedia and copying down the answers.

I'm surprised to find Georgina in class, sitting alone at her usual table, so I start to approach her to say hi, but Ms. McKnight interrupts with a clear of her throat. Georgina and I only manage eye contact and a smile before I'm forced to sit at my own lone table near the back. This teacher intimidates me way too much to ever challenge her, even in such a lackluster way.

Ms. McKnight immediately stands from her desk and hovers before us, wearing her traditional black pencil skirt ensemble with a pop of blue in her blouse. She is probably one of the best-spoken teachers here, and her lectures are always captivating and intriguing, despite the fact that I'm not a fan of Shakespeare, our first unit of the year. The lectures also feel quick, another pro.

An hour flies by in the drop of a hat, and Ms. McKnight takes a seat on her desk, as she often does, and glances us over.

"We still have a few minutes left, so you can work on your presentations for next week," she says, and I can detect just a touch of exhaustion in her voice. Nobody in the class moves, and she throws her hands in the air, chuckling. "Now."

Georgina is the first to move, clutching her backpack, and she appears by my side, drawing up a chair to my table. She moves more quickly than I even had a chance to react to our prof's words.

"Hey," she says, settling in.

"Hey!" I sound over enthusiastic, and I try to calm my voice, but I am happy to see her. "How are you doing?"

"Okay." She pulls out her notebook and her copy of *The Taming of the Shrew*. I chose *Hamlet* myself, because it's the most recent work I've read. I always adore the plots of the plays Shakespeare comes up with, but the reading is not my taste. At all. "How are you?"

"I'm fine." I open my notebook up to where I've been writing notes about *Hamlet*. "Have you been…I mean, are you feeling okay?"

Georgina pauses and bobs her head from side to side. "I think so?" She gives me a scrupulous glance. "I don't know. I'm really confused. I still don't know what happened. The more I think about it, the more it doesn't make sense. But then it also makes a lot of sense. Does that make sense?"

My mind wraps around her words and I nod through the webbed speech. "Yeah. Yeah, I get what you mean."

"Honestly, I just want to move past it," she says, so flippantly that I'm a little taken aback.

I want to pry, but I know it's not my place. She knows what's best for her, and I'm not going to question that, no matter how much I want to. I just don't think I could. "Good for you," I conclude, speaking slowly and carefully. "Just...do whatever feels right for you."

She smiles, pleasantly surprised by my reaction, and she sits up straighter. "Thanks...so, why *Hamlet*?"

My eyes follow her gaze to my book, and I slide it closer to us. "Oh, uh, I just like it." I don't know Georgina all that well, and I'm not sure if she'll judge my lazy attitude towards Shakespeare or not. It's not like I'm lying, I do enjoy the story.

She holds up her book, shaking her head. "I chose this 'cause it's my mom's favourite, so hopefully she'll help me."

Our quieted giggles are soon interrupted by Mrs. McKnight projecting the words, "you are dismissed."

Most of the staff here don't care if classes are finished early or not, but Mrs. McKnight is the exception. We all learned real quick that there will not be a second wasted in this class. This professor is very old school.

Georgina moves double time to get all of her books back into her bag.

"Hey, thanks again for everything," she says, scrambling to get her items away. I don't think she has another class, so I don't know the urgency.

"Oh, no problem." I stand to my feet, slowly putting my notebook back into my backpack. "Just glad you're okay."

Georgina nods, tucking her chair in beneath the table. "I'll see you around, okay?" She smiles sweetly and is off again, shooting through the class. Outside the doors, I see a guy and a girl waiting for her, and the three of them wander off together, already chatting away.

I'm glad that Georgina has good friends, and I'm glad that she's okay. I don't know what I'd do in her situation, but I don't think I'd be able to move forward so quickly. Anything the slightest bit mysterious sends my head spiralling.

I pack up my things, and, as usual, I'm the last one out of the class. I head towards the front exit, hoping to skirt past Ms. McKnight without a hitch, but she stops me.

"Ms. Clay?" her crisp voice presents itself in the classroom, and I whirl around to face her.

"Yeah?"

She smiles gently and uses one finger to coax me closer, holding tight gaze with mine. I respect the hell out of her, but she is a bit terrifying.

"I read your paper for Mr. Ace's class, your opinion of Seven Oaks." She watches my reaction as she speaks, expecting something out of me, but I stay the same straight faced I've been all class. I've been told that I don't have the most expressive face.

"What did you think?" I prompt, suddenly feeling nervous. I don't particularly want her opinion, but something tells me I would get it either way.

"It was very well written. I'm excited to see what you come up with for...*Hamlet*, was it?" There is something knowing in her smile.

"Yeah, *Hamlet*." I always bring on a blush when a teacher compliments my writing. When *anyone* compliments my writing. "Well, thank you, I appreciate that."

"However," she states, and then picks up her travel mug of coffee. It has an abstract giraffe wrapped around it, something unique that I've never seen before. "Next time, I'd like you to write more to your own style, not what you think we'd like to hear."

I open my mouth, about to protest, but then I remember some of the bogus lines I put in there. *The residents of Seven Oaks are almost as delightful as the magnificent natural curiosities sprinkled throughout the town itself.* Mentioning the absurd amount of people who are okay with kids being hospitalized due to drugs and alcohol in this town didn't seem like the direction expected of my essay.

My shocked jaw tightens into a grin and I nod solemnly. "I'll work on it."

Amused, Ms. McKnight purses her lips, and sips from her African styled mug. "Glad to hear it. Enjoy the rest of your day, Ms. Clay."

"You too." I resist the urge to add her name in case she takes it the wrong way, so I strut out of the class to the deserted halls. It amazes me how quickly students vacate the halls once a class is over.

I head down the empty hall, making my way outside to what will probably be the last of the nice days. I've heard a few warnings about the unprecedented cold weather coming, and this blazing sunny day feels like the end of the era.

The air still smells like freshly mowed grass, even though the grass hasn't been tended to in a while, and the flowers are emitting one last glorious scent before dying off in the fall. It smells renewed, like the end of one chapter and the beginning of another.

My stomach starts to growl from all the scents, now catching a whiff of some kind of food. I had breakfast earlier, but that was six hours ago now, and two pieces of toast can only go so far.

I slow down near the parking lot, catching one of my new friends approaching. I bet he'll come get food with me.

"Hey," I call to Owen. He doesn't notice me, or even look up from his straight path. I skip a little in front of him, waving. "Hey?"

He perks up and I see the headphones in his ears. He chuckles, ripping the buds out, and then wraps them around his neck. "Hey, Kim. How's it going?"

"Good," I chime. "You?"

"Pretty good." He straightens his classic green jacket; it's starting to become his staple.

"Do you wanna grab food with me?" I ask before Owen can say anything else. I also realize that it's four o'clock, not a time that people usually eat any meal, except old people who eat dinner early.

"I can't," he says to my dismay. "I normally would, but we have this workshop today before class. I'm sorry."

"That's okay," I chuckle, taken aback by his genuine disappointment.

He sighs and checks his watch, and is interrupted once again, but not by me this time.

"Hey, Kim!" Holly bounds up to me, looking fresh faced as always. The lowering sun shines brightly on their faces; I don't understand how Owen and Holly have perfectly clear skin. Do people in Seven Oaks just not get acne?

"Hey," I respond; maybe something is in the water that will lead me too to clear skin.

"Oh, Owen!" Holly turns to Owen. "Hey. You know Kim?" She steps by my side, crossing her arms over her chest. *I forgot that everyone knows everyone. Except me.*

"Yeah," Owen says, chuckling. I can hear the music feeding through his headphones, some sort of loud instrument medley. "And you do too?"

"Oh, yeah." Holly gives me a tight hug, as if we've known each other for years. I kind of love it.

"How do you guys know each other?" I ask stupidly, and immediately regret it. "School, obviously."

"Yeah," Owen mutters, his cheeks flushed.

"And we have a few classes together now," Holly adds. Her eyes are scanning all over the place, and I realize that ever since I've met her, she's had this childlike curiosity that I share as well. It's nice to relate on that front.

"What's your major?" I ask Owen. I like asking that, it sounds so grown-up, but I'm also shocked I've never asked Owen before.

"I'm in for engineering," he says to my surprise. "Mechanical."

"Wow, that's really cool." I place my hands on my hips. "Do they have a good program here?"

"Yeah, it's not bad."

"There's so much homework in this class," Holly grumbles, unzipping her maroon coat. Standing still in the sunlight is starting to roast us. "It's not even hard, there's just a lot. It's stupid."

"Apparently it lessens as the year goes on," Owen replies to Holly.

I start to zone out of their conversation when I feel a chill against the back of my neck. I swipe my high ponytail out of the way, thinking it's some stray hairs, but the coolness remains. I turn around, confronted with the school parking lot. It's filled, as usual, and most of the cars aren't any older than about seven years old. It's a drastic change from my twenty-year-old van back home.

Amidst the flashy cars, most of them being white, oddly enough, I find two people in the parking lot. Two men, standing by a black town car. Expensive, classic, and without a single speck of dirt.

Both men are facing each other, standing in front of the car. One of them looks older, dressed in a charcoal suit, red tie, and white button up. The other is that douche bag who ran into me from before. It takes me a moment to place his face, but once I do, my expression hardens.

"Who is that?" I ask, unsure if I'm interrupting any conversation or not.

Owen and Holly both fall in line next to me, looking over the parking lot.

"Who?" Holly asks.

"The mayor?" Owen says.

"No, the kid." I point towards the jerk just as Owen's words catch up to me. I whip my head to him. "Wait, what?"

He shrugs, staring back at the two guys. "That's Mayor Livingstone."

"And that's Mason," Holly supplies, her voice low and cautious. "He's a jerk, you're too good for him."

I snort, widening Holly's eyes, and I say, "No, not like that." I cross my arms. "So, he's the mayor's son?" That could explain the entitlement and asshole-like behaviour.

"Yep," Holly laughs. "He's terrible."

"Shocker." Back home, the mayor of our town had a daughter who was an awful bully at my school. Spoiled, greedy, threw a fit if she didn't always get what she wanted.

Mason's face screams that same personality. "Livingstone, that sounds familiar."

"Their family has been running this town since it was founded," Owen says, sneering. He looks unimpressed by Mason's mere existence.

"Weird," I note.

As if Mayor Livingstone can hear me, his head suddenly turns over to the three of us gawking. It's hard to see any discernable features, but he looks to be smiling warmly. The dissatisfaction radiates from Mason when he glances over.

I remember the name from when I was little, and I think Mom used to be friends with a Livingstone, maybe even the mayor. It's strange how these memories slowly come back to me.

"Is that not weird?" I ask, keeping eye contact with the mayor. He seems friendly, from what I can tell, but his son certainly does not. Mason has his head cocked to the side, like he's looking to fight.

"What?" Holly says.

I seem to be asking that question a lot. "That one family has been running the town for however many years. Is that not weird?"

"Never really thought about it," Holly replies. She swiftly pulls out her phone and checks her screen. I stare blankly in her direction, emptiness filling my mind. I don't know what to say. *Is this some sort of monarchy?* "Hey, Owen, class starts in five. We should hurry."

"Right," Owen says. "It was good to see you, Kim."

Holly gives Owen an odd look, and then she faces me. "I'll see you later."

"See you guys," I mumble, eyes fixed back to the king and prince of Seven Oaks. Mayor Livingstone finally turns away, back to his son, and they continue their conversation. I can't tell if it's casual or serious; the two men have solid expressions in opposite emotions. "Have fun in class." By the time I turn back to my friends, they're already walking away together, and my words have rung to empty ears.

Chills are running through my spine, electrocuting all the way up to my brain. I can't tell if it's my anxiety talking, or the fact that something strange is going on, despite the constant reassurances of everyone around me. Not to mention the whole Georgina thing has me on edge; it doesn't make much sense, but then again, nothing seems to make much sense here.

Small towns always have secrets, according to every TV show ever. What makes Seven Oaks any different?

I try to shake the thoughts from my mind as I force myself to finally turn away from the Livingstones.

I need to get out of my own head.

I find myself wandering towards the cafeteria, stomach growling. Many of the tables are vacant, only a few people inside, but I still walk away; I think today is the day I try the famous sushi I've heard so much about.

Heading to the sushi place, the walk is a lot less magical during the day than it is at night. The enchanted forest looks more like any other forest; still beautiful, but the warm glow is gone from the precariously placed streetlamps. The sun shining through the trees is changing the colours on the ground, contrasting extremes. This time, however, I see a squirrel, and seeing any animal makes a good day.

The little squirrel hops up on one of the benches, even as I approach, perked up on his hind legs. It looks like he has a small nut in his hand.

"Hi," I coo, slowing my pace. I stop just before him and he stares ahead, oblivious to my existence. I crouch down and see that he has a pistachio; he's no stranger to humans.

The little guy pays no attention to me and starts to munch on his current meal, and I search for any other woodland creatures around. I spot a few more squirrels hiding in the bushes, none as brave as my new friend, and some birds are dangling in the trees above.

In a possibly stupid attempt, I place my hand next to the squirrel to see if he'll let me touch him. He pauses eating, a tiny piece of the shell hanging from his mouth and looks at my hand. He quickly turns away from me and starts eating once again, his chubby cheeks inflating repeatedly.

"Well, it was nice to meet you," I say, standing back up. "Enjoy your dinner."

I wipe my hands on my skirt and make my way through the rest of the forest. There's a couple walking towards me, and they promptly avoid eyes with me as we walk by one another. They seem awkward enough that they probably watched me talking to the squirrel, but I don't mind. I like animals.

Walking through the bleachers, I find myself rushing more than normal. I already walk at a brisk pace, but these bleachers freak me out. I glance to my left, thinking that I hear some ominous sound, but the secluded grass is merely filled with empty beer bottles that must be rolling into each other.

I emerge from between the stands, a shudder rolling down my spine, and I catch the batting cages off in the corner. By the way the fields are designed, it looks like the batting cages were purely meant to fill empty space with *something*. It works for me.

The short trek to The Village ends, and with the birds singing and wind bustling through the leaves, it's a very peaceful ending. Not many people are eating outside, but the shops are busy. The Starbucks is fully loaded, as are the other coffee shops, and unfortunately, so is my sushi place.

"Darn," I mumble, but still fight my way inside.

All the tables inside, which is only about ten of them, are packed with extra chairs, and there are eight or nine of us standing in the doorway. The restaurant isn't much to look at, and just has white walls, given one wall plastered with photos, wooden flooring, and mostly windows. It's very minimal, but it's charming, too. The kitchen is set up in front for everyone to see, and there are four employees working on different rolls along the long cutting board. It must be ten feet long.

"Hello!" a woman hollers, and I search around to find her.

"Hello!" a few other voices join in, but I can't tell where any of them are coming from.

A perky and petite Japanese woman comes up to me, an apron tied around her slim waist, and she smiles.

"Hello!" Her expression drops. "You're new. Have you been here before?"

Even the sushi joint that's been here for two weeks knows that I'm new.

"No, I haven't," I mutter, hiding my bitterness.

She smiles and snatches one of the paper menus from a stack on her hosting desk. Along with the menus, there's a computer, dine-in plastic menus, and three different card machines. She places the paper menu in my hand.

"Wave me down when you're ready to order, okay?"

"Okay, thanks," I reply, observing the menu. It's only one page, but when I open it up, I find that there's about a hundred different options. I drop my voice to a whisper, "Oh, wow."

I observe the many, *many* items available for purchase. After about ten minutes, and scanning over the thirty specialty rolls about thirty times, I have it narrowed down to two.

"This is so hard," I whisper to myself, in my own little sushi zone.

"Sorry, just gotta reach past you," a man says, his voice strained.

My head perks up at the sound of someone else talking, and I find myself face to face with Damien. He's trying to arch around me and grab a menu, but when recognition dawns on him, he stops, his arm stretched out next to me, and his eyes widen.

I haven't seen Damien since the girls' party on Friday, not that I even expected to see him then, and he wasn't all that pleasant.

"Oh," he says bluntly, and then takes a step back. It takes him another moment to remember to bring his arm back with him, and then he solemnly puts it by his side. "Hi."

"Hi," I say. I'm a little uncomfortable, but mostly because he's making this so weird. "How's it going?"

"Uh..." He looks around him as if he's trying to find someone to save him from this situation, but he ends up facing me again with a sigh. "Okay."

I narrow my eyes at him. He could at least be polite. It hits me that I've probably seen Damien around campus a lot more than I thought, since he's a part of the varsity jacket club. I wonder what sport he plays. "Okay."

I go back to reading my menu, pretending like I haven't been contemplating between two dishes. I focus really hard on the words, the font, the letters, in hopes of Damien just walking away. I never understood why it's so difficult for some people to be the most basic level of polite or kind. I've learned that if people aren't going to positively influence your life, then–

"I'm really sorry," Damien sputters, and I nearly get a jolt from hearing those words.

"What?" I choke back. I must have misheard him.

"About Friday." He scratches behind his head, flexing the muscles in his arms. I'm mesmerized for a moment before his arm comes back down. "I'm really embarrassed. I was such a dick."

I debate brushing it off, but instead I pull a me, and I risk the potential of making things worse for a cheap laugh. "I mean, you weren't *such* a dick. Kinda, maybe, but not *such*."

My risk pays off and Damien does chuckle, but I think it's mostly out of pity. "Well, either way, I'm sorry. It wasn't cool."

I don't know Damien well at all, but I wasn't expecting this from him. He struck me as the jock type who didn't really care about anyone, and that was fine with me. It was only a kiss. I've gotten more remorse from Damien's one thoughtless statement than I had from years of…

"Well, thanks," I say, finding myself rather pleased with this situation. "I appreciate that."

Damien breaks his first smile of the encounter, and his shoulders relax immediately. He just took a load off. "To make it up to you, let me buy you sushi." I arch my eyebrows and he holds his hands out gently, his expression softening. "Just as a peace offering, not a date."

"In that case," I begin, and start my search for the hostess from earlier. I give her a wave and she nods, scurrying over to us from chatting away with the kitchen staff. I meet eyes with Damien. "I'll get both rolls."

He doesn't fully understand what I mean, other than the fact that he'll be paying more money, so he just rolls his eyes. I should have checked with him to see if he was ready, but I'm guessing like most students here, he's frequented this place.

"What can I get for you?" the woman asks, drawing a notepad from her apron and a pen from behind her ear, hidden by her fine black hair.

"We'll be paying together," Damien says, pointing to the two of us.

"Oh, so one of your regular," the hostess says, jotting it down. Makes me wonder why Damien even needed to grab a menu in the first place. The woman perks back up at me. "And for you?"

I open my menu back up, forgetting the names of the rolls already. "Um, I'll have a Sea Serpent roll, without the wasabi, and a Cowabunga roll, please."

She nods, jotting it all down. "Okay, no wasabi Serpent roll, one Cowabunga, one classic with extra sauce, two tuna, two California. Anything else?"

"No, thanks," I say, and then turn to Damien. He shakes his head as well. My stomach growls when she reads off all that sushi, reminding me that I really need a more regular eating schedule.

"It'll be about fifteen minutes." She rips the page from her notepad and sticks it to the bar part of the kitchen, along with a long line of other orders. They must work fast if it'll only be fifteen minutes. She quickly steps back to the computer and waves Damien over.

While he's paying, I watch the four staff members rolling in the kitchen, but I a few more workers hiding further in the back, preparing the hot cuisine, I imagine. I hear the faint sound of sizzling along with friendly conversation.

Damien returns, sliding his credit card back into his wallet.

"Thanks, by the way," I say, surprised at myself for not thanking him earlier. "You didn't have to do that."

He shrugs and places his wallet back in his pocket. "Don't worry about it. The least I can do." I smile; this may not be a date, but any time with free sushi is aces for me.

Damien and I find a place to stand out of the way, me nestled against the wall near the front door, him facing me. He has his hands tucked into his pockets, frozen, and he's glancing around him, once again searching the room.

"Are you waiting for someone?" I ask, a tinge of guilt spurting.

He flashes back to me. "No, sorry." Maybe it was just the party atmosphere and alcohol talking, but he seems a lot less confident in himself now. *That makes two of us.* "There's some cool pictures on the walls."

I follow his outstretched point and the two of us walk over to a far wall, awkwardly standing in between two tables. It's one of the two walls not made of windows, lining the side of the building. The wall itself is a collage of old photographs, none of which have any captions, but I'm immediately drawn to one black and white photo, blurred and aged. It depicts two people standing outside, in a forest, I think. The contrast is very strong, leaving little gray, only black and white.

It looks like the two people are standing in the middle of a circle of trees, and there's something in the ground below them. Their faces are difficult to make out, but I think they're both men, and one of them is holding a shovel. One of them, the one at least three inches taller, has an arm around the other, draped across his shorter friend's shoulders.

"What's this one?" I mumble, placing my finger on the wall. I feel a slight shock when I touch it.

Damien peers over my shoulder, his minty breath filling my senses. "That's the founder of Seven Oaks, Manfred

Livingstone. It's apparently the first day he decided to do construction for our town."

I look at Damien, bemused. "Wow, you sure know your town history." I don't know a single thing about Vancouver.

He rolls his eyes. "I should, they've shoved it down our throats for twelve years. These pictures are everywhere."

Damien steps back and I fall back with him. Despite that we're blocking access to a lot of the restaurant, nobody seems to notice or mind. Everyone sitting over here has their sushi anyway.

"Who's the other guy?" I press.

"His brother. Clint, I think." Should *I know things about where I grew up?*

"And what's that?" I step forward to point at the dirt in the ground jutting up before the two brothers. There's a pure white spot in the darkened soil, a perfect flash.

Damien leans in closer. "Dirt?" He chuckles, crossing his arms. "Those are the Seven Oaks, there." He points to the seven saplings circling the two men. "They wanted to dig up right in the middle of the circle as their first ground breaking." He laughs again and holds my arm, tugging me back further away. A couple enjoying their sushi get up in the now free space, and sneak by us to get to the cash register to pay. "Trust me, you'll learn all of this at our Seven Oaks Festival this winter." *How appropriately named.*

"Can't wait," I mutter, still stuck on the white dot. I search along other pictures, finding a similar white dot in a picture of the pristine beaches; must be a lens flare. "This is really cool, having all these pictures up."

"A lot of stores do. Most that were constructed by the government have a wall dedicated to our town history."

"Is that weird?" I ask genuinely. A lot of things have struck me as weird so far, but I'm sure most things that I'm used to would strike everyone here as odd, too. I don't even think twice about the blunt query anymore; I just need to know what's normal and where I stand on things.

"Not in Seven Oaks. It's not always pictures, sometimes it's a mural, wood made from the oak forest, stuff like that."

Damien suddenly whips around behind him, and the tiny hostess from earlier appears, holding two plastic bags. I don't know how he noticed her, or how she just appeared out of thin air, but the thought of sushi now has me salivating.

"Soy sauce and chopsticks inside," she says, handing the bags to Damien.

"Thanks," he replies, nodding graciously.

The hostess without a nametag beams widely before returning to her post. It looks like she might be the only hostess and server working here; she must be constantly busy, but she seems so cheery.

Damien signals to the door, and I follow him out, sliding past all the other students waiting for their sushi. I don't recognize most of the people waiting, but I remembered that The Village is shared by all the campuses, which means us first years are not the only ones impatient for raw fish.

Once we're outside in the fresh air, Damien hands me the smaller of the two bags, the one containing my rolls. The area is still deserted, with only a few students entering and leaving shops. There are some picnic tables and benches set up in the middle, but nobody is sitting on them today.

"Thanks again," I say, and he begins to slowly walk away, nodding towards me to follow. I fall in step next to him.

"No problem," he says, his fingers wound tightly around the plastic straps. "Have you had this sushi before?"

"Nope." I try to catch a whiff of my food, but the smell of sushi isn't always exactly potent. "I have high expectations, I've heard it's delicious."

"It is, it's really good." I can almost hear his voice quiver with anticipation. "We have Sushi by the Sea back in town, too, but the chef actually moved to this location."

It takes me a minute to realize that the restaurant is called "Sushi by the Sea." Everyone up until now just referred to it as "the sushi place."

"Are you serious?" I gawk. The love of fish is apparently strong in this town.

Damien laughs, flashing his perfect teeth, but something about it feels forced. "Yeah, I think some students petitioned it."

"Wow." I chuckle, scanning around the campus. "Impressive."

"That's one word for it," Damien scowls.

I'm taken aback by his tone; as far as I know, everybody loves it here. Am I starting to find a tear in this perfect painting of a town?

"What, you don't think having a sushi restaurant built is worth a petition?" I half mock. We round the corner at the batting cages, heading towards the fields. The soccer field on the right is empty, but the football field has two dozen players lining along, next to a single man wearing a hat and a gray ensemble. I knew we had a football team, but I'd never seen them practice.

"It's all just so self-serving," Damien says, his tone dropping again. "Back in high school, everyone would throw a big fit about something stupid, like our broken frozen yogurt machine, and we would get it fixed. Like it's some big victory." *They had a frozen yogurt machine?!* "It would just be nice if we cared about actual problems."

I stop in my tracks, so dumbfounded by his words. Everything I heard about Seven Oaks was the charmed lives of the students here, no one dare criticized. Or, maybe I'm just finally fitting in enough to understand their lives.

Damien halts, realizing I've stopped, and then turns around. He looks ashamed. "What?"

I find myself pointing to the bleachers overlooking the football field. I'm not entirely sure why I ask, but I think it's because Damien is really piquing my interest right now. I think I want to pick his brain. "Want to eat with me on the bleachers?"

He arches an eyebrow. "Bleachers?"

"Stands," I correct. I forgot how language can differ from coast to coast.

He glances at the football stands, then back at me, and nods. "Yeah, okay."

I lead Damien and myself up towards the metal bleachers, find the first stairway, and head up. My boots clang loudly against the silver metal, so I try to step lighter, and we make our way to two rows from the top. I slide in on the bench, leaving plenty of room for Damien and his food, and we start to unpack our takeaway.

I open both my Styrofoam containers of sushi, and I am not disappointed. It looks incredible. However, I did not pay attention to how much it costs, which may be my downfall.

"So, what else can you tell me about this town?" I ask, settling into my seat. I lean against the bench behind us and set one of the rolls on my lap. I pull out a packet of soy sauce and drench the raw fish and rice.

"What do you mean?" Damien says, already beginning to devour into his meal.

"I mean, I don't know very much about it. I was born here but left when I was young." Thank goodness nobody has asked why I moved away yet.

"*That's* why you got accepted," he chuckles and meets my eyes. He says it more as a confirmation than anything else. "You're the only first year who didn't go to Seven Oaks High."

My suspicions have been confirmed. "Yeah, I figured."

"What do you want to know?" Damien has already finished one of his tuna rolls before I have even taken two mouthfuls of my first roll. He must have been starving.

"I don't know." *What* do *I want to know?* "Any other petitions?"

He sighs, taking a break from eating. "Yeah, sorry. I want to go into environmental law, so looking back, we wasted a lot of time on stupid shit."

"Environmental law." I'm in awe. I continue eating, the roll occasionally slipping from my chopsticks, thanks to my rusty skills. "That's really cool. What made you wanna do that?"

"My mom is an environmental lawyer, I've always been into it with her. We're lucky here, Mayor actually gives a shit about the trees, ocean, animals. Lots of protected forests, but there's still more we can do."

"But, I mean..." I clear my throat, swallowing my delicious bite. "Think of the yogurt machine." Damien snorts, and I fear I've gone too far, so I add, "But good for you. Could always use more people looking out for the world."

"Thanks." He straightens his back and sets his shoulders, like a peacock showing off his feathers. "What are you here for?"

"Writing." I finally gaze down towards the field, watching grunting players perform drill after drill. "Well, English, I guess." I find my eyes stuck on the field, each carefully and meticulously painted line, number, each filed blade of grass kept at the perfect height. Frankly, I'm not super interested in giving Damien my life story; I more want his. "What else should I know about Seven Oaks?"

Damien shrugs, chomping so viciously that a grain of rice falls from his mouth. He wipes his lips and glances up at the football players. "What you see is what you get." Out of all the answers I expected, that was not one of them. "Most people are pretty well off. Lots of parties, booze, weed, ex." That must have been what the girls were taking the other night at our girl's party. "Hey, uh…is Georgina okay?"

I cough on my sushi but force it down my throat, swallowing roughly. "What?"

He bites his lower lip, narrowing his eyes. The sunlight gleams in his buzzed dark hair, glowing on his rich skin. "Georgina. I know you're the one who helped her out, right?"

"Yeah…she's doing okay." I don't know how much I should say, so I try to hold back on many specifics. "She's back in school now."

"Oh, really? That's good." He smiles calmly to himself, opening his second box of rolls. It must be the classic roll the hostess mention, unless it's a really fancy California roll.

"Are you guys friends?" I pry, sensing something deeper.

"Kind of. I mean, we talk sometimes. Glad she's okay." His eyes are focused on his meal, not that I can blame him.

"Me too." I decide to push this further, craving more information about this school, these students. Before my brain can fully catch up with my words, I find myself saying, "Do you think she was drugged?"

Now it's Damien's turn to cough on his food, except he actually starts choking. "What?!" His voice is hoarse, so I wait for him to calm down. *You pushed too far, Kim.* "*Was* she drugged?!"

"No, I'm just asking." I probably shouldn't spread news around like this. I delicately eat another piece of sushi with Damien fuming next to me. *Way too far, Kim. Way too far.* I face him again. "I don't know this town, okay? Kids didn't overdose at my school and then act like everything was fine. It just seems weird to me. We have lots of dispensaries in Vancouver, so it's usually safe, so..."

He shakes his head, the tension slowly leaving his face. He coughs one last time. "We don't have anything like that. There's a grower just outside town, we get our shit from him. Only place to get it, he's been growing and dealing for years, and he wouldn't do that."

"Okay." I sense his defensive tone, so I try to diffuse the situation. "Sorry. It was just scary seeing someone like that, I've never seen it before."

"Well, it happens." His words are certain, but his tone is not. I feel bad for striking a chord with him. "You should have seen our grad, at least four people got way too fucked." *Lovely.* "What do you expect? Small town, not much to do."

"That's what Georgina said," I say, hoping to lighten the mood. I have a bad tendency to overshare; I need to keep that in check. I decide to change the subject. "You know, I'm still so surprised how fast this place got built, and how it runs so well. It's crazy."

It's hard to believe that it was only two short years ago when the mayor announced he would be building this school.

"Yeah, but we know why it was built so fast." He looks smug and arrogant, an expression he wears shockingly well. It gives me knots in the pit of my stomach. Even so, that's another thing I've seemed to notice; it's very easy to get people onto a different topic. Definitely a double-edged sword.

"We do?" I urge.

Damien nods, exchanging his second empty box for his third and last one, the two California rolls. I start into my second roll as well. "For Mason."

A shiver runs down my spine, my bare arms suddenly chilled. "Mason?"

"Yeah, he *is* the mayor's kid. You met him?"

I'm not sure if him running into me and giving me dirty looks constitutes as meeting him. "Kind of."

"He's not bad." *Had me fooled.* "Entitled, being daddy's little boy and all, but most of us are."

My mind is trying hard to keep up with Damien's thought process, but I'm getting all turned around. "Wait," I stop. "You're saying that the mayor built a whole university so that his kid wouldn't move away?"

"Yeah," Damien replies casually. I wait for more, but he just continues eating. I pop a piece of sushi into my mouth, mulling this over.

"Isn't that insane?" Sugar coating times are over.

"Yep." Damien's eyes are fixed on the hustling football players, but not focused on any one of them in particular. I feel like some young padawan being regaled with wisdom from an elder. "Apparently his brother moved back, too, can't remember his name. He's fourth year."

"Wow." I can't think of anything else to say. It's starting to feel more and more like I'm in some bizarre dream.

Damien finishes his food and stows the empty containers into his plastic bag, picking up all his trash. "Look, I gotta get going, but it was nice talking to you." I'm not sure if he means it, but I let it slide. I have other things on my mind now.

"You too," I say, smiling. "Thanks again."

"No worries." He places his hands on the bench and leans down close to me, his lips only a few inches from mine. I can smell the mint on his breath, and his coffee eyes are something I could get lost in any day. *What is happening?* "You're pretty cool, Kim. You just seem...real."

"Thanks," I sputter, hoping he doesn't catch the blush that I'm letting on. "And thanks for telling me about Seven Oaks."

He smirks his signature smile, the one that spikes my heart a little, and swiftly pecks my cheek. "I'll see you around."

"Bye." I hold a hand up to wave, but he's already trotting down the stairs. I watch him down and he disappears behind the bleachers, and...what was I thinking about?

...

"...Mason," I remind myself, getting my mind back on track. "Mason..."

I contemplate the facts I have, slowly picking at my second delicious roll. I think this one is even better than the first one, fully earning the Cowabunga title.

I definitely got the entitled vibe from Mason, and it's all making a little more sense. His dad apparently built an entire university for him so he wouldn't move away. It must be overwhelming to have a father do that for his kid. I can't even imagine going to that kind of extreme.

Still, I can't shake the feeling that there's something else going on, something unspoken, but maybe that's my creative side talking.

I finish up with my sushi, enjoying watching the bulky football team fulfill their practice needs. It's hard to see any familiar faces with all the helmets on, but when I trot down the bleachers and toss my trash away, one of the players waves at me.

He looks to be the same height as the people around him, maybe shorter. Other than that, there's nothing distinguishable about him. I still wave back, bearing a grin, and he returns to his practice. Their coach, an older man with a clipboard and a gray track suit that looks like it's from thirty years ago, starts making the team run lines back and forth on the field. *I might make it across one end of the field before I keel over.*

I walk past the bleachers, avoiding the dim pathway in between, and I head back into the enchanted forest. The lamps have turned on now, but it's still too light out to feel the magic glow. As I enter the narrow walkway, I find somebody else approaching me. I return to staring back down at the ground, until I notice his features.

Speak of the devil.

Mason is walking towards me, a fire in his eyes. He's dressed in his football jersey, shoulder pads, the whole nine yards. He has his helmet beneath one arm, and his cleats are stomping violently on the concrete. It's an uncomfortable crunch that makes me squirm, but I try not to show it.

Passing Mason, he once again nudges me in the shoulder, but it's much more forceful this time because he has giant shoulder pads on.

I stop in my tracks, thinking that I should let it go, but instead, "What the fuck is your problem?"

I'm not facing him yet, but I hear the squeamish sound stop. My shoulders relax, one of them sore from his touch, and I whip around. He too turns around, slowly, less than impressed.

"Excuse me?" he says.

I must show surprise at his voice, because he immediately looks offended at my reaction. I can't help it; I didn't expect his tone and pitch to sound so…weak. I think I pictured a deep voice to match his intimidating demeanor. I'm a lot less afraid of him now.

I try to think about why he's so stuck in my head. I barely know him, and a stranger like this shouldn't bother me so much. It hits me all at once, like a ton of pretentious modern bricks; I don't understand him. He's a mystery, and I am not good at letting things go unsolved.

"Why are you such a dick?" His eyes widen and his jaw sets. He steps a little closer to me, showing his not-much-taller-than-me height. I wish I had my bat right about now. I try to keep my voice calm, despite being alone in a forest with nobody else within sight. That was always the best thing about walking home from baseball practice, always having a faithful defense with me. "Stop running into me, I don't even know you."

His eyes are an icy green, stone cold, and his lips have much more colour than the rest of his pallor. "Then why don't you stay out of my way?"

A snake. He sounds like a snake.

I scoff, purely out of anger, and take two steps backwards. "Why don't you fuck off?" I retort back, holding my hands out. I whirl around on my heels and continue through the forest, listening for that awful sound of concrete beneath his feet. After a few seconds, his strut starts up again, but it's only getting quieter.

Feeling brave, I turn around and he's walking away, his head held high, like nothing happened.

I face forward again, exhaling a breath I didn't even know I had been holding. Mason Livingstone, son of the mayor, daddy's boy.

Potential future mayor.

I shudder at the thought. A lot of things confuse me about Seven Oaks, and Mason is starting to climb to the top of my list. Something is definitely not right about Mason Livingstone, and I'm going to find out what.

Chapter 7

Even after all this time, the most satisfying sound in the whole wide world to me is the sound of a bat successfully smashing its target. *Smaaaaash*; it is truly the most freeing feeling on the planet.

I've hit nothing but homers tonight. I've been on such a roll that it's been almost two hours. My arms are starting to feel like jelly, along with my twisting hips, but it's such a release.

I came out to the batting cages around sunset, expecting their constant vacancy. This time, however, I opted for a different pitcher, and it didn't give me any problems. No bruises that are now a massive ugly circle of yellow and brown, and no balls inexplicably flying off at a right degree angle.

No nonsense. Just perfect hitting.

After my fourth set of one hundred, I approach the machine to set it up again, only to find that my arms are quivering from exhaustion.

"Better call it quits," I mutter to myself, patting the small control box. I approach my duffel bag and slide my bat inside it up, nearly finished zipping when the bag begins to vibrate violently. I fish around the giant space and pull out my brick of a phone.

I'm expecting it to be my mom, since we talked on the phone earlier, but it's…Carolyn?

"Hello?"

"Hey, it's Carolyn," she confirms. Her voice sounds different than I expected on the phone, higher pitched, but so does mine.

"Hey, what's up?" I stand up and throw my bag over my shoulder, leaving the secluded batting cages. It's gotten dark out now, so I follow the zig zag pattern of the alternating lights above, always straying in the path of light.

"Are you busy right now?"

"Um…" I search around me, thinking I hear a noise, something rustling around me, but I can't find anything. *Damn nerves.* "I will be in, like, fifteen. Why?"

"Me, Brit, and Jay are going into town. Wanna come?"

Jay.

Jay?

Jay!

"Sure!" I chuckle, until I notice I'm approaching the bleacher path. I make a quick divert to the right, opting to use the bright football field lights at my guide.

"Have you been to town before?" Carolyn asks. I can hear someone in the background, probably Brit chatting away.

"Not to explore, not since I was a kid." A small gust of wind chills the back of my neck, a shudder rolls down my spine.

"Huh?" She pauses. "Oh, right. Okay, well, cool! There's this really good dessert place, we're gonna go there, maybe go to the beach. Meet us in the parking lot when you're ready."

"Okay!" I'm not sure about going to the beach, since I'm chilling down quite quickly in my long socks, but I'll be sure to dress warmly. "I'll see you soon."

"Thanks, Kim," I hear Brit yell into the phone. After some short rustling, her voice becomes crisp and clear. "I owe you."

Before I can ask what exactly Brit owes me, she hangs up, and I'm left alone in the magic of the forest.

My walking speeds up, now excited to go into town. The only time I've been there was to visit Georgina, and that was a short hospital visit and then to the grocery store. I'm wondering how much more of the town will come back to me this time.

I get to my dorm room, stumbling inside, body shivering from the cool night. I chuck my duffel bag onto my bed, and immediately strip down. I fancy wearing a dress, but knowing how cold it's going to be, I choose a traditional fall outfit. I fit snuggly into some leggings, grab some flannel, and fix my hair in the high pony tail it was in. After ensuring my makeup has not failed too much, I snatch my purse, sticking my phone inside, and I head out the door. I tug it shut twice, just to be extra safe, and I head towards the parking lot.

I can't help but speed towards the parking lot, partially because I'm excited to explore more of my old town, and partially because the campus at night still gives me the creeps. Nobody seems to be out and about on this fine Wednesday evening; it's a ghost town.

When I get to the top of the stairs leading down, I spot four people hanging around an older looking car. I can't tell who the fourth person is, but three of them are my companions for the night.

I trot down the steps, finally able to focus on their features. Owen is the mysterious one, and he's dangling a set of car keys in front of Jay, looking very serious.

"Kim!" Brit calls, looking more ecstatic than ever to see me. She throws her hands in the air and then charges at me, tackling me into a hug.

"Hi," I spit out, shocked by how such a tiny person can knock the wind out of me.

"Thank you, oh, my god," she whispers. We're mostly out of earshot of the other three.

"For what?" I whisper back.

"Saving me."

I'm about to question her further when she releases me, clutches onto my hand, and drags me towards the silver…car. I don't know anything about cars, all I know is that it's not a truck.

"Kim's here, we can go!" Brit chimes brightly.

I'm still confused what's going on, and Owen matches my level of surprise.

"Hey," I greet everyone, gripping onto my purse. "Um, thanks for inviting me." I briefly make eye contact with everyone, though I'm not quite sure who to thank.

"You're coming?" Owen asks, looking more than a little surprised.

I blush and nod, feeling a bit guilty. Judging by their reactions, Owen and Jay seemed unaware of my invitation. "Yeah, if that's okay."

"Of course it is!" Carolyn chimes in. She and Jay are standing pretty close together, and with the help of Jay's awkward expression, I think I'm starting to figure out what's going on here.

Date gone wrong.

"In that case," Owen says, a grin appearing on his lips. He faces Jay and clutches his car keys tightly in his hand. "I'll drive."

Jay gives him a nasty look but agrees with the roll of his eyes. "Sure."

"Whose car is this?" I ask meekly, checking out the back seat. Looks like the girls will be squished in the back seat.

"Mine," Owen confirms, walking around it and unlocking the doors.

"Mine's in the shop," Jay grumbles, taking initiative to snag the passenger seat.

I turn to Brit and we exchange a knowing glance; enough said.

Carolyn opens one of the back doors, holding it open for us. She asks the question that's on my mind, "Who's going in the middle?"

"Brit," I reply, turning to her. Wide-eyed and confused, Brit drops her jaw at me. "You're the shortest, it only makes sense."

"Agreed," Carolyn says, grinning.

Brit reluctantly shuffles into the car and I walk around the other side, reaching for my door. Before I can open it, in a pleasant gesture, Owen grabs the handle and pulls it open for me.

"Thank you," I say, offering a small curtsy. "What a gentleman."

He rolls his eyes, ensuring I'm safely inside before shutting my door, and then gets into the driver's seat.

Us girls struggle to get all of our seatbelts done up, but once we do, there's actually a surprising amount of room. It's a nice car.

"So, Benny's first?" Carolyn wonders aloud.

"Yeah," Jay says and clears his throat.

"I want to go to the beach afterwards," Brit says. Carolyn and I can make clear eye contact over Brit's head; I never realized just how short she is until now.

"That sounds like fun," I add. I'm not sure if I'm allowed to contribute to the group consensus, considering I might just be a tagalong, but I offer my opinion anyway.

"Sure!" Owen says, his enthusiasm greatly higher than it was before.

Jay sighs, leaning his head against the passenger side window. He tries to catch Carolyn's eyes, but she doesn't notice, being in the seat directly behind him. The question is, did she know it was supposed to be a date?

The drive into town is significantly different in a car, and extremely peaceful at night. There are seldom lights along the secluded road, so Owen keeps his high beams on most of the time. Back home, Mom and I used to go on drives all the time growing up, and my favourite drives were like this, surrounded by darkness. I always kept my eyes stuck on the road, just in case any wildlife decided to pop out in front of us. There were lots of deer and coyotes back home; I have yet to see anything but birds and squirrels here, and Carolyn's unconcerned warning of cougars briefly enters my mind.

Seeing a cougar would be terrifying.

My eyes are fixed to my window the entire time, my head resting on the frame. I watch the trees go by in a charcoal streak, hearing remnants of the conversations I'm not a part of. The evening feels calm.

Soon the streetlights appear again, and the Zen is gone. The trees turn back to dark husks of green and brown, and the car begins to slow at our first stoplight into civilization.

"Why are we even stopped?" Carolyn says, squeezing past Brit to lean towards the front of the car. I catch Jay briefly catch her attention before he blushes and faces forward again.

"Typically, red means stop," I mumble, not even really thinking. My eyes grow huge when I realize what I just said, and I have Brit, Carolyn, and Jay all staring at me, jaws dropped. I guess I shouldn't start sassing people yet.

"Fuck off," Carolyn says with a chuckle, and the rest of the gang break out into laughter. I'm met with so much relief that I can hear my heart beating. I giggle along with them, pushing away the urges that this is a trap, and I regain my cool. "I meant, why is the light red? There are no other cars around."

"Sensor isn't working here," Owen states flatly. He points at orange and white pylons along the crossroad, and construction tape marking the area. There's a lot of loose concrete on the ground, but no tools around, as if someone stabbed the road with a giant drill and let the pieces fly where they may. "Doing construction or something."

"Looks like a crack in the road," Brit says, leaning back in her middle seat.

"Drilling for oil," Jay jokes.

"Looks like lightning struck it..." My voice trails off, staring at the oddly shaped markings on the ground. I've never seen a tool that could create such a distinct crater, but I also know little to nothing about construction.

Owen thrusts the car forward, the light finally turning green, and we are led into a sea of green. All the lights as far as the eye can see are green, accenting each and every little shop on this strip in a minty haze.

"It's so pretty," I find myself saying, head pressed against the window. The streetlamps have that same soft glow as in the enchanted forest, and they look more like tall garden lanterns than anything. There are trees planted on both sides of the street, thriving in their minimal environment, and they look to have some Christmas lights in them. None of them are lit up, but it's only September.

"I guess," Carolyn says. I debate arguing, but instead, I lose myself in the small-town charm.

I didn't go so far into town when I visited Georgina, but a few shops are triggering some memories. Laney's Ice Cream, where my mom and dad would take me out for ice cream. If I remember correctly, there were some other ice cream parlors, but Laney's was the best. They had this delightful waffle cone bowl that they filled with ice cream and a hot brownie, and it's still one of the best things I've ever tasted. Harold and Son Hardware, where my handyman of a father used to buy his tools. He built me this little treehouse in our backyard, and I don't remember him building it, but I remember going inside of it.

I didn't even think about the old house…it must only be a few blocks up from here.

Owen takes a swift left into a parking lot, and we park in one of the empty spots nestled between a restaurant and plain brick wall of the Frugal Foods I was in not too long ago.

The five of us exit the vehicle, the chilled air tickling my skin. Definitely a good thing I bundled up.

I scan the building, a large light-up sign reading "Benny's" hung above us. It's a diner, and hints at familiarity, but I can't be sure. Inside, it looks like a typical fifties style diner. I suppose that's any diner nowadays, and nostalgia is super "in."

"Can't wait," Carolyn says, marking the leader of the group. We let Jay and Owen go ahead, and Brit and I trail behind the group.

"This was supposed to be a date, right?" I ask, keeping my voice low.

"Yeah. Carolyn is an idiot." Brit crosses her arms over her chest, shivering.

"Wait, she didn't know?"

She meets my eyes, smiling. "Again, Carolyn is an idiot." We wait until the three of the others have gone inside, and we stop just outside the door. "I didn't think Owen was coming, that's why I invited you along. Didn't wanna deal with this alone."

"What about Marla?" I'm not convinced that Brit sees the irony in all this.

"Busy. Studying or something." I grin, amused, and Brit calls me on it. "What?"

I bite my lip, briefly distracted by the cozy town. We're directly across from a childcare facility called Mimi's. I guess when every business is run by one person, they name it after themselves.

"Doesn't Carolyn third wheel you and Marla all the time?"

I don't mean to overstep my bounds, and I ask the question laughing, but Brit is not as amused. She appears shocked at first, but it quickly fades away to guilt.

"Am I a terrible friend?" she pleads.

"No, no." *Whoops.* "Of course not. I didn't mean it like that." I reach for the door, holding it open for the two of us. Brit doesn't enter right away, so I let the door close again.

"I guess since we're all friends, I forgot it can be kind of awkward." She chuckles, sticking her hands inside the tiny pockets of her jeans. She's usually so bubbly and confident, so it is a rare omission to see her like this. "It's still weird, dating Marla. Haven't fully gotten used to it."

"When did you guys start dating?" I ask. I peer inside the window, wondering if the trio are wondering where we are, but they're still standing and waiting for a table.

"Only since grad. Like, three months. I dated this guy for a bit in high school, until I realize that I have no attraction to men whatsoever. And he took it well, he was really nice about it. He went to college in Alberta." Brit gazes off into the night, looking majestic in the moonlight. The sky is clear, and the moon is shining bright, reflecting in her eyes. It's illuminating her already near-platinum locks in a way that makes it look like her hair *is* the moonlight. "I don't know. Now I feel bad."

"No, don't, I'm sorry." I step into her view, forcing eye contact. "I get it, being a third wheel sucks." Most of my high school experience was spent being a third wheel, the few times I went to group outings, and it was not always the best.

Brit smiles, her teeth flawless. "I'll have to remember to thank Carolyn for putting up with me and Marla."

I grin, reaching for the door once again. "What are friends for?"

Brit enters the building, following up to meet Owen and the group. I spend an extra second breathing in the sweet and salty air before catching up with my friends. My heart skips a beat at the thought of having nice friends, like it's too good to be true. I try not to let the fear sink in too deep.

I step inside, Brit and I rearing up the group, and Owen turns around to face us.

"You guys okay?" he asks, scanning between us. A chill runs down my spine from how warm and cozy it is inside. I start to take off my coat, immediately starting to get warm.

"Yeah, it was just so nice out, wanted to look a bit," I lie. Brit gives me a knowing smirk, and then stares down at her delicate flats.

Benny's looks pretty much like a Denny's, but with an old-fashioned flair. There's a bar in the middle of the restaurant tied up with the kitchen, and all of the tables are booths, except for two lone tables near a jukebox in the corner. The floor is black and white checks, and I step my foot on a square to see if I can hear that perfect tap sound.

Tap.

"I think we're supposed to just sit down," Carolyn notes, looking around the diner. There are only two other customers here, a couple, seated in a booth near the back. I see two people working in the kitchen, a man and a woman decked out in gray shirts and greasy aprons.

A scattered woman suddenly appears from the back, wearing ratty jeans and a tank top. Her graying hair is hastily thrown up into a messy bun, and she's rubbing a towel in between her steady hands.

"Oh, sit wherever you like!" she says, smiling. Her teeth are a little crooked in her toothy smile, but that only adds to her charisma.

"Can we get..." Jay checks around at all of us. "Five slices of apple pie?"

"Oh, yeah!" The woman laughs and tosses her washcloth onto the counter behind her. "What kinda ice cream you want with that?"

"What kind do you have?" Brit asks, though she's now a lot more preoccupied with her phone than anything else. That shy and insecure girl that was outside is a very unusual sight, and I have to admire how quickly her confidence returns to her.

"Chocolate, Vanilla, and Strawberry."

"Chocolate," Brit and Owen say in unison. They exchange a comical glance before Brit returns to her screen.

"Vanilla," Carolyn says.

"Vanilla."

"Can I get vanilla, but is it also possible to get caramel sauce on it?" I ask, my love of food shines brightly. Once again, neglecting to eat is catching up with me.

The other four hungry teens all look to the woman, and she grins, setting her hands on her curvy hips.

"Three vanilla, two chocolate, caramel for all?" The smiles speak volume. "You got it. The booth in the corner over there," she points to one of the larger booths near the wide windows overlooking the street, "should fit you all nicely."

We give our thanks, and Jay takes it upon himself to lead the gang over. The five of us squeeze into the booth, Brit and I making sure that Carolyn is next to Jay. Maybe if we drop enough hints, she'll figure out what's going on. I don't know where she stands, or where she wants to stand with Jay, but I guess tonight will tell.

"Have you been here before, Kim?" Owen asks, leaning over texting Brit to see me.

"I don't think so." I look around at the ceiling, the booths, the tacky neon glow signs plastering the walls. None of it triggers any recollection, though the overwhelming sense of familiarity is quite present.

"Well, they have the best pie," Carolyn says. She turns to Jay and places a hand on his arm, grinning from ear to ear. "This was a great idea, Jay."

The deer-in-headlights expression that Jay gives is priceless. Carolyn disappears into her own little world, admiring the décor, and Jay is looking to all of us for help.

Maybe subtle hints aren't gonna do it.

"I'm gonna run to the bathroom," Brit says, starting to shove her way out of the booth. I slip out, giving her easy access, and she turns to Carolyn. "Carolyn?"

"Oh, yeah, me too," Carolyn responds after pausing for a moment. Carolyn nudges me a little towards Brit, and I guess I'm going, too.

The two girls lead me to the back of the diner, into a closet size walkway, the entrance to the men's and women's bathroom. Brit forcefully pushes Carolyn inside the women's room, not surprisingly empty.

"What?" Carolyn says, stumbling through the door. I trail after her, my purse still tangled around my body. I hadn't even been seated long enough to take it off.

"What the hell are you doing?" Brit says, now blocking the door. She places her hands on her hips and stamps her foot impatiently. I bare my teeth, definitely glad that I am not the recipient of Brit's wrath.

"What do you mean?"

While the girls begin their conversation, I slip into one of the aggressively red four empty stalls; I might as well.

"Are you serious?" Brit squeaks, her squeal echoing in the room. "You invited me on your date."

"I...what?!"

I hear Carolyn pacing around the bathroom, her sandals clapping against the tile.

"Jay obviously likes you."

"No way." Carolyn sighs dramatically, turning into a small scream. "Really?"

"Yes, really!"

"Wait, then why did you invite Kim?"

On cue, I step out of the slender stall, the blood metal walls giving me a headache. *Who decided that this red would be a nice colour for a bathroom stall?*

"She didn't want to third wheel," I say, stepping towards the sinks. Despite the faded floor, the countertops are exceptionally clean, and the three sinks are nearly sparkling. I drench my hands in soap and lather them under the cool water.

Carolyn laughs ferociously and whips back towards Brit, her ginger hair flying frantically. "Oh, my god, Brit, I am *always* a third wheel for you and Marla!"

"That's what I said," I chime in, but shut my mouth immediately; *not helping.*

"I know, I'm sorry," Brit whines, walking towards Carolyn. "I am, really. I didn't realize it was that bad."

"Brit, it's not." Carolyn sighs and sits up next to one of the sinks, rapping her fingers against the porcelain. "I like hanging out with you guys, you're my best friends. I don't usually feel like a third wheel..." She growls, thrusting her hands into her hair. "Can we discuss this later? Did I actually invite you on my date?"

"Yeah." Brit is blunt, something I really appreciate. I've always admired upfront honesty.

"What happened at that party?" I ask, leaning on the wall next to the hand dryers. The bathroom is a bit trashy, in need of a thorough and deep clean, but at least it's well stocked.

"Huh? What party?" Carolyn wonders aloud. Her eyes narrow, trying to remember. I couldn't forget that party if I tried, frankly.

"When you and Jay were dancing," I reiterate. "Almost two weeks ago."

"We just danced." The wires in her brain cross and she winces. "Oh."

"I think most people are oblivious when it comes to people liking them," Brit says, and for a split second, I swear she shoots me the look. *Who would like me? Damien?* "Do you like him?"

"I don't know," Carolyn weeps. I can tell she's starting to panic. "I haven't dated anyone since,"

"Fuck face," Brit supplies. I turn to her and she shakes her head at me; sounds like a bad breakup, and a story for another time. "But Jay seems nice."

"He *is* nice. But..."

Brit is about to say something, but I interrupt her. "There's no pressure, Carolyn." She meets my eyes, hers drenched in that puppy dog look. "Do what's right for you. You don't have to date someone just because they like you, a relationship is not the be-all, end-all. That being said, if you're into him, give him a chance."

Brit and Carolyn stare at me, and I fear I've said something wrong, until Brit says, "You give great advice."

"Thanks," I reply hesitantly. I can't tell if she's being sarcastic or not, but I choose to believe the latter.

Carolyn's spirits seem to be lifted, and she slides off the counter. "Okay. Yeah. No pressure."

"No pressure," Brit reiterates, glancing my way for approval. I nod gently; I have to admit, it warms my heart a little that I actually gave good, listen-worthy advice.

"No pressure," Carolyn whispers.

Carolyn is the first to leave the bathroom, Brit and I trailing behind back to our table. The couple that was sitting near the back is gone, and they've been replaced by two police officers sitting at the bar. They each have mugs of coffee, chatting away about some vandal in Seven Oaks High. I believe the word "hooligan" was tossed around, bringing a small smile to my lips.

Carolyn sits back down next to Jay and gives him a big smile, eyeing him carefully. Now that the shield has been broken, she's going to be looking for all the signs that he likes her. It's hard to tell in the atmospheric lighting, but he might be blushing.

Shortly after we sit down, before we can even begin another conversation, our server approaches, managing to hold all five pieces of pie on her large plastic tray, and their ice cream counterparts.

"Let me see if I got this right," she says, holding the first chocolate ice cream and apple pie. She places them all down correctly and then stands back. "How did I do?"

"Perfect," Brit says, beaming. "Thank you!"

We all thank our lovely waitress, whose nametag reads Shelly, and she returns behind the bar. We dig into the pie, the warm and flaky crust, the savoury apple slices, the cool ice cream and caramel flows together perfectly.

"Fuck, this is good," Carolyn moans happily.

"It really is," I confirm. I have to check around to see how fast everyone is eating, just to make sure I don't devour it down too quickly. Brit hasn't even touched her pie.

"Brit, get off your phone," Carolyn nags, reaching across the table. She nudges Brit's plate closer to her, and Brit swiftly picks up her fork.

"Sorry, Marla has my car," she says with a heavy sigh and shovels a giant piece of her pie into her mouth. "Wanna make sure she hasn't totaled it."

"Why does she have your car?" Owen asks; he's the only one keeping pace with my fast eating. I'm normally a slow eater, but this pie is something else.

"Just drove home with it, she knew I was getting a ride in with you guys. She'll pick me up later." Brit shrugs it off, subtly checking her phone one more time before tucking it back into her purse.

"Hey, so, Kim," Jay begins, holding a hand to his mouth. He finishes his bite, swallows, and then continues. "You and Damien?"

"Me and Damien what?" I ask, eating another bite. *Fuck it, if they can't keep up, that's their loss.* I'm honestly astounded by how big these pieces are, it seems like it's four hefty pieces to a pie. I meet Jay's eyes and he holds contact, waiting for it to sink in. *Wait, what?* "What?"

"I saw you guys together the other day, football practice."

"Um..." *Oh, he was the guy!* "Oh. Oh! No, no." I laugh, tempted to take another bite, but shoving my face with food is not currently the answer. "No, we're just friends."

"Really?" Brit says. I arch an eyebrow, about to lay down the law, when she adds, "Marla said that..."

"Oh." I chuckle. *Relax, Kim. You've steered clear of the rumour mill thus far, keep at it!* It makes sense that Marla would have mentioned it to Brit. "Yeah, he was actually apologizing for what happened, bought me sushi."

"What happened?" Owen asks, leaning closer to me. It's like he forgot Brit was in between us, and she quickly recoils back into her seat. She nearly disappears into the cushion.

"He was just kind of a jerk," I admit. "But it's fine now."

"Good," Brit says forcefully, and inserts herself back into the conversation. She must sense that I don't want to share anything more, and she prompts, "So, hey, beach after this?"

"Sounds good to me," says Carolyn. Jay and Owen silently agree, and we eat the rest of our pie slices in near silence, only the sounds of chewing and forks scratching filling our ears. I finish first; no shame.

When we're done, we head up to the front to pay, and our server takes it upon herself to hop up behind the cash register. The two cops both look up at Jay, and the three of them exchange a hearty nod and smile. My first assumption is that they're being sarcastic, like they're skeptical of his mere youthful existence, until Brit leans over to me and whispers, "his dad's a cop."

"Ah." I clear my throat and fall further back into the group. I've never felt comfortable around policemen. I know that's the point, to protect and serve, but I haven't had positive experiences with them. Must be different here on the East Coast. Everything is different here in Seven Oaks.

"I'll pay for me and her," Jay states, approaching the counter. He signals to Carolyn who whips her head around to look at us. Brit rolls her eyes and physically pushes her closer to Jay. She stumbles into him and then meets his eyes, startled.

"Thanks," she sputters, beaming.

Jay smiles, pulling out his wallet. He holds up a gold credit card, and our waitress hands him a card machine.

"And how are you guys paying?" Shelly asks, drawing up another bill.

"Debit," Owen says, diving into his pockets. "And I'll get these two."

"Awe, thanks, Owen," Brit glees, clinging onto Owen's arm. She gives it a tight squeeze before releasing.

"Are you sure?" I ask.

"Yeah, don't worry about it." Owen flashes me a smile and Shelly hands him a second card machine. I seem to have a knack at getting free food in Seven Oaks; this could work really well.

"What fine gentlemen," Shelly says, placing her hands on her hips. "What are you kids up to tonight?"

"Going to the beach," Brit boasts. She really strikes me as a beach body, despite the fact that it's no more than ten degrees outside and pitch black. I hope the beach has some lighting.

"Well, you be careful," Shelly adds, taking back the approved card machine from Jay. She rips off the receipt and hands it to him, and he stuffs it in his pocket. "Those waves can get pretty wild."

"We will," Carolyn says, smiling. She seems much more relaxed now and can hardly take her eyes off of Jay. It's like she never even considered that he would like her, and now that she does, her whole view has changed.

"Thanks," Owen says, handing Shelly the card reader back. "I don't need my receipt."

"Well, thank you, and you have a good night. Be safe." Shelly bows her head for a moment, and then leans back against the bar. "And don't go climbing near the cliffs, got it?"

"Got it!" Brit drags me out the door, and the rest of our group follows.

"Cliffs?" I mimic back. There's the mountain, and I guess with a mountain comes cliffs, but I thought it was a more gradual slope.

Brit laughs. "Yeah, don't worry, we're not going there. It's on the east end of the beach." I nod, as if I know which direction is east from here. Wouldn't the ocean be east? "To the beach!"

"Man, it's cold," Carolyn says, rubbing her arms once we're outside. I can't imagine her cardigan is protecting much against the ocean air; I once again thank myself for bundling in something warm.

"Do you want my jacket?" Jay asks timidly, and I have to physically turn away from them. It's just too cute.

"I-if that's okay," Carolyn stammers. Jay removes his letterman jacket and holds it out for Carolyn. She sticks her thin arms inside; the jacket is more like a dress, making this moment even more adorable. I live for this romantic shit. "Thanks."

Jay smiles, and Brit grabs onto me, dragging me forward. "Let's go!"

We check carefully that the deserted road has no cars driving on it, and then we trot across the clear street to another line of shops. We start walking towards the direction we came in, eventually towards the mountain. I keep trying to see the beach, but most of the shops are blocking my view.

"It's so nice out," Brit says and takes a deep breath. She dramatically spins around, arms flailing. "I love the smell of the ocean."

I inhale some of the salty air; it's not as prominent as the West Coast, but it's a comfort nonetheless.

"Me too," Carolyn says. She and Jay are leading our group, with Brit, Owen, and I falling behind. The three of us are staggered because the sidewalk doesn't hold enough room for all three of us to walk side by side.

"There's beach access just at the light," Owen murmurs to me, pointing ahead. The crossroad of Main Street and Lighthouse Way looks like it might lead into a beach parking lot.

"Oh, okay." The whole walk through town feels like a weird dreamscape, where it feels like déjà vu, but I can't recall seeing any of it before. It's like a comforting hug from a stranger.

"Oh, this is so sad," Carolyn says, slowing down to a halt. She stops next to probably the only dingy looking shop here. It's an abrupt change from the quirky and colourful atmosphere, like biting into the most beautiful apple to find a rotten core.

I step closer to this beacon of darkness and take a look inside the dusty windows, placing my hands at either sides of my eyes. The store is filled with beautiful antiques and furniture, along with a few handmade items at the front desk. The lights don't even appear to have bulbs in them, and the open sign looks like it hasn't been turned on in quite a while. The floor is covered in a thin layer of dust, and the front door is sealed shut with a ginormous padlock.

It's reminiscent of any given horror movie; I feel a chill on my neck.

"What have they been doing?" Brit asks, stepping away from the eerie store.

"Grieving," Jay contributes, shifting uncomfortably in the street.

"What is this place?" I ask, the disturbance in my voice riding high. I can see a small iron metal sign on the aged wooden front desk; *One in a Million Antiquities.*

"Veronica's parents own this place," Carolyn says.

Veronica? It takes a moment for my mind to register where I'd heard that familiar name before.

"Wait, that girl who went missing?" I feel bad for speaking so bluntly, but Carolyn just nods.

"Yeah. Her parents closed the store like a week later. I don't know why."

"Her parents wanted to focus on finding her," Jay says.

All eyes turn to him, and Brit asks, "How do you know?" Her hands are on her hips, her tone accusatory.

"My dad told me," Jay mumbles, his cheeks flushing. I'm guessing he's not too keen on spreading that information around, judging by his expression.

"That's so sad," I mutter to myself, scanning the store again. It's been completely abandoned. My heart flickers when I see a small mouse scurrying around near the back of the shop. "When did she go missing?"

"June," Owen replies.

"Around our grad, I think," Brit confesses. She seems the least affected out of the bunch, but none of them seem all that down. It strikes me as strange.

Carolyn quickly latches onto Jay's hand, tugging him forward. Pleasantly surprised, completely forgetting why she's holding onto him, he follows along next to her.

"I guess you've seen the missing posters," Brit says, and points to the door of the antique shop. They're very faded, but at least twenty posters of Veronica are plastered all along the door. When I first saw the door, I thought it was spread in an odd design choice, not prints of a missing girl.

"Yeah," I mumble. The picture they chose of Veronica is just as ominous as her disappearance. Her eyes look wide and tired, her lips neither smiling nor frowning. It looks like a beautiful mugshot. "Kind of scary."

"Honestly, she probably just ran away." Brit crosses her arms over her chest, a breeze coming in from the sea. "She actually talked about wanting to move to Vancouver a lot, funnily enough."

"Really..." Despite the appeals of the West Coast, this is a very blasé attitude to have towards this subject.

"Yeah. Well, hopefully she's there and happy."

I'm about to question Brit, but she keeps on marching ahead; I think what bothers me so much about Seven Oaks is that nobody seems to think these serious things are a big deal. It's one whole town in straight up denial.

Everyone is distancing themselves from the shop, from me, so I jog to catch up.

Let it go, Kim. It's not my place to involve myself in stuff I know nothing about. Try to let it go...
  We get to Lighthouse Way and take a sharp left. Like I thought, there's a giant parking lot hidden by the storefronts, stretching several blocks down. There are a few extra shops facing the sea, one of which has a giant surfboard that I saw last time I was in town, and the rest look like small food places or beach rentals. The beach is as expected at this time of night, a sea of black reflecting the moon's light. It smells much more salty and fresh than it did back on Main Street, but there was also the barricade of stores blocking it off. The waves are about a foot tall, rushing in, receding back out. They're much more naturally larger than I thought they'd be.
  Part of me is scared open water and what's underneath, the unknown lurking. I can swim just fine, enough to survive, but I've never enjoyed swimming. I like standing in the water, floating, feeling the liquid flow between my fingers.
  I stop in my tracks before stepping off the sidewalk and onto the road, the hairs on the back of my neck standing up. My legs have stopped working, and all I can do is watch what's going on around me.
  "Yay!" Brit squeals and runs ahead, throwing her hands in the air. She runs so freely, without a care in the world.
  "Oh, my god, Brit," Carolyn mocks, but still runs along with her. She releases Jay's hand, and he walks on behind them. Even from back here, I can feel his smile.
  "Haven't been here forever," Owen notes, chuckling. He trots into the parking lot, tagging along with Jay.
  "Me neither," Jay replies. His voice starts to trail off as they walk away. "How do you think it's going? I think she might actually be into me..."
  They're all walking away. They haven't noticed that I'm immobile, standing near the edge of a curb, stuck.

And suddenly, all of my new friends disappear. Suddenly, it's sunny out, and I'm a lot shorter, and it's hot. I'm soaking wet, and I taste salt on my lips.

The beach is alive. Golden sand is being thrown everything, kids howling with laughter, teenagers flirting away, adults just relaxing and smiling. There is no stress here; stress doesn't exist in this world.

I have to squint, holding my hand above my eyes, blocking out the bright sunshine. There isn't a single cloud in the blue sky, except for my blurred vision.

"Are you okay?" a young-looking woman asks me. She places a hand on my shoulder, leaning down towards me. I wipe my small hand across my cheeks, cleaning the tears away.

I'm five years old again.

I'm wearing my favourite pink swimsuit, my favourite pink sandals, and I'm dripping ocean water. I don't know how I've managed to wander this far from the water, but finding my family is currently like finding Waldo.

Seven Oaks is popular in the summer, I remember now. The perfect beach getaway.

"Where are your parents?" the woman repeats, holding the hand of her own son. He's my age too. She looks around her and I face forward. My eyesight is fuzzy and my entire body is shaking, cold but melting in the sun.

"Kim!" a familiar voice yells, and I see my father emerge from the crowds of people. He bulldozes in between a couple and collapses on the ground before me, wrapping his arms around me.

"Thank god," the woman mumbles, and starts to walk away. I can see the judgement in her eyes, but I don't say anything.

"You were gone," I find myself saying to my father. He draws away, just enough to look into my eyes. He's crying, too. . His caramel hair is close shaven for the summer, along with his constant stubble. I haven't looked at him in over twelve years.

"I'll never be gone," my dad says to me, gently stroking my sea salt hair. "I just got lost. I'll always be with you. Always."

"Kim?"

Owen is standing before me, matching my height, only a few inches away. I step back a little, shocked by how close he is, and I hit the lamppost behind me. My eyes travel down to the ground; Owen is in the parking lot, on the curb below me.

"Are you okay?" Owen presses, now stepping up onto the curb; he doesn't leave much room between us.

Liar.

"Yeah," I spit out. I can feel my eyes widen, frightened; I haven't even seen a picture of my dad in years. Seeing him like that, so vivid and clear...

Owen looks skeptical, but I stand up straight, clearing my throat. Jay and Carolyn have returned closer, holding hands again. Brit is still far off, I think I see her by the ocean. "Sorry."

"What's going on?" Carolyn calls, and I can't quite tell if it's concern or annoyance in her voice.

"Nothing," I laugh, forcing myself to hold the smile.

My cheeks are dry, but I still feel five-year-old Kim's tears streaming. The girl who cried from losing her dad for five seconds, the last time I cried about him. The only time I cried about him.

The odd feelings around Seven Oaks finally start to fade, the veil dropping. It all makes sense. In a world of bad things, it's so much easier to imagine the best. Georgina wasn't drugged, she just had too much of her own volition. Veronica isn't missing, she's off partying it up in Vancouver. My dad didn't leave, he's just lost. Seven Oaks is one big happy show.

It's so much easier to believe the things that might not be true, to spare the raw emotions. Human beings are capable of anything, but in a small town like Seven Oaks, that's hard to believe. When you know everyone all your life, where you not only watch your own kid grow up, but every child, it's hard to believe anyone in this town would betray others in that way. It's hard to believe a student would drug their peer, a teenage girl would be taken, and a father would willingly leave the child he claimed to care so much about.

The whole god damn town is wearing rose-coloured glasses.

"Kim," Owen begins in an insinuating tone, but I cut him off.

"I'm fine," I force a laugh, and I dig through my purse to put on my glasses for the night. I don't wear them at the batting cages, and I haven't put them on since; I think it's time for a bit more clarity. The small details of my night suddenly come into focus, and I can see just how much apprehension is in Owen's gaze. "Just a trip down memory lane." I sweep past Owen, Carolyn, and Jay, managing to gain serious ground on Brit. "So, where are we going?"

"I'd just rather sit and watch the water," Carolyn says, biting her lower lip. She looks to Jay.

"Yeah, that sounds great to me." Jay beams just at the sight of her.

"I want to walk along the water," Brit yells over the crashing waves. She's just within the cusp of earshot.

"Why don't we go walk, and you guys can hang out here?" I ask, checking with Carolyn to make sure she's okay with it. She mouths her gratitude and nods.

"Sounds good," Owen says. Carolyn and Jay begin their trek off to the right, and they take a seat on one of the many logs lining the surprisingly sandy beach.

Brit runs up to me, smiling. She splashes me a little, her feet soaked from the water. She's taken off her shoes, holding them in one hand, and her jeans are rolled up above her ankles. "By the way, those are the cliffs."

I follow her outstretched arm, past where Carolyn and Jay have settled. "Cliffs" are not an understatement at all. The entire mountain that the university campus has one road that leads on and off the mountain, but I didn't realize how abrupt the bluff was. It must be three hundred feet high, all rocky edges along the side of the mountain, and then the beach immediately below.

"Holy shit," I marvel.

"Yeah, all the logs along the beach are trees that fell down," Brit says, and whirls around to head back towards the water.

"Wild." I adjust my purse on my body and follow Brit, allowing her to be my guide for the evening.

I walk parallel to Brit, Owen straggling at my side. The sand is becoming finer, scratching against my boots, but as long as I stay in the perfect position between wet and dry sand, I think I can spare wreckage.

"Hey, I'm sorry about..." Owen says. He lifts his head up from the ground and sighs, defeated. He has his hands thrust into his coat pockets, his right hand fidgeting with something. "I don't know, I didn't mean to–"

"No, oh, no!" Owen whips his head to me, and I continue. "Sorry, I just remembered being here as a kid. It was kind of trippy." I don't want to expand more on my obscure past; I hope he doesn't pry.

"Yeah, you were born here, I forgot." I don't even remember if I told Owen about that.

"I was actually here for kindergarten. So maybe I met some of you guys before." Before coming here, my mom reminded me of that fact. She said I even had a best friend, and that we both cried when I left. I have no recollection of her, and there aren't any pictures either.

"Really?" Owen meets my eyes briefly before facing forward. "That would be weird. What do you remember from kindergarten? You must have gone to Cherry Wood Elementary."

I wait for the name to trigger a memory, a moment, *anything*, but I have nothing. I don't remember any teachers, any school, any students. I don't remember any of it. My mind is hazy with school in Vancouver, as if it completely overwrote my year of education here. "I actually don't remember it."

I think it's weird since I was five years old, but Owen thinks anything but. "Well, makes sense, you were pretty young."

I sigh. "I guess."

I take a deep breath, feeling the tiny bits of salt tickle the insides of my nose. My mom hates the smell of sea life, but I can't get enough of it. I would bottle it up and take it with me everywhere if I could.

"You guys should come walk in the water," Brit offers, kicking her legs against the shallow waves. She has stayed on the tail end of the surf, only catching the calmed seawater brushing the shore.

Taking one look at the water, I start to feel queasy. It looks like miles and miles of oil gleaming in the darkness, very off-putting. Not to mention the giant pie I devoured.

"No, thanks," I chuckle, placing my hand on my stomach. "Way too cold."

"It's actually not that cold," Brit says. The cuffs of her jeans, even though hiked up, are still getting soaked from her tromps.

"Right," Owen laughs. His mind seems elsewhere as we're walking, like he too has gotten lost in some distant memory. *But maybe not so distant.*

"No, really!" Brit protests.

I strategically wait until the waves have retreated and I trot near the ocean, touching the freezing water.

"Liar," I mock, sprinkling some water at Brit. She giggles and tries to kick some water back at me, but I swiftly hide behind Owen, using his body as a shield.

"Thanks," he quips after taking the brunt of the splashing, wiping the salt from his pants.

"Sorry," Brit coos.

I stray further ahead, partially to escape the potential of getting drenched, partially trying to catch a clear reflection of the moon in the water. It's cloudy tonight, so the moon isn't crisp as usual, and I can't find a single star.

"Watch out, big wave," Brit warns, her voice shaking.

Half of her body is soaked in the wave, up to her slim waist, and she screams while Owen jogs backwards, away from the onslaught.

"Shit," I mumble, trying to step away. I lose my foot in the deep sand and I don't make it far enough. I stare helplessly down at my unsteady feet, knowing the inevitable demise of my combat boots. I focus on the water, biting my lips, squirming at the impending wave, and I hope that my boots won't be permanently ruined.

But, in an odd turn of events, my feet aren't soaked. The flooding water forms a circle around my feet, flowing around my boots but not touching them.

"Woah," Owen marvels, and I catch him gawking at my confusion. It's like there's a force field around my feet. It must be some weird lump on the ground, like I'm elevated over the uneven terrain.

"What?" Brit says, stumbling out of the water. She runs over to me, the water now flowing back into the ocean. She growls and stomps one damp foot, slapping on the wet sand. "How did you not get wet?!"

"I...don't know," I say. I search the sand for any rocks that could have diverted the water, but I don't see any. *What the fuck?*

"That's weird," Owen notes, also stepping closer. He leans down towards the ground, scanning around, but there's nothing. Nothing explainable.

"You're like a superhero," Brit adds.

I laugh, shaking my head. "Right, my powers are to keep my feet dry."

Brit shrugs, uselessly and furiously trying to ring out her pants. "Just saying, that was weird. *I* got fucking soaked."

"Yeah, are you okay?" I try to change the subject away from myself and this weird occurrence. This isn't even the first time something inexplicably weird has happened like this...*this town, man.*

Brit whines, growing frustrated. She pulls her phone out and violently texts someone, ignoring both Owen's and my concerned expressions. She stows her phone back into her purse, thankfully dry, and then plants her hands on her hips.

She is completely drenched from the waist down, and completely unimpressed. "Can we go back?"

"Yeah, of course," I say. I would offer her something if I could.

Our walk back goes a lot quicker now that Brit is rushing to get back. I don't blame her, she must be freezing, and her clothes make an uncomfortable tugging sound when she walks. It's like her jeans are being peeled and replaced back onto her skin with every step she takes. When we get back to our original entrance, Jay and Carolyn are still sitting on the log. They have shifted positions, but it's hard to tell what exactly they're doing.

"Hey, Care!" Brit screeches; her annoyance has yet to fade.

Carolyn suddenly shoots up, and from this angle, it looks like she was on top of Jay. Owen and I exchange a glance, Brit definitely being the oblivious one now.

"Uh, yeah?" Carolyn calls back hesitantly. I can see her darkened figure scrambling to stand up. She snatches Jay's jacket off the log, making sure Jay is behind her, then walks over to us. She gasps at Brit, recoiling away from her. "Oh, wow, you're soaked."

"Yeah. Marla is coming to get me." On cue, Marla pulls into the parking lot, driving what I assume to be Brit's car. It's small and surprisingly orange, a little bug.

"Oh, that was fast," Carolyn says, now frantically trying to soothe her teased hair. She's avoiding eye contact with Brit, and only gives me a quick glance before returning to using her fingers as a comb.

"She was nearby," Brit says, already skipping towards her girlfriend. Something tells me that Marla was actually a lot closer than we thought; learning that Marla and Brit have only been dating for three months, they are most assuredly in the honeymoon phase. I wouldn't be surprised if Marla was just waiting around town for her girl. "I'll see you guys at homecoming!" Brit tries to throw her arms around Carolyn, but our dry friend hops back into Jay's chest, shielding her own body with his arms wrapped around her.

"I'm already cold enough, thanks," Carolyn jokes. In Marla's headlights, it's now easy to see that all of Carolyn's lipstick is gone, and most of it has transferred to Jay's lips. Looks like the date went well.

Brit pouts but obeys, jogging towards her car. "See you guys!"

We all bid our goodbyes, and Brit makes a beeline for her girlfriend. From her, we watch her dive into the passenger side and try to hug Marla, but she playfully shoves Brit away from her. Soon, the two girls are giggling and disappearing from the parking lot.

"We should get heading back too," Carolyn says, running her hands through her still disheveled hair. "It's already midnight."

"Really?!" I pull my phone out, confirming her words. Just after midnight. "Well, shit."

"Time flies," Jay notes, and Carolyn nudges him teasingly.

The four of us return back to Owen's car, still lonely parked by the diner. The policemen are long gone, and the diner appears to be closed. Only the jukebox light remains on inside.

"Kim, you wanna ride up front?" Owen asks after a lengthy visual exchange with Jay.

"Sure," I grin, checking with Carolyn. She nods subtly, smiling widely. It's nice to see her so giddy about Jay after her earlier panic.

The rest of the night feels like a blur of shops, sea, and scenery. I'm fixed on the trees, their stature and magnificence, my head once again pressed up against the window. There isn't much noise, other than Owen's small car running up the subtle slope, and Carolyn and Jay whispering in the back seat.

The town of Seven Oaks and the rose-coloured glasses are so new to me. It almost doesn't feel real, and I don't know how to process it. It always feels like something suspicious is going on, because there is, but the constant–

"You tired?" Owen asks me.

"Yeah," I mumble, my voice feeling light. All my thoughts dissolve away when I open my window a crack, breathing in the crisp air. "But tonight was nice. Thank you for driving."

"Oh, anytime. If you ever need a ride or anything, just let me know." I shared a car with my mom back home; I miss being able to go on night drives to clear my mind.

I rest back into my seat, tilting my head towards our driver. He's a good driver, very careful, very calm. He doesn't have road rage like me. "Thank you. That's really nice, you're a really nice guy."

He chuckles a little, adjusting the heating vent near him. He doesn't respond to my compliment, so I lose myself in the forest once again.

Owen pulls into the first year parking lot, finding a single spot nestled against the far wall of the lot. We all exit the car, a wave of exhaustion hitting us all.

"We'll walk you guys back," Jay says, now slinging his arm across Carolyn's shoulders. She blushes but nods, grinning to herself.

The campus is once again eerily empty; I've quickly learned that during the week, the grounds become nearly abandoned, as opposed to the lively weekends. I'm glad to be walking with other people for once.

We get to the walkway of the girl's dorm, heading up the few stairs, when heavy footsteps fill our ears. I stop in my tracks and turn around, spotting a dark figure looming just beyond the streetlamp overhead.

"How you kids doing tonight?" the shadow calls, his voice gruff and deep.

Carolyn squeals, whipping around into Jay's open arms. He's more focused on the girl clinging to him than the fact that some guy is behind us.

The man steps into the light, revealing himself to be one of the security guards introduced at the assembly. He's donned in what looks like a police uniform at first glance, minus the gun at his waist. However, it looks like he has a taser...

"Good," Jay says after the initial panic has faded.

"Hmm," Mr. Bryers says, locking his thumbs into his belt loops. He's smiling, but I can sense an air of suspicion around him. He's the army veteran of the group, I recall by his daunting gaze. "You're all going in there?"

My friends grow silent, clearly intimidated by this guy, and so am I. Still, I respond, "the guys were just walking us in."

"Just making sure they get in safe," Owen adds, reaffirming my point.

"Can never be too careful," Mr. Bryers shoots back, eyes narrowed.

I bite my lips, now crossing my arms over my chest. Drugs are all fine and good, but they draw the line at boys entering the girls' dorm?

"Stay safe." Mr. Bryers whirls around on his heels and walks back towards the main pathway like a cowboy, head held high. He stops once he's about ten feet away, and then faces us once again, reminding me of Sheriff Woody.

"He gives me the creeps," Carolyn says, not even bothering to ensure the door has sealed us inside the building. I guess she doesn't care if he hears her.

"Me too," Jay says, and slips his hand into Carolyn's. It's a smooth motion that makes my friend smile, and the two of them skip ahead towards the stairs. *Maybe Mr. Bryers was onto something.*

"Goodnight," I mock after them, nearing to a halt at my own close door. They seem to have forgotten that Owen and I exist.

Carolyn turns back around, all smiles before jogging up the stairs with her new guy. I can hear her giggles echo through the stairwell and into the hall.

"They are really cute," I mutter to myself and begin to dig through my purse for my key.

"He's liked her for a while," Owen confesses to me, and immediately goes white as a sheet. "Well, I mean–"

"Really?" I press on. "That's sweet. He seems like a nice guy."

"He is." He clears his throat and stands up taller. "He'll be good to her."

I smile, baring my slightly crooked teeth. Owen seems to know exactly what a girl wants to hear about a friend's new beau. "Good, I'm glad. Thanks again for the pie, by the way." I finally draw my key out from my purse and start to head inside.

"Oh, yeah, no worries." Owen stretches his arms, drawing out a yawn from both of us.

"Definitely time to sleep," I moan, opening my door.

"Yeah..."

I turn around and flop into Owen's arms, giving him a tight hug. He must be getting used to my random hugs by now. "You're a really cool guy, Owen," I mutter, sleep really catching up with me. He wraps his arms back around me, relaxing his body into mine.

"You're a really cool girl, Kim," Owen retorts back.

"Right." I laugh pull away from him, smiling, and lean against my doorframe. My eyes start to lose focus and I think about Veronica once again. I'm not sure why my mind makes the jump and connection, but… "This place is really weird," I think aloud.

"Yeah?" Owen looks dumbfounded, but I *have* been all over the place. I sometimes forget to connect the dots between what I'm saying and feeling. The sleepiness doesn't help.

"Yeah." I sigh, squeezing my eyes shut. Tonight was not what I expected, and not necessarily in a bad way. In a strange, dreamscape sort of way. "Sorry. I'm gonna go to sleep. Thanks for walking me back, Owen, and have a good night." I hop inside my room, now clutching the door.

"You too, Kim." He smiles brightly, although a bit frazzled, and heads out the door. Once I hear him open the exit door, I shut my own, pressing against it hard to make sure it sticks.

I flick the light on and turn around, placing my hands on my hips. For once in my life, instead of overthinking everything that's happened, with Georgina, the beach water, the ball from the pitcher that flew into an opposing fence, the untimely sight of my father, I lay down and slip my glasses from the bridge of my nose. For once, I don't think. I close my eyes and accept this town for what it currently is.

One big enigmatic mystery.

Chapter 8

The big day of homecoming has finally arrived, and I am actually excited. I never had the chance to attend a pool party since nobody I knew back home had a pool. I barely had a yard, let alone a pool. Needless to say, I'm pumped.

Four rhythmic knocks rap upon my door, and I open my room up to Holly, the best friend I never expected at Seven Oaks.

"Hey," she coos, drink in hand. It's a pink reusable cup with a straw, and the purple drink inside is already half empty. She shoves the cup at me. "Wanna try?"

I take it from her as she sweeps past me inside my cozy room. I'm so enthralled in being impressed by her lipstick staining her lips and not the plastic straw that I nearly choke from the abhorrent taste entering my mouth.

"What is this?" I spit, handing the cup back to her.

"Grape juice, rum, and champagne." *Jesus Christ.* "Mostly rum."

"Yeah, I can tell." I resist the urge to vomit, placing a hand over my mouth. "That's disgusting."

"Excuse you, this is great." Holly sticks the straw into her mouth and gulps down another large sip. "Gonna be nice and lit for tonight."

"There's gonna be drinks there too, right?" I ask, throwing a cardigan over my outfit. I have my bathing suit on underneath my shorts and tank top, something easy to take off in a hurry.

"Oh, yeah. Don't you worry, you'll never have to pay for your own booze anymore." Holly smiles and glances down at my outfit. "Is that what you're wearing? You look so cute."

"Thanks," I sneer until I realize that she's serious. I quickly begin to fix my hair, "accidentally" using it to cover my flushing cheeks. "Um, do I need to bring anything? You said they have towels there, right?"

"Yeah, I just like my towel," Holly says, smiling gently, patting her pink towel inside her bag. It's like she knows what just went through my head, but also knows not to say anything about it. "So, no, you're good. I'm bringing my phone, though, but that's just for pictures. Oh, I got this new bikini, what do you think?" She sets her cup down on my desk and rips up her shirt, revealing her brand new pink bikini top.

"Wow, I love it." The pink is a bright and vibrant neon, but is somehow subdued by her tan skin tone. "You look hot."

She giggles, putting her shirt back down. "I don't know about that, but it was a hell of a deal." Looks like I'm not the only one who can't take a compliment. "Remind me to take you to the mall here one day, do you like shopping?"

"Do I like breathing?" I joke, heading towards the door.

"You are fantastic," Holly smirks, sweeping past me into the hall. She clings tightly to my arm for a moment before tensing her entire body. "I'm so excited!"

"Me too." I tug the door shut behind us, making sure that it's locked. I will never not double check that my door is shut and locked from now on. "I've never been to a pool party. Do you know what the pool is like here? Hopefully it's warm." I'm not in the mood to freeze my ass off trying to get in the pool.

"Oh, I'm sure it's fine." We start our way through the dormitory, heading towards the exit. "You've really never been to a pool party? Didn't you party in high school?"

"No," I confess. I'm just about to brush it off, like I'm joking, that *of course* I've been to all the parties in the world, but I ride with it. No sense in pretending. "I didn't have the partying friends."

"What, so you weren't invited?" Holly scoffs, pushing the door open into the cool outdoors. It's very cold, and I am extremely eager to get in that pool, or even better, the potential hot tub. I'm surprised that it gets so cold so quickly at night. "That's stupid. Everyone is invited to everything here."

"And how many people were in *your* grad class?" I remember my own graduation and not knowing a solid sixty percent of the names announced, strangers walking across the stage.

I watch Holly do the math before she admits, "Good point. Still, you're so friendly."

"Making up for lost time now." My eyes travel up towards the sky, my heart fluttering at the sight of the stars. It's cloudy again tonight, as it is most nights, but not enough that I can't see some major constellations. "You guys are a lot nicer here, anyway."

Holly squeezes her face together, beaming. "Well, I hope so. I was gonna ask before, do you talk to anyone back home?"

I pause for a moment. Most people don't know anything about me, but Holly seems like a good person to open up to. I actually *want* to open up to her. "No. No, not really." The few friends I made throughout my last hurrah of high school were short-lived; I think one of them goes to school in Alberta. We barely talked over the summer, so I doubt I'll be contacting any of those acquaintances now. I'm not sure if any of my "friendships" back home were meant to last. In fact, I am certain they weren't.

"Do you miss them?" Holly asks.

I meet her eyes, sensing some raw emotion from her. She's *trying* to get me to open up. I don't know if anyone back home did that. The only people I really opened up to ended up spreading rumours about me and using my weaknesses against me, so this is foreign to me.

I must pause for a long time, because Holly adds, "Sorry, I don't want to pry."

"No, it's okay." *Relax, Kim. She isn't Rose, she isn't Toni.* "Um...I don't know. We weren't meant to be friends, I don't think."

"I get it." The only sound I hear is our sandals flopping against the cement, along with the excess chatter of the students floating through campus. "I mean, I don't totally get it, but I get when you stop being friends with someone, and you kind of realize that they weren't your friend at all." She sighs, slowing down her eager speed. "I had a friend like that, but in a bad way."

I stop dead in my tracks and stare at her. I've never met anyone else who was hurt this way like me. Nobody would ever talk about it, at the very least. My heart beats a little faster; maybe I'm not alone in this.

Holly looks embarrassed and starts rubbing her delicate hands together, picking at the remains of her cracked pink nails.

"Me too," I say. She shoots up at me, smiling a little. She has a bittersweetness surrounding her, the same one I'm emitting.

"Really?" she asks, too excitedly. "I mean, not that it's a good thing. But it's nice to know that..." She sighs, losing her train of thought.

"Maybe we're not alone." I vocalize my thoughts, hoping it lands.

Holly grins and nods, small beads of sweat lining her hairline. This is uncharted territory, and definitely not easy to talk about. Maybe we can help each other. Holly, near tears, wraps her arms around my neck, drawing me against her. I encircle her waist and we both squeeze tight.

"I'm really glad you moved here," Holly says, her voice breaking.

"Me too," I whisper. I'm worried that if I try to speak any louder, my own voice will fail me. I find my eyes drifting closed, lost in the comfort of a friend I didn't think I could truly feel. Nagging thoughts enter my mind, reminding me that it has only been a short time, and I can't really know someone like this. I'm finding it hard to sink into those thoughts right now.

"Hey, Holly!" a man calls, breaking Holly and I apart. We both turn to find one of our fellow peers shirtless, waving one tanned muscular arm this way. He's wearing blue swim trunks, and has a duck floatie around his narrow waist. He has a swimmer's body for sure. "Will I see you inside?"

"Uhh..." My friend hesitates, looking to me for help. I just shrug; I don't know who he is. "Yeah. I guess."

"Who's that?" I ask while Duck Floatie waddles away, inside the pool building. I can see the budding party from here through the glass walls, the splashing, the drinking, the dancing, the screaming. The music is not as loud as expected; maybe it's a party where people are supposed to talk. Or maybe the speakers in the pool area don't go so loud.

"Robin," Holly replies, staring off at him.

"Are you guys friends?" I press, now starting back on our path to the party.

"Kind of. Not really. He's friends with Landon." *Landon...right, the guy Holly is into.* "I haven't talked to either of them since school even started. I wonder if he'll be here tonight."

"Only one way to find out." I grip onto Holly's hand and drag her inside, giggling all the while. Long live the nights of hopeful romantics.

We walk down the hall of the building, identical to every other hallway on campus. The orange emergency lights are on, adding to the mysterious ambience. There are less doors along these halls, since there are less and larger rooms, and Holly shows me into the girls' change room. We pass by the few girls getting changed into patterned and colourful swimsuits, and one girl doing cocaine off the benches lining the walls, *holy shit,* and we enter into the pool area.

The nauseating scent of chlorine mixed with the bitterness of hops explodes inside my nose. After the first few repulsive seconds, it starts to fade away, and I observe the party. Two giant stereos are on tall tables near the pool, which is a lot bigger than it looked outside. The stereos still aren't playing very loudly; it seems like they're more there for the rumble-in-your-chest bass effect, but quiet enough to actually partake in a conversation. There's a diving board about ten feet high against the window, and a girl jumps from it, screaming. Her splash is small as she splits right into the water, and she pops up, looking refreshed and happy.

There is no indication whatsoever that this is a homecoming party, except for one single banner along the back wall, hastily thrown up, slanted, and reading, "Welcome Home!"

Any excuse to party.

"This is so great," Holly says, scaling the wall. I trail behind her and she puts her beach bag down with a few others, next to one of the security guards, Ms. Dahl.

"Evening, ladies," Ms. Dahl greets us, nodding professionally.

"Hi," I say back, hearing the hesitation in my speech; I do not handle authority well.

"Be safe tonight," she warns, focusing her gaze back to the pool. There doesn't seem to be a lifeguard on duty, so I guess it's everyone for themselves tonight.

There are only about fifteen people in the pool swimming, or making out, and the small hot tub nearby is packed to the brim. The water is almost at ground level from all the people crammed inside.

"Drinks first?" Holly turns to me, pointing towards the coolers lining the windows.

As we get to the table carrying at least twenty different bottle openers, I recognize some more familiar faces lounging by the drinks.

"Hey, Owen," I greet, and then turn to Leslie. "Hey, Leslie. How's it going?"

Leslie's short curls nape her neck beautifully, shining in the faint pool lights. She has one hand placed on her petite hip, and the other is holding a beer, relatively untouched. Her black bikini is killer.

"Hi," she quips and then turns away. I guess she's in a mood.

"Hey, Kim," Owen smiles; he's wearing navy swim trunks with tiny gray sharks patterned across. He holds up his bottle of beer. "Drink?"

"Cooler," I reply.

"Make it two," Holly adds. She pries the lid from her cup and chugs the rest of her drink.

"You got it." Owen crouches down and fishes through the first coolers. "Palm Bay?"

"Yes!" Holly reaches over Owen's shoulder and grabs two different flavours in one hand. She begins her concoction on the table, mixing the sweetened vodka together inside her pretty cup.

Owen holds a can up to me and I thank him before cracking it open.

"Enjoying the party?" he asks, finishing off his bottle of beer. He places it behind him, next to two other empty bottles, so it's safe to say he's been here a while.

"Just got here," I admit, taking a sip of the fizzing goodness. "But it's cool so far."

"You like swimming?" Leslie asks me. When I look at her, she does not look impressed at all. Her tone is light and calm, but there's something condescending about it.

"I guess." I don't really, but muttering some excuse seems easier than explaining yet another backstory.

"You guess?" she mocks and scoffs, taking a sip of her beer. She purses her lips at the taste; it doesn't even look like she drank any.

"I don't," Holly says, now sipping Palm Bay through her pink plastic straw. "I like being in the pool, but not like laps or anything."

"Same here." I shoot her a grateful glance. I get the impression that Leslie isn't too fond of me...

Leslie doesn't respond, and she doesn't even look at us. She's off staring in the direction of the hot tub, clearly bored by our existence.

"Oh, shit, hot tub opened up," Holly says, shoving me towards the tub. I almost slip on the wet ground, but she stabilizes me. "Come on."

"See you guys later," Owen says. He has a look of disdain on his face; Leslie *does* seem a bit snarky tonight.

"Definitely," I call behind me, following Holly. I inch closer to her, doubting we'll snag the apparently rare availability before someone else, especially because, "I still have my clothes on."

"Take them off there," Holly mumbles without missing a beat.

We get to the hot tub where there's only a gap for about one person. In one smooth and impressive motion, Holly slips out of her shirt and shorts, tossing them to the side. She slides right in, unfazed by how hot it is.

"Can we fit one more?" Holly asks and looks up at me. A few people have their eyes on me, and I have the incredibly awkward task of stripping down before them. I try to replicate Holly, going as quickly as possible, and I sit on the ground and dip my feet in.

"Fuck, it's hot," I say, shocked at how fast Holly got inside.

"Come on," she laughs, her face turning red. Something tells her she doesn't feel the heat as much with the alcohol numbing her, but her body is still soaking it all in.

I cross my arms over my stomach and try to slip inside the cramped space, hiding my insecurities. It's dark enough and everyone seems drunk enough that they wouldn't even notice all the things I'm trying to hide.

The water burns me, but sort of feels nice. By the time I'm seated next to Holly, we are nestled in between two girls, both distracted by their own conversations.

"Lots of lovely ladies tonight," one of the guys on the other side of the circle says. He has longer black hair, reminding me of a greaser. He scans over the girls, and I can't help but feel overexposed. It doesn't help being squished together, my breasts tightly packed. His eyes briefly fall onto my chest and moves onto Holly's.

"Why don't one of you girls come and sit on one of us?" a blonde guy pipes up. He's the only guy in the tub wearing shorts that aren't black or blue, but a vibrant red that sticks out beneath the water. "I don't think any of us would mind."

"Okay," the girl next to me says. From the one word she speaks, I can tell she's out of her mind. Her ginger hair is tied up onto her head, and her white swimsuit leaves little to the imagination. I'm worried she'll pop out at any moment. She sits on top of the greaser, and he places his hands on her thighs. She turns around to make eye contact with him and bites her sultry lips. "This okay?"

"Oh, yeah," the guy chuckles, checking to see his buddies grinning.

I'm conflicted. It shocks me how easy it is for girls and guys to get together like this. At the end of the day, most of the guys I've met here, forgetting Mason, have been quite kind. I don't think it's even possible to grow up with people so closely for your whole childhood and then not care about them, so I'm sure the hookup culture is a little different here.

However, I'm not convinced that this classifies as "care."

The guy in red shorts lunges across the tub, filling in Ginger's seat, and he stretches his arms on the outside of the tub, around me and another girl.

"And how are you girls?" he asks, scoping us out.

"Fuck off," the other girl snipes, inching away from him.

"My apologies." He retracts his arm, being careful not to touch her, and then his eyes fall to me. "How are you, new girl?"

"Thirsty," I mumble, searching for my Palm Bay. Red Shorts produces it from behind him and hands it to me. I don't know if he thinks he just grabbed a random drink, but I recognize my lipstick staining the can. "Thanks."

"What's your name?" I hate to admit it, but I'm a sucker for a killer smile. And he has the deadliest one I've seen in a while.

"Kim," I reply, feeling a little flustered. I finish half the can of the cool drink, hoping to calm my nerves, and I glance over to Holly. She's chatting with the girl next to her, who I soon recognize as Gretchen. It's hard to tell in the low light.

"I'm Matt." *Of course you are.* I smile a little and he pries. "What?"

I roll my eyes and face him, and suddenly, he's a lot closer than I remember. I grin madly; boys like this will one day be my undoing. "You're very handsome, Matt."

Matt's eyes dilate for a moment. He clears his throat, chuckles, and leans in closer. "Is that so? Well, Kim, you're pretty easy on the eyes yourself."

"Hm." I've never been the best at accepting compliments, but I'm excellent at giving them. I sip at my Palm Bay, once again checking on Holly. She's too enthralled with her conversation to be my wing-woman.

"I think I recognize you," Matt says, inching closer to me. I face him, his face once again a lot closer to mine than I recall. He has incredibly attractive features, chiseled jawline, high cheekbones.

"Really?"

"Yeah. Think I saw you at football practice the other day." *Oh, my god, who* didn't *see me there?* "Must have been there to watch me, hey?"

A few of the other guys in the hot tub chuckle, enjoying the little show. There's only about twelve of us in here, and we were almost split in half with the boy/girl formation, until White Bikini shifted.

"You play football?" I chuckle to myself, my eyes drawing themselves to the giant windows outside. There's water streaking the glass along with steam, and it really hits me how hot I am. I could go for a dip in the pool.

"I sure do." Matt licks his lips and leans closer to me, and I, in turn, chug the rest of my cooler. I place the empty can down, being sure to avoid any altercations with his nearing lips. "You want another one?"

"Oh," I mutter, surprised. "Sure. Thanks."

"Save my seat," he says, leaning in close again. His lips graze my ear when he speaks, sending chills through my body in the heated tub. It feels nice.

He hops onto his seat and then steps out of the hot tub, snatching up my empty can along the way.

"Look at you," Holly says to me, drawing my focus back to her. Gretchen is chatting with her other friend, paying no care to us. "Matt's a hottie."

"Seems okay," I admit. Unfortunately, the goofy and cocky charm works with me every time, not to mention my thing for blondes. I take care to keep my voice low; I know there are vulturistic listeners in Seven Oaks, myself included. "Anything I should know?"

Holly considers this for a moment but settles on a half-hearted shrug. "I mean, he's hot, but you can see that."

"I do have eyes, yes," I joke, bringing Holly to a giggle.

She brings one arm out of the water, laying it down on the tub's edge. It must be cool because her arm flinches a little when she touches the ground. "Nothing serious."

"Fine with me," I mumble.

"Hey," Matt says, and I draw my eyes up to him. He's slicked his blonde hair back, and there's something extremely sexy about it. He signals down towards his feet, my cooler in one hand, a beer in the other. "Fair trade, booze for a spot."

I didn't even realize that upon his absence, the other hot tub dwellers had slowly taken over his spot. Everyone has slightly more room now. I sigh, standing up to my feet, and I enter the middle of the circle. I place one hand on my hip, self-consciously sucking in my gut. "I guess we'll have to share."

Without an ounce of hesitation, Matt slips into my spot, still holding out my drink. He opens his legs, inviting me to sit on one of them. Holly has already joined back into Gretchen's conversation, but I catch her offering some quick glances to make sure I'm all right. Or maybe just to be nosy.

I position myself onto Matt's lap, keeping my thighs pressed together to maximize space; this idea was much better in theory than in practice. He hands me my can of juicy vodka, and I open it immediately.

"Thanks," I say, taking a sip.

"My pleasure." He grins, his arm snaking around my waist. His eyes travel down to my boobs, and I pretend I don't notice, nursing my Palm Bay.

I scan the pool area; there are still so many people I don't know, but I'll know them soon enough, hopefully. Leslie is still standing by the refreshments table, very displeased. Owen has left her and she's all alone, and I feel bad; I don't think Leslie is a bad person, despite the snarky vibes, but I've only ever seen her talk to Owen. She takes a seat against the glass windows, hunched forward, staring off into space. I think she's still holding her barely touched beer.

Carolyn and Jay are in the pool, my attention drawn over to them when I hear Carolyn scream. Jay is splashing her, and she is trying to retreat, holding her hands in front of her face. She quickly submerges beneath the water and pops up behind Jay, clinging onto his shoulders. She moves so gracefully in the water, like a mermaid, so she must be a strong swimmer. Jay seems purely happy, grinning madly with Carolyn holding onto him. It's hard to tell, but I think he's taken her legs into his arms, holding her on his back.

Owen and Cam are also with Jay and Carolyn, chatting away about something. A girl I've never seen before approaches the two of them, slowly wading through the water. She has bright pink hair piled on top of her head in a bun, and she looks extremely uncomfortable in the water. Her shoulders are tense and rigid.

Cam, the friendly guy he is, immediately smiles and welcomes her in. He reaches off to the side of the pool, snatching a bottle of beer, and takes a swig. He offers it to the girl and she denies, turning to face Owen.

Leslie suddenly appears in the pool, somehow teleporting from her previous spot, slipping in between Cam and Owen, and smiles widely at the girl with pink hair. It doesn't seem genuine, though.

I'm starting to figure out what's going on with her.

"You're really hot," Matt says to me, snapping me out of my haze.

I meet his eyes, and he glances down to my breasts again. I'm not sure why I get such a strong urge, but I put my can down, take his cheek into my hand, and proceed to kiss him.

The boys watching the show start up, as if they've never seen a girl and a boy kiss before, and Matt shifts, his body tensing. His arm draws me in tighter, pressing my body against his chest. One hand finds its way up to my breasts and squeezes, latching on tightly.

I don't know how long we kiss for.

The peanut gallery calms down after an unknown amount of time, but Matt and I keep kissing. He pulls away briefly to whisper, "You're a really good kisser."

"Thanks," I say, stroking my nails against his cheek, and I dive in to kiss him again. It's good to know that I'm not terrible at this, despite my inexperience.

I shift on his lap, turning more to face him, and one of his hands grips onto my thighs, pressing them closer to him. We only stop when some guy starts chanting a word throughout the pool area.

"Paella," a male voice, deep and gruff, begins yelling throughout the pool. "Paella, Paella."

Matt suddenly pulls away, turning his body so abruptly to find where the voice is coming from that I nearly fall off his lap. He turns back to some of the boys in the tub who are swiftly exiting the water.

"I gotta go," Matt says. I stand up, placing my hands on my hips. I don't mind that he has to go; if anything, I'm more intrigued by why he has to go from the word "paella." Yet another mystery to add to the books.

"Okay."

Matt stands and looks at me again, holding my cheeks in both hands before shoving his tongue down my throat one more time. I nearly gag at how forceful he is.

"It was nice meeting you, Kim. Maybe I'll see you at another party."

"You too," I say, already sitting back down in my seat. "See you later."

He thrashes out of the tub, splashing the hot water around. I notice Jay leaving the pool too, so it must be some football team thing, since those are the only students leaving. I haven't seen Mason around all night, so maybe he's already where the players need to be...

The water level has significantly fallen since the boys left the tub, but soon rises again when other students take their place. I guess the hot tub is the "hot" place to be.

At least I make myself laugh.

"How was it?" Holly asks, turning to me. She slurps at her pink cup, despite it being empty, and shakes it violently, the plastic straw rapping against the inner plastic.

I pause for a moment to understand what she means, and then shrug, gazing around. "It was okay." I sigh, feeling a little empty inside. Trust issues run deep. "I just don't want anything serious, you know?"

She nods, chuckling. "Oh, I know. I get it. You've come to the right place for that." She holds up her drink to cheers, but then sneers once again realizing it's empty. "Wanna go to the pool? It's getting hot."

"Yeah."

Holly and I climb out of the hot tub, two other scoping girls taking our place. The air outside of the streaming water feels chilly and dry, despite the humidity of the room. The two of us snatch our clothes from the ground, and we maneuver our way back to the drink table to pile our stuff onto Holly's bag.

Holly soon crouches down at the multitude of coolers and pulls out a Smirnoff Ice, quickly cracking it open and pouring it into her cup. She offers me one and I take it. I can already feel my alcohol tolerance increasing from merely attending this school; Holly's must be through the roof. She doesn't even seem affected.

"You're a heavyweight, eh?" I comment, following her to the ladder leading into the shallow end of the massive pool. It looks a lot bigger now that we're about to go inside.

"I don't know," Holly says. She can hold quite a bit considering her delicate stature. "Never thought about it." She grabs my opened bottle from me and places it on the pool's edge, alongside her own cup. She starts into the water and immediately retreats. "Fuck, it's cold."

I dip my toe in, confirming her suspicions. My arms cross over my bare stomach, chills coursing through my veins. "Want me to go first?"

Holly nods, and I slowly inch my way down the ladder into the chilled pool. I know that I will adjust shortly, but fuck, it is *cold*. As soon as it hits my belly button, I want to pop right back out, but I press on. The next problem area is the chest, but the water ceases rising at my waist.

"How is it?" Holly asks timidly, sitting down next to our drinks. Her knees are pulled up to her chest, arms wrapped around.

I count to three inside my head before submerging to my neck, and I let out a small howl. "Could be worse," I choke. After my teeth stop chattering and my body adjusts, I paddle over to her, snatching my bottle from the edge. "You should just slide in from there. I think it's easier to get it over with at once."

Holly moans but takes her cup in hand, and in one fluid motion, slides into the water. She bares her teeth, emitting a high-pitched squeal that I can't help but laugh at. She soon ducks down to my level, shaking her head. "This was a mistake."

"Drink," I say, pressing on the bottom of her cup. She brings it to her lips, sipping it quickly. I'm impressed how quickly she's adjusted.

I scan the pool, only about fifteen of us in here, a few straying in the deeper end. Looks like some guys showing off for the girls, and vice versa, and then Owen and his friends. Robin is in the deepest end with some of his friends, and I have to wonder if one of them is Landon. There are two girls hanging off of two guys along with Robin, so for Holly's sake, I hope not.

"Is Landon here?" I ask, my curiosity getting the best of me.

Holly glances around towards Robin and his friends; he offers her a small wave and she smiles back, but she looks melancholy.

"No," she grumbles.

"His loss," I comfort, and she manages to bring her usual smirk back to her lips. I would press, but I get the feeling that she doesn't want to talk about him. Another time.

We float along over to the familiar crowd, popping up just behind Carolyn.

"Hey," I chime.

"Hey, Kim." Owen smiles, holding his beer bottle up to me.

Carolyn turns around, bearing a huge grin. "Hey, girl. You're getting busy, hey?"

I laugh, Holly and I filling the empty gaps in the circle. Carolyn is clinging to the wall, despite it being shallow enough to stand, and then Holly, the pink haired girl, Leslie, Owen and I complete the rest of the circle. Cam is with the group, but just beyond the crowd, staring off at the giant diving board. He has ambition in his eyes. I can see his feet dancing beneath the water, so he must be too deep to touch.

"Are you guys having fun?" I ask, ignoring Carolyn's prying question. "Where's Brit and Marla?"

"They wanted to have a date night," Carolyn says, reaching for her beer on the pool's edge. She draws the can to her lips and takes one quick sip. "Plus, they both swim all the time, so they're kind of sick of it."

"Really?" Holly says.

"They're on the swim team."

"That's cool," I say; I learn new things about this school every day.

"How you doin', Holly?" Cam asks, drawing himself from the hypnotic diving board.

"Not bad," she replies, and hands her cup over to him. He takes a sip and nods as he returns it to her. "Math is a bitch."

"Tell me."

Leslie and Owen are having their own quiet conversation, and I focus my attention to the girl with pink hair. I didn't recognize her until now, being up close.

"Oh, hey, you're in my bird class, right?" I ask, leaning in front of Holly to get a better look at the girl's familiar features.

The girl looks to me and smiles, nodding. "Yeah! I'm Emma."

"Kim," I reply. "You dyed your hair, that's why I didn't recognize you."

She laughs nervously, patting it gently. "Yeah, I did it yesterday. Can't get it wet, though, not in this water."

I notice the top bun on her head is completely dry, untouched by the chlorine. "It looks really good."

"Really?"

I nod, unable to tear my eyes away from it. "Yeah, I think that might be my favourite shade of pink." If only I could commit to my hair colour being anything different. I'll stick with mousy brown for now.

Emma smiles genuinely, biting her lips. "Thanks. I was really nervous, it was my first time dyeing my hair."

"Looks so cute," Holly chips in before focusing back on Cam. She's really good at that, managing to listen to several conversations at once.

"Thanks!" Emma is beaming from the compliments, the dimples in her cheeks gleaming. "Carolyn actually gave me the idea."

Carolyn looks startled, and she chugs the remainder of her beer before questioning. "Really? I did?"

Emma laughs, nodding. "Yeah, but a while ago. At our grad, I think you were drunk, you told me I should do something crazy and dye my hair pink. It's a few months later, but you were right."

Carolyn smiles, shrugging dramatically. She stands up straighter, revealing her black and white polka dot bikini. "I'm an intelligent drunk."

"Right," Cam teases, and Carolyn glares in his direction.

The conversations continue, but my mind gets pulled in a different direction when I see Georgina. She's standing with two friends, the same two people I've seen her with a few times around campus, all of them fully clothed. As expected, her plaid is draped across her shoulders, but her blonde hair is tied up today. She must be getting hot with the party going on.

She looks happy.

She meets my eyes for a moment and tightens her smile a little before hysterically laughing with her friends. The girl she's with looks kind of like Brit, but with jet black hair, and the guy looks like a modern punk; curly blond hair, wild sideburns, rock band t-shirts. Looks like a cool guy.

"Hey, where did Jay go?" Emma asks, drawing me back to the conversation.

"He and the football team have some prank planned," Carolyn admits, and glances back to our security guard of the evening, as if she'd be watching us and only us. Carolyn inches closer. "It sounds stupid, but you'll hear about it tomorrow."

"How are you two doing?" I ask, regretting not biting my tongue. I'm not sure if they're public, or if they are anything at all.

She must see the pain on my face because she eases it all, "We're really good. It's only been like a second, but I really like him."

"That's so cute," Holly gushes. I can almost see the cartoon hearts in her eyes.

"He's so fucking smitten," Cam says, and Owen shoots him a dirty look. Cam starts floating on his back, staring up at the piping running along the ceiling.

"Good for you," Emma says, and I realize that she's the only one not drinking tonight. "It's so hard to find nice guys like that! Until then, looks like the university one nights will have to do." Emma looks a bit embarrassed, her cheeks flushing, as if she accidentally revealed too much.

Leslie then decides to join the conversation, offering up the least helpful advice, and rolls her eyes, judging hardcore. "Maybe you should try *not* giving it up right away."

Emma looks mortified, Holly and Carolyn both staring at Leslie in a peculiar way. It takes me a moment to process what she even said.

What the fuck?!

Before Leslie can add anything else, I jump in.

"Or, everyone should do what makes them happy and mind their own business," I snip, glaring at Leslie.

Leslie's face flushes instantly, and she turns to Owen for help, but he's busy chugging his beer. *As if Owen would be helpful in this situation.*

I didn't used to be like this. I didn't used to be so outspoken and honest; I used to hide my feelings and keep my mouth shut. I was never great at it, but it's what I was accustomed to, and I never really thought I'd have the chance to start fresh like this again, away from Rose, away from Toni, where I can stand up for myself and others, and say what I want to say.

It's scary.

It's *exciting*.

"Unless you're, like, murdering someone," I add for comedic effect, my crutch, and then to seal my point, "or just straight up making other people feel bad about themselves."

Leslie stares down at the water, and for a second, I think she might just submerge herself and sink away. I hear Holly cackling quietly, a savage statement on her part, and Carolyn looks away in discomfort. Emma just smiles a little.

"Right on, Kim!" Cam paddles towards me, still floating on his back, and then lands gracefully on his feet. He holds his hand up until I give him a high five. "You're so cool." *If only they'd seen me a year ago.*

The girls, excluding Leslie, begin to converse, Emma stepping further from Leslie and towards Holly and Carolyn.

I'm now certain that I'm not the only one who isn't a huge fan of Leslie.

"Also, you won't have to walk me home tonight," Cam jokes, waving water in my direction. "And thanks again. I seriously owe you."

I had honestly forgotten about walking Cam; it wasn't anything big for me, just making sure he got some safely. Things that are big deals here are not what I expected.

"You don't owe me anything," I retort, disbelief in my voice.

"Is anyone else turning into a prune?" Carolyn says, holding up her fingers, disgusted at the sight of them. "I'm gonna get out."

"I could use another beer," Owen says, finally breaking his silence. I'm not sure why he's been so quiet tonight. Now that I think about it, he's been still and not very talkative at all; this might be drunk Owen.

"I'm gonna head home," Leslie says, her arms crossed over her chest. "I'm tired."

"Okay, well, make it home safe," Owen says, very clearly to her dismay.

"Have a good night," I say genuinely, but she takes it very wrong. She rolls her eyes and leaves the pool, using insane arm strength to pull herself out without the help of a ladder. She stomps away, dripping wet, and disappears into the changing room, launching the door violently open.

"Yikes," Holly chuckles, looking uncomfortable, and then starts to drag me over towards the ladder we came in on.

"Is she always like that?" I ask, wondering if I did something to offend her. I could see how she could misconstrue what I said, but I really meant no harm.

"Are you serious?" Holly asks, meeting my eyes. She pauses on the ladder, halfway out of the pool, and then turns to me.

"Yeah? I barely know her."

"But, oh..." She suddenly snaps her mouth shut and smiles, shaking her head. She knows something, but seems to have no intention of giving it up. "Right. I keep forgetting. She's not usually that rude, maybe just had a bad day."

"Well, I hope it gets better." I curse under my breath, exiting the pool. I search around for a promised towel, but no dice.

I cover my belly with my arms, and return over towards Owen and Cam, who are lounging by the drink table. Carolyn and Emma are chatting it up, and Holly quickly joins them.

"Hey," I say, approaching Owen.

"Hey." He smiles, finishing off the last of his beer.

"Are you drunk?" I ask bluntly.

I'm met with a deer-in-headlights look, and his body tenses. "What? Oh, no. Do I seem it?"

"You're just really quiet..." My voice trails off when I hear a sharp static sound, and I whip my head around to see Ms. Dahl listening intently to the garbled noises on her radio. She sweeps past the students, striding alongside the pool with a stern expression; something tells me it has something to do with the alleged football prank.

"Oh, I just had a test today," Owen says as Ms. Dahl exits the room. "My brain is kind of dead. Sorry."

"No, don't be sorry." I laugh, realizing that I had left my drink back by the ladder.

Before I can head back, my ears filled with the sound of thrashing and splashing, and everyone's eyes turn to the pool. It's completely empty now, with a few students staggering out, except for a single girl flailing in the water.

"Oh, my god!" somebody screams, their echoes filling the gym, and soon the girl in the water starts screaming.

"She's drowning!" another spectator states.

"Oh, shit," Carolyn says, and begins to search around. "Where's the security?"

"She just left," I say dumbfounded. My heart is racing; why isn't anyone jumping in? Why aren't *I* jumping in?

"Someone find security!" Carolyn yells to the gym. Most students are out of their minds and half of them aren't even listening. The woman continues to struggle in the water, her head bobbing up and down from the surface. She's not too far from us, and a few guys start towards hopping into the pool, until, "Nobody go in the water! It's not safe for anyone to jump in unless you're trained."

The few men about to pounce and save the girl hesitate back, and instead make their way towards the exits of the pool to presumably get help.

"What?!" I scream, and Carolyn turns to me.

"Kim." Her serious expression only hardens. I have never seen her look so dire before, and I get embarrassed for even yelling at her. "I was on the swim team in high school. You learn that people who are drowning like that will only take you with them, because they can't help it. She needs–"

"She's fucking drowning!" My body is shaking, all the hairs on my arms and back of my neck standing on end. Maybe Carolyn is right, and she has a valid point, but that's so far different in practice than theory. "Fuck."

"People are getting help, she'll be okay," Carolyn says. Her voice is hesitant, and she steps towards me, knowing what I'm going to do. I may be the most sober one here, and if I don't do this…

"Kim, don't!" Owen reaches after me, but I leap into the water, not realizing how deep it is until I feel nothing but water beneath my feet.

"Fuck," I gargle, water already filling my lungs, and I kick off the wall.

Splashes hit my face from the panicked arms thrashing in the water. She's not too far from the wall; I summon every swimming lesson I ever took.

I try to grab onto her arm, her black hair covering the entirety of her head. I narrowly deflect one of her hits, and it sinks in that this is so much more dangerous than I thought. I need to regulate my breathing.

"Get help!" Holly screams, reaching an incredibly high pitch. "Kim!"

"Holy shit," a guy mumbles, and I think it's Cam.

I finally grab a hold of the girl, but my touch only makes her scream more. I hear one more call of my name before she pushes me under the water, as if I'm the pool's edge, and getting above me will help her. Chlorine flows down my throat, and I resist the urge to take a breath to clear it away until I'm back on top.

"Kim!" Holly screams. "Oh, my god, Kim!"

I turn back towards the screams, finding my friends all crouched by the water, holding their hands out to me. I can't see them all clearly, but I know it's them. I know that they're there for me. I continue kicking beneath the girl and me, and just as I'm making it to the side, she pushes me under again.

I hear her and another girl screaming, muffled by the water, and suddenly all the pressure on the top of my head alleviates. I pull myself to the surface, gasping, unable to properly breathe.

Cam and Carolyn have pulled the girl up to safety and have her lying down on the ground. My hands fumble for the edge, but I can't focus, and I end up all turned around, my muscles already aching. Two strong hands latch onto my arms and draw me out of the water seamlessly. My footing slips and I almost tumble to the ground, but the hands set me down gently.

"Kim?" Owen panics. I can feel him hovering behind me, but I can't see anything anymore, my eyes burning. He places one hand on my shoulder, and the second his other hand makes contact with my back, most of the water I swallowed comes right back up my throat and onto the ground before me. "I need a towel!"

My words slip out of my mouth along with the chlorine and come out as gibberish.

"It's okay," Owen comforts, and he soon has a warm towel wrapped around my shoulders. "Kim, it's okay."

I look up at the violently shaking woman, Carolyn still by her side. She is alive, breathing, and has severely calmed down. Her black hair is a mess over her eyes, and the most I can consciously recognize is that she looks tall and lean. Ms. Dahl comes rushing back in and slides into a kneel next to the girl. She yells something into her radio, but I can't understand it.

A looming figure catches my eye, my head spinning, my chest heavy and expelling the liquid in my lungs. I try to keep focused on the man, but my eyes are stinging from the chemicals.

It's someone I know.

It's someone familiar.

It's...*Mason.*

All at once, everything comes into focus. While all the other students seem concerned and panicked, Mason appears unusually calm. He's standing still, observing, his hands resting by his sides. He's much too settled for this situation.

I speak again.

"Don't talk," Owen instructs. He's knelt beside my quivering body, one arm stretched across my back and the towel, his other hand gripping onto my shoulder. "Just breathe."

I take his advice the best I can, but then Mason sees me. His head turns in my direction, and the moment it does, he starts his way out of the building. I find my body crawling towards him, and another mouthful of water rushes back up.

"It's okay," Owen says. I close my eyes, coughing and crying, the sting of vodka and chlorine never ending, and I try to stand up. In the process, I lose my footing and slip back into Owen's chest. I give up and rest against him, finding something sturdy and reliable as a comfort. He wraps his other arm around me, cradling me in his arms. His warm embrace is soothing. "It's okay. Just breathe."

Mason has completely vacated the building.

"We need help *now*!" Ms. Dahl ushers into her radio. My eyes travel to the girl, convulsing on the ground. There's vomit next to her, and she looks completely vacant. "She's overdosing on something. Tell the ambulance to hurry up!"

Upon hearing the word overdose, I immediately search for Georgina. When I find her, huddled with her two friends, she is staring at me. Shock does not even begin to describe the expression.

Owen rubs my arms gently, warming my body that I realize must be in shock. I can't move a single finger without my head feeling inexplicably sick and cold. Owen has settled behind me, comfortable, planted on the ground. His legs stretch around me, containing me in one place, which might not be so bad right now.

I finally let loose a sob, the fear and panic all catching up to me, and Owen tenses against my back.

"Just relax, it's okay."

Georgina and I regain eye contact, and she looks just about how I feel. Even from here, I can see her gulp. Her girlfriend clings tightly to her arm, petrified, and her rock band t-shirt friend hovers behind glumly.

I don't think it's just me anymore. I don't think there will be anymore of me being shut down just because I'm new, because there has officially got to be a problem now. This isn't normal anymore, and this school can't pretend that it is.

No more "normal," no more "it happens." No more me believing all the bullshit being spouted about how safe and great this town is.

It looks like the rose-coloured glasses are starting to come off.

Chapter 9

In an even odder turn of events, Seven Oaks University has a Saturday assembly in light of last night's incident. It was announced all over campus today that at 4:00pm, there will be another safety assembly. Nobody heard about it until it was passed around by ear, since the dorms are seriously soundproofed, but there is a decent sized turnout.

I didn't hear about it until noon, which is when I woke up with a slight headache, and a throbbing throat. When I first woke up, I thought I was getting sick, but then I remembered all the water I swallowed last night. The awful sensation of water filling my lungs threw me out of bed, gasping for the air all around me, like I was drowning all over again.

Last night.

I remember the girl, whose name I learned is Patricia, was carted off in an ambulance while I was still choking. I recall the listless look in her eyes, the same that was in Georgina's when I found her half-conscious in a bush, and how Georgina started crying and had to leave the pool, her two friends trailing after her.

The prank that the football team played was very short-lived; one of the player's girlfriends called him and told him that something bad had happened, so their plan was thwarted. They had started to spray paint our lightning bird mascot on the side of one of the buildings, and desperately tried to cover it up when they heard what happened. I'm not sure why they bothered to clean it up, and I have yet to see the failed masterpiece, but apparently there are shabby remnants on one of the pristine buildings.

Ms. Dahl is nowhere to be seen at this point. She got reamed out pretty bad by Mr. Bryers, who appeared on scene shortly after Ms. Dahl, and just today on my way to the auditorium, I saw a new security guard, Ms. Almanda, according to her nametag, making the rounds. I can't confirm nor deny whether or not Ms. Dahl was fired, but it does not look good.

"It's already 4:15," Holly mumbles, checking her phone for the fifth time since we sat down. She slaps her hands down on the two arm rests and readjusts her position, now leaning forward. "My god, is this ever gonna start?"

"Holly..." My voice is extremely hoarse from last night, and in a permanent state of parched. It has never hurt this much before. I didn't expect her to be so impatient considering there's something potentially terrifying going on. But then again, I didn't expect any of what university has been like thus far.

The auditorium is nearly filled to the brim, and I suppose there was an email or automatic calling program, because a lot of parents are here too. An odd number of them are wrapped in pea coats, something that must be the fashion here. I spot Georgina's parents, sitting on either side of her, facing forward. All three of them are tense, even from only seeing the back of their heads. Georgina's plaid is a giveaway.

"No, not like that," Holly defends, slipping her phone back into her pocket. "The longer Mr. Wolfe waits, the more mad people are gonna get." She points to two parents now standing in the aisle, having a very heated discussing about something. One of the women seems like her insides are on fire; I can almost see the steam blowing from her ears. It's so strange seeing parents strolling in here, talking to their kids. Seven Oaks University is its own little city, where all the residents are my age, where *we* are the adults. Seeing parents waltzing in, talking to their kids like this, it's like taking a peek behind the curtain of a famous show; you know it's there, but it's still weird when you see just how much is going on behind the scenes.

If anything, it just reminds me that I need to call my mom.

"You're not wrong," I admit.

"They should also give you a fucking prize." I snap my head to Holly as she says those words. "You're like a hero."

"Superhero." The joke lands and Holly giggles a bit, returning her focus to the arguing parents.

I didn't expect so many parents to so willingly drop their schedules to come to a school assembly on a Saturday, but this involves their kids' safety. I guess it would be stranger if nobody showed up.

"Though, I did hear Carolyn give you shit," Holly says with a wink.

Last night feels like such a blur. It shocks me to know that so much happened within the span of two minutes. It was right after Patricia was carted off on a stretcher, several paramedics hooking her up to a heart rate monitor, even going so far as to give her a shot of something.

I was wrapped in Owen's arms when Carolyn came storming over to me.

"Kim, that was so fucking dangerous," she yelled at me. I remember looking up at her, my vision blurry, and just coughing. "That was so stupid."

"Carolyn, chill," Owen snarled, using a tone I hadn't heard before.

"Yeah, she saved her life," Cam chimed in, and he crouched down next to me, checking my teary eyes. "Just take it easy."

"She could have *died!*"

"I didn't," I managed to choke, and Carolyn let out a frustrated growl, throwing her hands into the air. She stomped off after that, and I didn't see her for the rest of the night.

Holly then appeared with our clothes, and she and Owen helped me to my feet. Holly walked with me to the bathroom to get changed where I choked up even more water, and then we started back for the dorm rooms. Before I could go, I had to make another statement with the police. It was a different officer, thankfully, and he didn't ask many questions, just like my previous experience. My answers were short, considering I could barely speak, but at least this cop seemed a little more invested in what I had to say. Both Owen and Holly waited with me and helped me back to my room; Holly and I were both so spooked that she ended up crashing on the couch, stealing one of the two blankets from my bed.

The story goes that Patricia got a little too high, fell into the pool, and started tripping real hard. I pulled her out, she went to the hospital, and as far as I know, she's still there. I hadn't seen her around campus, so I can't be sure she's not here. Apparently, Ms. Dahl was caught off-guard, and had briefly left the room after she gathered wind of the football team's prank. Patricia "falling" into the pool just when there wasn't anyone senior to save her? It's too big of a coincidence to believe.

"Yeah, that was fun." I sigh; Carolyn ended up apologizing this morning, meeting up with me in the cafeteria, but not before insinuating how reckless I was. The conversation ended in a hug, which was nice, but I couldn't help but feel like I'd be scolded by a parent.

The empty stage suddenly fills with the stress carried on Mr. Wolfe's shoulders, and he saunters to the centre, stopping just behind the centralized podium. His hands are tense, stuck on either side of the wooden stand, and his gaze is harsh. He's unhappy.

"Thank you for your patience," Mr. Wolfe begins, taking an exasperated breath. The audience still flows with murmurs, but most have been silenced by his presence. "I truly appreciate everyone's effort to attend this meeting, the parental participation of Seven Oaks always inspires me."

"Oh, Jesus," Holly groans, and nudges me. I follow her head nod up towards the stairs, finding a disgruntled man and woman searching the crowds. Their happiness, or lack thereof, is oddly similar, though presenting itself quite differently. "My parents."

I do a double take at Holly's parents; her mom looks similar to my mom, a high-class business woman, but Holly's mom is wildly taller, partially due to her expensive pumps. Her dad matches her mom's height, but is wearing jeans and an old, ripped t-shirt. He looks about ten years younger than his wife, but from watching my own mother growing up, I'm sure the age on Holly's mom's part is due to hard work.

"Did you know they were coming?" I turn back to Holly, who has now sunk into her seat. Her hand is covering over her eyes, attempting to hide.

"No. My mom texted me saying she could maybe make it, but usually 'maybe' means no." She growls, sliding so low in her seat that she's nearly on the ground. "Especially not together. My dad moved out last week."

"I'm sorry." I drop my voice as her parents skip by on the stairs, finding seats lower down. I hear Holly's mom mumble something, and her dad stops in his tracks, glaring down at her. He ducks into a single seat on his own, and she struts a few rows down, sitting next to another couple. She doesn't seem in the least bit bothered by the fact that her ex hasn't followed closely behind her; she almost seems relieved.

"It'll be an awkward dinner," Holly half-heartedly jokes, sitting up straighter.

"Bullshit!" a student yells in the crowd, drawing our attention back to the assembly. We all search around the room until the girl stands up, only a few rows from the front. "How can you even say that?"

"I assure you, Ms. Nelson, that safety is our top priority," Mr. Wolfe replies, and the light starts to reflect from the forming beads of sweat on his forehead. "Nothing means more to us than the safety of our students. I would like to remind students that no drugs of any kind will be tolerated at this school."

The standing student hesitates, and an uncomfortable silence fills the room. Mr. Wolfe holds himself higher, about to continue speaking, when another student interrupts.

"It's not because of pot," a girl yells, standing up. She's only a row down from us, far to the right side of the auditorium. "These girls are being drugged."

I gulp hard, and Holly whispers a hearty, "Holy shit."

"We have no confirmation of that," Mr. Wolfe says, wiping his brow. "All we know–"

"All we *know*," a third girl screams, her voice much higher and frustrated than the others, "is that Patricia has never done drugs of any kind. She didn't just OD."

"And nobody overdoses on pot," the first girl says again. The echoes in the auditorium are shockingly amazing; I can hear everything. "Not like that."

"Ladies, please–"

"My daughter does not do hard drugs," a timid voice enters the room. Mumbling ensues until a man who I recognize to be Georgina's father stands up. Georgina is nestled in between him and her mother, slightly mortified, but another part of her is beaming. "This was no accident."

"How are we supposed to trust you to keep our daughters safe?" an older woman shouts from the crowd.

The mob mentality is almost too overwhelming to me, and I'm only sitting and watching. I can't keep track of where it's all coming from anymore. This isn't Mr. Wolfe's fault, but he does have the unfortunate task of trying to fix this. I do not envy him right now.

"Please, if we can all calm down," Mr. Wolfe says, holding his hands out. "I know this is a scary time for us all–"

"Um, no, not all of us," the first girl chimes, her tone growing more tantalizing. "I don't recall any *boys* being drugged thus far. I don't think any *guys* here are scared to walk around campus as night. I don't think *men* have to worry about being accused of 'overdosing'," she even uses the air quotations, "if this kind of thing happened to them. Not to mention, I don't think any guys helped with Georgina, or Patricia, *at all*. And frankly, I highly doubt that a girl is drugging other girls for shits."

"Oh, my god," I whisper, in awe of how quick and articulate she is. I pray that she's not going to bring me up in her speech, at least not any more than she has.

"She was our debate captain in high school," Holly informs me. I can see a small fire in her eyes sparking. "She's not wrong."

This is starting to get intense.

The girls in the auditorium cheer along with the first girl, filling the room with a thunderous applause and hoots and hollers.

"Our children are scared," Mrs. McIntosh stands up, and Georgina hangs her head low, eyes permanently to the floor. "What are you doing to do to help? Are there even cameras installed?"

"We do have cameras, yes," Mr. Wolfe says, puffing out his chest. This is the one break he's caught so far. He's not a very tall man, and he's shrinking by the second. "We have not been able to install them all over campus yet, as this is a privacy risk, but–"

"I'd rather my kid be slightly uncomfortable than dead," a man shouts in the crowd, and receives mixed feedback.

The line of security versus privacy is a very fine one, and not easy to decipher.

This is such a shit show.

"Nobody is dead," Mr. Wolfe says. "The police are currently conducting an investigation into these events, until then, I want everyone to stay calm." Shouts fill the room, but the dean presses on. "I know we are all scared, but we must remain calm and rational."

"This is ridiculous!" a middle aged man yells, standing up. He's a business suit, sitting next to an enraged looking Emma. She stands up after him, throwing her hands in the air.

"What are we supposed to do?" Emma screams. I can see the resemblance.

"Please," Mr. Wolfe pleads, his voice now quivering. "If we could all..." he sighs, shaking his head, and his head drops.

In an eerie turn, the auditorium slowly quiets. I search around until I spot a familiar man standing. He's wearing a charcoal suit this time with a navy-blue tie. His hair is dirty blonde, combed neatly, and he has the overall presence and charisma fit to be mayor of Seven Oaks. I'm disturbed by how quickly he's silenced the room.

"We are all scared for our children," our apparently beloved mayor states, his voice echoing through the room. I see Mason seated next to him, staring up at his father with adoring eyes. I did not expect the mayor to show up. "I have known Mr. Wolfe for many years, a trusted friend, and there is no greater want from him than to keep our children safe."

Mr. Wolfe smiles politely, and Mr. Livingstone offers a courteous nod.

"We know this town. We know our neighbours, they are our friends. It is tragic that these events are happening, whatever they may be, but we will get to the bottom of this."

I don't know what it is exactly, I can't quite place it. The cool demeanor, the soothing tones in his voice, even the constant familiarity I feel with him, despite hardly knowing him, the odd urge to trust him. But it calms everyone down in a heartbeat. And it suddenly makes a lot of sense why he's the mayor.

"I suggest the students of this university be dismissed, while the parents discuss a plan of action to keep our children safe."

His words spark some gentle debate, and my dear friend Holly swiftly hops to her feet. I could tell she was antsy to speak up and add to the chaos from earlier, but she resisted up until now.

"With all due respect," she begins, drawing the audience's attention. Her mother's eyes are on fire, while her dad actually looks kind of proud, "the only person who has helped anything at all is a student."

My cheeks start to flush, and Holly's tone grows sour, her eyes narrow, and she even signals to me. "A student who didn't even grow up here and who barely knows anyone is doing more than anyone else."

"Holly, shut up," I hiss, latching onto her extended hand.

Mr. Livingstone's expression remains the same, except for the heavily arched eyebrow above his left eye. He skirts onto the stairway and waltzes up the steps, each step a tender rumble on the smooth floor. He stops at our row, hovering just beyond the unclaimed seats that separate us.

"I've heard about you," Mr. Livingstone says, and I finally get the chance to meet him up close. He was fuzzy before, but now up close and with my glasses, I can see the man who runs my hometown. He is tall and well built, with perfectly tailored suits. He's intimidating but friendly, with a strong "manners maketh the man" vibe. He extends his left hand towards me, past a shy Holly. "I'd like to shake your hand and welcome you to Seven Oaks."

My gulp is audible to at least a few rows around me, but I still stand up, straightening my skirt, and I shake his hand. Electric shocks pulse in my hand, all the way up my arm, and soon start to travel throughout the rest of my body.

"Kimberly, is it?" My name rolls off his tongue so smoothly.

"Yeah," I squeak, and clear my throat. "Kim."

"It's a pleasure to have you back, Kim." It strikes me as peculiar for a moment, but I remember that, as mayor, it's his job to know everyone. I wonder if he was the mayor when

I first lived here. "Though, I apologize for these unfortunate circumstances. We have been very lucky to have you here."

"Thanks." There's a permanent catch in my throat preventing me from speaking more than one word at a time. The weight of the eyes staring in our direction becomes unbearable, and I release Mr. Livingstone's firm grip. He offers one last smile and nod, and then turns back to the rest of the room.

"I believe the students here have been through enough," the mayor continues. He has a natural character that helps him capture an entire room in the drop of a hat. "I propose, if I may, that we dismiss the students, and that the parents and faculty continue to discuss this issue."

Without hesitation, the parents all agree and send their kids away, gazing over the younger crowd until they very willingly shuffle up the stairs and out the auditorium door. I stay seated until Holly stands up, and she latches onto my arm.

"Come on."

"That's it?" I question, shocked by how quickly everything changed. I'm pulled to my feet, and I grip tightly onto my purse at my side. "What's gonna happen?"

"They're gonna talk," Holly replies, dragging me towards the stairs. Mayor Livingstone has ducked back into his seat, Mason now heading up the steps. "And hopefully they'll figure this out soon."

"We're not allowed to help anymore?" I watch the shambling students go by, most of them looking unfazed. It's eerie, how relieved some of these students look. I'm shocked by how easily all the teenagers got up to leave, like Mayor Livingstone has some kind of mind control over them. I didn't expect this kind of abrupt change; one minute there's an army of girls yelling at Mr. Wolfe, the next they're all going back to their rooms.

"No need," Holly reassures.

I forcefully tug against Holly's pull until we're stopped in the row, dozens of aggressive students trudging by us.

"Holly,"

"Kim, trust me." She faces me dead on, her expression apologetic and clever. "The parents in Seven Oaks are like sharks. They'll think of something."

I hesitate; it doesn't feel like anyone truly understands the potential severity of this. I don't even understand it myself, but I don't have my mom here to pass the problem off to. I've never been good at letting sleeping dogs lie.

"Kim?"

I meet Holly's gentle eyes. "Holly, I don't like this."

My new friend doesn't know how to respond. Instead, she takes my hand and leads me with all the other students. The two of us stomp up the lengthy steps and immerse ourselves in the great gray outdoors. My stomach has a strange sinking feeling, wallowing deep within me, aching. I try to push away the discomfort I feel; I'm starting to get scared.

"It's so sad what's going on here," Ronald's soft voice echoes beneath the shaded area of the auditorium. He's holding onto a dandelion, one he must have plucked from his feet, and he's observing it carefully, turning it around to catch all the petals.

"We don't know what's going on," Charles replies in a gruff, hushed voice.

"Still." Ronald sighs and crouches down, placing the flower delicately on the ground, and the two men resume watching guard over the sea of students flowing from the stage area. Ronald and I smile upon eye contact, and Holly and I head on our way.

Ronald seems to be the only one who has any semblance of the darkness behind the blinding light of Seven Oaks. It's beginning to feel sinister. Though, Charles does have a point, that nobody really has a clue what's happening. I would like to believe it's the local grower just fucking up and adding something intense to their marijuana strains, but...

"Hey!" Carolyn's projected voice calls to Holly and me. We find her, Jay, and Cam wrangled up in front of the cafeteria doors, about to go inside. I didn't see any of them in the auditorium, but I could barely focus on any one person at a time. "You guys hungry?"

Carolyn is tightly gripping onto Jay's hand, Cam staring off in the general vicinity of the hidden sun, sunglasses on. Jay holds the door wide open for us, and Holly starts to walk towards the door.

"Starving." After a few steps, she turns back to me, puzzled. "You're not coming?"

"I'm actually not that hungry," I say, feeling nauseated more than anything. I press a hand to my stomach and sigh, forcing a smile. "I'll catch up with you guys later."

Carolyn beams and she and Holly start chatting it up, Cam and Jay trailing behind. I catch Carolyn sneak Jay a subtle wink, and he grins wildly.

They are way too cute.

In the cafeteria windows, I see Owen and Leslie seated at a table, now greeting their new guests. Owen's head quickly turns outside, and I swiftly avoid the potentially awkward eye contact, ducking behind the building, out of sight.

I still have to thank him for what he did last night, but I don't feel good enough to do that right now.

On my way to my dorm room, I decide that I should do something with this strange feeling inside of me, and the batting cages seems like a good idea. I feel restless and impatient, though I'm not sure what for. I feel like I have all this pent-up energy; swinging my all too familiar bat sounds like a cathartic way to get rid of this agitation. More than anything, I think I just feel helpless.

What am I supposed to do about a situation that I don't understand? How can I continually claim what is or isn't normal when I'm not the one that's lived here my whole life?

I pause a moment before entering my dorm room, trying to gather my thoughts. I give up after a solid minute and storm into my room, and immediately change into my now traditional socks, shorts, and whatever t-shirt I grab first; in this case, it's a band shirt, black and yellow.

The path to the batting cages is fairly populated today, with many more people than I'm used to seeing. After leaving the assembly, it's a safe bet to assume that most students are on their way to get something to eat. It does seem like a great day for sushi, but what day doesn't?

I get a few peculiar glances on my way to the cages, given my unique choice of style and large black duffel, but I lose myself enough in the Enchanted Forest that I don't mind too much. I spot the squirrel I had seen before, I think, eating another nut, not a care in the world to the students rushing by him. He's seated on his bench, watching.

"Hey, little guy," I whisper as I walk by. He continues chewing, his cheeks moving a mile a minute, but I spot the tiny flick of his ears. If I talk to him enough, he'll really start to remember me.

The walkway in between the bleachers is a lot less cagy during the day, as well as with other people around. I'm surprised that a chill still rolls down my spine when I walk through, despite the couple of guys in front of me, and the charming melodies of the girls behind me. There are remnants of joints and cigarettes further beneath the stands, along with broken bottles, crushed cans, and even a crumpled shirt. Strangely enough, the sex appeal of underneath the sports benches is not working for me.

I veer off from the minor crowds to the batting cages, and I catch some people staring as if they had never noticed them before. Baseball isn't exactly popular in Canada in general, and no one other than me has even used the cages, as far as I know.

As I'm settling into my usual cage, two from the right, just hidden enough to feel like I'm in my own world, my duffel bag starts to vibrate. I dig around and find my phone; there's only one person who ever consistently calls me.

"Hello?"

"Hey, Kim," Mom's chipper voice rings through the phone. "How's it going?"

"It's okay." I take a seat on the lining benches within my small cage. Looking at it sideways like this, it feels more like a prison cell than anything. "How are you?"

"Concerned."

Oh, god. "...concerned?"

She sighs, and I hear the familiar sound of her home office chair squeaking; she never did get that fixed. "Well, I got an e-mail from the dean of your school today regarding two students that overdosed at your school?"

"Oh." *Right. That.* "Yeah."

"*Yeah?*" she repeats. "*Yeah?!*"

"Well, it actually seems more like they were drugged." My attempts to comfort my panicking mother have failed immensely. I squeeze my eyes shut, wincing at my own stupidity.

"Oh, well, that's just great, Kimberly." *The full name. Yikes.* "What the hell happened? Seven Oaks was safe when we lived there, I send you there for three weeks on your own—"

"I'm being safe," I interrupt. "I don't really know what's going on. Nothing is actually, like...but, I..." I think of the people I've met here, Mason and Rian, and my heart rate speeds up. But then I think of others; I think of Owen pulling me out of the pool, Holly making sure I was okay, Carolyn yelling at me for my own safety, Georgina's trusting conversations. I calm down. "I have good friends."

"So, you're not going anywhere alone?"

I scan my surroundings; it doesn't help that everyone is now out of sight, enjoying their stellar sushi and Starbucks. "...right."

"Kim."

"Mom." I chuckle. "I'm okay. And the girls are physically okay, too. They both had *tests*, and apparently nothing happened." I'm trying to downplay it for my mom, but the thought of losing a chunk of time and not knowing what happened will continually terrify me. I can't imagine how scared Georgina and Patricia must be. I know my mom is already scared enough, and I know if I buy into it, she'll be sent into a frenzy.

"Hm." I roll my eyes at Mom's tone; she always gets this snark in her voice on the rare occasions she disapproves. "You just better be safe."

"I am." I debate telling her of my heroics in almost drowning, but I shut my mouth again. Time and place.

"You actually sound really happy," my mom says, slightly disbelief in her voice. She knows better than anyone the struggles I had in high school. She doesn't know much about this Kim, the one who is immediately forward and outwardly witty, but she has nurtured her well. "You're making friends well?"

"Surprisingly so." *Has it only been three weeks? Not even?* "I think I mentioned Holly before. She's really awesome." I've never felt so comfortable with someone so quickly. I think I see part of myself in her, part of the same past. Part of the same coping mechanism.

"Was that the girl that just came into your room one night?"

I smirk. "Yeah, her. And some other girls, most people are pretty nice, except for a few."

"It's like that everywhere you go," Mom reminds me. Not only has my mom been my anchor ever since I can remember, I like to think that I'm hers too. I might not be, but it's always a pleasant comfort.

"Yeah. A lot of the guys are pretty nice, too."

"Whatever happened to that one boy you kissed?"

I try to remember telling my mom about Damien, I assume, but I can't pinpoint the exact time. I tend to tell her everything. I haven't mentioned Matt, not that he really needs a mention. "We're just friends."

"What about those other boys? Owen, is that someone?"

"Yeah, I really like him, he's really sweet." My mom pauses, or the phone disconnects, causing me to prompt, "Hello?"

"Do you like him?" *Of course.*

"As a friend." Another long pause. "I'm not looking to date anyone." Not to mention that I haven't even considered Owen as anything more than a friend. A super nice friend. I giggle a little. "Boys suck."

"You're not wrong," Mom mutters, something wistful in her voice. I can picture her expression exactly right now, one that I've inherited, with the skeptical brows, the subtle soft smile, her blue eyes gleaming. I know her all too well. "Well,

I'll let you go, I guess I've bothered you enough for today. Be safe, Kimberly."

"I will," I reassure, though I'm not sure if it's more for her benefit or mine. I definitely don't want to freak her out with my own worries. "I love you."

"Love you too. Bye."

"Bye."

"Wait!" Mom calls, and I wait patiently before hearing some intense rustling.

"...hello?"

"Hold on." More silence. I tap my fingers on my thigh, my invisible piano, and pause until I finally hear what she's doing. A small meow echoes into the phone, and before I can call on it, a rather loud cat call fills my ears. "Bailey says hi!"

"Oh, my god." I laugh it off, but I actually find it adorable. The apple doesn't fall far from the tree. I decide to play along, "I'll talk to you both later."

"Bye, sweetie," Mom chimes, chuckling to herself, the cat purring directly into the microphone, and it all suddenly cuts to silence.

I hang up the phone; as corny as it sounds, every single time I get off the phone with my mom, no matter how long or short the conversation is, I always feel melancholic. It's weird being so far away from her, and I often wonder what it's like for her. I can't replace her with a cat, since there are no pets allowed in the dorm rooms. Maybe a cute plush.

I grin at the thought and throw myself into action, refocusing myself on the sport at hand. The last time I was here, I learned more about the settings on the ball pitcher and perfect the amount of baseballs and time in between. I set it to 500, eighty kilometers an hour, fifteen seconds in between. It's longer than I'm used to, but I like to watch how far the ball goes before hitting another one. It's always satisfying to see the wave through the net above, or the crunch if it hits the fence directly across.

I miss the first few balls, kicking myself after every miss. The most disappointing sound is the anticlimactic whipping of the bat, so forceful and strong, only to have nothing to follow.

I grip tightly onto my bat, and I start to channel my energy into my hands, buzzing through my fingers. I feel electric. Surges flow through the bat with each perfect hit. I attempt to do the crazy thing and shut my eyes, trusting my other senses to help me out. The machine *plops*, and I can hear the air being split by the ball. I can almost taste it on my tongue when it's close enough, and I strike; I only open my eyes when the vibration of the fabric netting sends chills down my spine.

"Wow," an uncomfortable voice echoes behind me. I whip around clutching my bat, ready to attack, to find Mason Livingstone in all his glory. *What the fuck is he doing here?* "You can hit a ball with your eyes closed. Good for you."

I can feel a small fire burning within me, and I am tempted to charge at him. He's somehow managed to get inside my cage, despite my swearing that I locked the gate, and is tucked along the side, safely away from the baseballs. A ball swipes by us, and surprisingly, I don't flinch. Mason, on the other hand, has a minor heart attack.

"If you're scared, you should probably leave." I try my best to calm the anger in my voice, but it comes out arrogant and condescending.

Mason doesn't like that, and he glares at me, stepping closer, still along the fence. His well-tailored clothes are completely pristine, except for his overly expensive shoes that have begun to gather dust from the cages. Another ball shoots in between us, smashing flat against the matted gates. He stands across from me, face to face, and my fingers adjust on the bat.

Studying his face, I start to let my guard down. him so close, so vulnerable, he looks like a puppy, lost and confused. His eyes can't seem to focus, and it feels like his mind is working a mind a minute just to remain this calm.

I chuckle, releasing my bat down to my side.

"You have some issues," I state bluntly, and one of his eyebrows perks up. "I don't like being stalked."

"Oh, please." He crosses his arms over his chest and rolls his eyes.

"Then why are you here?" I start to get scared again, and I instead draw my courage to the front lines. "Like, actually. It seems like you've hated me since before we even first spoke."

"I don't hate you," he shoots back, and I refrain from cringing at how defensive he gets.

"Had me fooled." Every ball that flies by us, his eyes twitch a little, but he seems to be getting used to the abrupt splitting. I rest my bat on the ground, leaning onto it a little. I don't like Mason; I don't like the feeling I get around him, and how he's putting off this cryptic attitude. I don't know why I feel the need to press, but maybe it's because I get the sense that he doesn't really know what he's doing, despite the tough guy act. Seeing him like this, he doesn't seem capable of having any sort of deviant plan. "Maybe it's because I didn't grow up here. And I don't buy into the whole 'daddy's boy' thing."

I inadvertently set him off and he dares to take a step closer to me, blazing eyes. I swear they even turn red for a brief moment. "You have no clue about anything in this town."

"Enlighten me," I snarl, challenging him further. There's only about a foot in between us, and a baseball zips in between the two of us. I feel the air against my waist, my shirt blowing in the wind. "Like, what's happening to the girls here? Who's drugging them?"

"You think they're getting drugged?" He spits, laughing. *Looks like I'm the only one here who thinks these "overdoses" are intentional.* "You're fucking crazy."

Keep going. "Mayor's son, convenient excuse, isn't it?"

Through gritted teeth, Mason growls, "Shut up." For a moment, I feel something inside me shaking. I start to feel scared again. It's almost like Mason can sense this, because he steps closer, in the path of the baseballs, and gets way too close for comfort. "If you know what's good for you, you'll shut your fucking mouth."

My heart rate skyrockets, and my own vulnerability finally catches up with me. I feel out of breath, terrified, and I stumble backwards towards the fence. Mason steps closer until I'm pressed against the chain links, trying my best not to show my fear.

"Anything else you want to say?" he presses.

I clutch tighter onto my bat, fancying the thought of hitting him with it. Instead, my courage flares again. I turn to the ball pitcher finding a ball heading straight for me, despite my not being in its way anymore.

These fucking pitchers!

I clench one fist, preparing for impact, and I hold my free hand out towards it, as if I can catch it. I'm not sure why I'm doing it; it's a panic impulse to keep it from breaking any other bones in my body. The setting is much faster than before, and I know this could leave more than a bruise.

My eyes shut on their own; I'm not sure why, but not seeing the horrid impact will make the hurt more bearable.

But that doesn't happen.

The flawed leather baseball slips gently into my hand, and my held breath escapes my lips. I don't fully process that I'm holding the inanimate ball in my hand, somehow not in agonizing pain, my fingers wrapping around the tight material.

Mason stares in horror at my hand, and I hold the ball up closer to my eyes, observing the lack of marks and pain in my palm.

Does it hurt so much that I've gone numb?

I meet Mason's eyes, catching his terror, and I grin, catching him off-guard. "Leave me alone." I pause theatrically between each word.

I chuck the ball flatly to the ground before whirling around, smashing my potentially pained hand against the control panel. It shuts off, and I swiftly snatch my bag from the dirt and leave the batting cage. I don't look back until I've spotted another person, another possible witness to this insanity. I thought Mason would be dramatically staring after me, but his eyes are fixed on the ball I had caught and dropped at his feet.

I bring my hand up to eye level, observing my same old, if not slightly dried from the crisp weather, hand. It was like time had slowed down just so I could catch the ball, or, or...

My head starts throbbing and I stumble on my path, garnering the attention of two passerby. Instead of offering to help, they skirt around me, walking on the grass. I drop my bat but catch it just before it hits the ground, the near-clanging sending my head spinning.

I need to sit down.

The nearest seats are the bleachers facing the empty soccer field. I fall onto the first row and lean over, caressing my head in my hands.

I don't know what's happening. I don't know what just happened, if that was even real. The more I think about it, the more my head aches.

How could I catch that ball coming straight for me at eighty kilometers an hour? How did it stop? How is my hand not broken?

I search my hand again before squeezing my eyes shut once more. Nothing makes sense here, it's like I'm in some backwards, alternate universe. My head is going a million kilometers an hour, and there's only one single thought that I can thoroughly focus on.

What the fuck is going on here?

Chapter 10

Despite my absolute adoration for our feathered, furry, and scaled friends, I always found their dissection fascinating. Today is the first of our few dissection days in Ornithology class, all birds who have died of natural causes, I've been assured.

Because of the immense lack of people in this course, everyone got to dissect their own bird. We went up in alphabetical order, my name being second, and I was assigned a robin. I had dissected rats and fish in high school, but birds hold a special place in my heart, so it was a little rough at first. My morbidity got the best of me after a while, and it started to get easier.

I got through it quickly enough, identifying the organs, writing them on my corresponding worksheet, and finally writing my report on what I find to be the cause of death. I did not expect to be learning causes of death in birds, but here we are.

My robin friend, who I creatively named Batman, simply passed away from old age. His heart stopped beating, and his wings stopped flapping. I tried my best not to get too philosophical with it all, pondering life and death.

    I finish my paper, adding that his slightly irregular heart size could potentially have something to do with his marginally premature death, and a small scratching sound captures my attention. I turn to the window, finding a live robin perched outside, staring inside the classroom. His eyes are directly on his deceased friend, and my heart aches a little. With my one gloved hand, I reach over to Batman, gently stroking his fragile feathers. His features are so tiny, his eyes, beak, nostrils. Logically, I know that he didn't suffer, and that one day, he just went to sleep and didn't wake up. No pain.

    My eyes begin to feel warm and I immediately shut them. The circle of life can be so horribly sad.

    "Are you okay?" Emma's voice suddenly pops into my head. My eyes shoot open, slightly blurry, and I force a startled smile.

    I lean back on my stool, observing Emma's hesitant expression. The only other time I talked to her was at the homecoming pool party, and she seems particularly friendly. I glanced over at her station earlier, and she was dissecting a stellar jay. She looked a bit pained too.

    "Yeah," I reply, clearing my throat. I face my robin again and then turn back to her, beaming harder.

    "I get it," Emma says, her eyes drifting down to Batman. She has both of her gloves on still, her hands hovering in the air so they don't touch anything. Her pink hair is tied up on top of her head, thoroughly wrapped around into a perfect knot.

    I open my mouth and attempt to say something witty or clever, but I come up blank. I shut my mouth once more, staring at my nearly completed paper.

    "Yeah."

"Just to let you know," Mr. Evans, our professor, declares, eyes fixed on his desktop computer. He has a habit of looking elsewhere whenever addressing the class. "Class is officially over. You can leave once you're done."

"Shit," Emma says, offering a courtesy smile before skipping back to her station. Emma is the only person I kind of know in this class, but I do recognize another student as one of Georgina's friends.

I slip my left hand into my other glove and pick up Batman's dissection table. It's easy to get distracted when you feel as if the outside world doesn't exist; it's easy to get lost in the moment and forget the harsh realities beyond your own views. I quickly take Batman up to Mr. Evans, who is patiently seated at his desk.

"No need to rush," he announces to the scurrying class. "Take all the time you need." He looks up at me, and grins a little, probably at how stupid I look. I have my glasses on beneath my safety goggles, my gloves halfway up my forearms, and my hair thrown hastily into a lopsided ponytail. I would feel embarrassed, but as a college student, I'm sure I will have much worse days. "How was it?"

"Good," I say through gritted teeth, carefully placing Batman in the plastic container on Mr. Evans' desk. He told us at the beginning of class that we should dispose of all "sensitive" materials in the large bin so that it will be properly taken care of.

"I'm almost done the worksheet. There was also a partially digested worm inside him."

"Really?!" The excitement in Mr. Evans' voice surprises me, and he hops to his feet, observing Batman very carefully. I never noticed how tall he was until now, standing next to me. He's a tower.

"Yeah." I point to Batman's stomach and carefully pry it open, revealing the sliming decomposing creature. "He had a good last meal."

Mr. Evans looks to me and smiles, nodding. "Indeed, he did."

"What are you going to do with him?" I remove my gloves, tossing them in the trash bucket next to the professor's desk. I dread the thought of Batman being just thrown into the garbage or discarded like he didn't matter.

"We have a special facility in the senior campus," Mr. Evans says, producing his own pair of thick gloves. He pulls out an empty plastic bin and pries off the lid. "Science building. They take all the dissected animals and..." as if sensing my own sensitivity, Mr. Evans chooses his words carefully, "well, to be quite honest, and none too graphic, it's a form of composting. I like to think of it as the circle of life, they become the soil that nourishes and feeds other forms of life."

I nod, smiling bittersweetly. That is probably the best response I could have hoped for. "That's really cool."

"I agree." He carefully lifts Batman from his metal plate and places him into the container. Another student arrives at the desk, and I smile politely at my professor before skirting off back to my station. I don't think I can stomach watching Mr. Evans put all the birds into one container.

Ten minutes flies by in an instant by the time I'm finished cleaning, sanitizing, and putting everything away. I say goodbye to Emma and Mr. Evans, only catching the smallest glimpse of the filled container.

Circle of life, Kim.

I check my phone, running late for my meeting up with Holly and Owen. I still have a few hours before English Lit, and the three of us have decided that after Ornithology, we should all start getting meals together. It turns out that I'm not the only one who's bad at keeping track of when they eat, or even remembering to eat. It seems to be a common problem as a student.

 The unfinished prank catches my eye, and I nearly jump out of my skin. The lightning bird, in all its hasty glory, looks absolutely petrifying on this wall. There are scratches all over the pristine brick of the science building from the desperate attempts to wash it all off. The body is relatively intact, but the wings are scrubbed away and faded. Its eyes are a piercing black, and are the most cohesive thing about this piece. The bird is about four feet tall and wide, wings spread, and the words "SOU 2K" are scribbled below the intimidating creature. Somebody managed to garble the numbers into an ugly gray mixture.

 Thoughts of the footballers desperately trying to fix their prank after hearing about Patricia sends chills down my spine.

 A tall body suddenly crashes right into me, my phone digging into my chest.

 "Oh," I express, steadying my balance. In my way is someone who I have seldom had the great pleasure of conversing with; Rian. Still, I begrudgingly say, "Sorry."

 "Watch where you're fucking going," she says without missing a beat. She bares her small teeth at me, her gums exposed more than her teeth. We are just outside the main building, the first dreary day of the year upon us. I suppose it's quite foretelling.

 "I don't get it," I mutter to myself, trying to get away, but she snatches my arm in her feisty talons and whirls me around. She is certainly aggressive.

 "Excuse me?"

I arch my eyebrow; I do not like being randomly touched like this. I hold my free hand up to her, and her fingers unlatch my arm, shooting away. She even winces, as if I burned her.

"I don't get it," I repeat, louder. She sways backwards and then comes in forward again, narrowing her pale eyes at me. I glance at her eyebrows, noticing the abrupt difference between them and her hair colour. They don't quite look drawn on, and they're nearly filled straight above her eyes, almost down to a geometric pattern. I try not to focus on them. "Why you're just so senselessly rude." I forget who I'm talking to for a second. Flashback to locker talks next to Rose's locker, and how she can make me feel so small, yet so large, at the same time. All the things I never said, all the things I never dealt with. "I don't get why you like being mean."

Her whole body sets on fire and she exhales smoke like a dragon, and I snap back to where I am. "You don't know anything about me. You're just some bitch who doesn't know shit all, who—"

"I have to go." I strut past her, my heart starting to beat ferociously. I can't believe how Rian can transport me right back to high school, right back to those shitty moments. I couldn't even think when I was speaking to her; all I do is say the stuff I wish I'd said to some other "friends."

My breathing is shaky, and my head feels like a mess, ignoring the thoughts of Rian, being confronted with Rose.

Ignoring the thoughts of Rose, *being confronted with* Rian.

I stop in my tracks, unsure if I'm even out of Rian's sights, but I can't find it in myself to keep going. I take deep breaths, my stomach churning in knots. The same panic, the same self-hatred, the same feeling of false sense of security; they're all there.

Something tells me that my interactions with Rian are plenty to come, though I sincerely hope not.

"Hey!" Holly yells my way. I look up, finding her and Owen standing only a few feet away. I hardly remember walking to the cafeteria, but I'm apparently here already. High school nostalgia can do that to a person.

Holly waves dramatically, baring her beautiful smile, her hair wavy and dramatic over her delicate shoulders. Owen has an equally happy grin plastered onto his face, his goofy and comforting face.

I smile; maybe I will have issues with Rian in the future. But I also have real friends. It might be naïve to think of these people I've known for three weeks as my best friends in the whole world, but...well, here we are. There's just something about them.

"Hey," I chuckle, catching up to them.

"You're late!" Holly screams, garnering a few stares. "Where were you?"

"We dissected a bird today, took a little longer," I admit.

"Um, ew." Holly shakes her head, her hair frizzing in the humid air. She pats it down viciously. "Let's go eat, I am starving."

"What kind of bird?" Owen asks as he and I follow Holly's lead towards the cafeteria.

"I did a robin." A bird swoops down from the cafeteria building, and for a moment, I think it's a robin, but it turns out to be a crow. He flies down above the door, and then perches back on the side of the roof. I add this part, just to bug Holly, "his last meal was a worm."

"Okay, enough," she squirms, grabbing onto the double doors. She throws them both open behind her, very theatrically, and slips inside. "We can discuss this later, like, when we're not about to eat."

"Sure," I quip. I catch a whiff of the delicious smelling pasta brewing, and I understand better why Holly wanted to postpone the chat of digested worms until after we've eaten our spaghetti. "How was your guys' day?"

"Okay," Holly says and snatches up three plates, handing one to Owen and one to me. "Pretty boring. My mom called today, so that was fun."

I bite my tongue before speaking, giving Owen a hesitant look. I'm not sure if he knows, or if he's supposed to know what's going on with her parents.

"How was that?" I press.

Holly sighs, filling her plate with spaghetti. I was going to opt for a sandwich but looking at the steaming pasta heaped onto her plate, I think my mind has changed. "It was...what it was. At least Mimi is okay."

"Mimi?"

Holly drizzles sauce onto her pasta and then beams in my direction. "My dog, my baby. She'll be living with my mom, which is good, 'cause my dad is moving into this tiny place." Holly pauses and glances at Owen herself. With a roll of her eyes and the shake of her head, she's decided that she doesn't care if he knows. It's not like he's listening anyway, he's enthralled in the wrap section of our elite kitchen, piling ingredients high onto his tortilla.

"Are you doing okay?" I ask, confident that Owen is out of earshot.

Holly sighs and watches as I toss noodles onto my plate, going directly for the cheeses and butters. Pasta and cheese; who can argue with that?

"I think so. It makes sense, at the very least. I think back to when I was a kid, and I don't know if my parents were ever happy. I guess it just feels sudden, because they never talked to me about it."

I really admire Holly and her bravery in speaking about this so openly. It might seem easy or simple, but being so outright about this subject can be extremely difficult. I know Holly and I share past experiences together, and maybe we've handled them the same way too, by being brutally open and honest. I don't know if she's always been that way, but I have certainly not. I can learn a thing or two from her.

"I mean, why would they?" Holly adds, chuckling to herself. Thinking back, my mom never mentioned my dad unless prompted by me. But, as just stated, why would she?

"Yeah," I sigh, mixing the pasta around on my plate. I wait for the cheese to melt beneath it before stirring again. "Makes sense. I'm glad you're doing okay."

She smiles, filled with glee. "I'm just happy I have someone to talk to about it. Most parents don't get divorced here."

"Really?" I state, capturing Owen's attention just as he rolls his tortilla shell into a perfectly formed, if not busting, wrap.

"A lot of them met in high school, you know? People stick within town."

"What?" Owen says.

"Marriage, divorce," Holly says bluntly, and the three of us walk towards one of the few empty tables. It's a prime time to be eating lunch right now, but I don't fully recognize any of the students in the cafeteria, except Matt briefly catches my eye. We both look away immediately. "I want to get married one day, but I don't want to get divorced." She laughs and adjusts her statement, "Well, nobody *wants* to get divorced, but I really want it to stick. Divorce isn't an option for me."

"I wouldn't mind," Owen mumbles as we sit down. Holly and I look to each other before staring at Owen. I think neither of us have ever heard a guy's opinion on marriage before. "If it needs to happen, it happens." He quickly looks at me and then begins devouring into his wrap.

"Fair enough." I pick at my food, swirling the long noodles around my fork. "To both of you. If I ever wanted to get married, I think I'd be okay with divorce, too. It's just a fancy breakup."

"You don't want to get married?" Holly says, stunned. Her jaw is gaping, eyes wide. "I totally pegged you for a girl who's looked at wedding dresses, planned her dream wedding–"

"Oh, I'd love a wedding," I start to joke. I'm surprised Holly nailed my personality so quickly. "I'd love to have a fancy party where I wear a beautiful dress and tons of food. But I don't even want a relationship, so a marriage isn't even in the question."

"Honestly, boys suck!" Holly slams her fork down on her plates, picks up some pasta, and stuffs it into her mouth. With a full mouth, she mutters, "No offence, Owen."

"Just as long as you know that girls suck, too." He takes another bite of his wrap, avoiding all possible eye contact.

"Okay, everybody sucks," I state, giggling. "Equality."

My jibe gets a small laugh before the three of us delve into our food again.

"Hey, did you guys hear anything about Patricia recently?" Holly asks, glancing between our gazes.

"No," I reply flatly. Patricia has been a sore topic for me; between Carolyn's concerned cries, Livingstone's awkward introduction, and the fact that my throat still has a numbing itch, I haven't been inclined to talk much about it. I highly doubt Patricia would want to be the buzz of the school either, at least not for this reason. I debated trying to contact her, like I did with Georgina, but I decided against it. It didn't seem right for some reason.

"I heard her parents pulled her out of school for now," Holly continues, oblivious to my discomfort. "And that Georgina's parents might do the same again."

"Really?" I inhale more of my pasta, the salted butter burning as I swallow. I hope this sting goes away soon.

"Do you blame them?" Holly looks relatively calm, but her voice is reaching higher and higher. "It's basically confirmed now, girls are getting drugged and potentially going missing."

"Missing?" Owen and I both say the word in unison and then glance at each other.

"Yeah. Patricia's friends said they didn't see her for a few hours, and same with Georgina's."

"Are you sure?" I lean in closer, my heart starting to beat louder. This dreamlike town is quickly spiralling into a nightmare.

Holly shrugs casually. Her blasé attitude is something I have yet to master, but has been a recurring theme in Seven Oaks. "It's just what I've heard. It's freaky, that's for sure. I know that I don't have to worry, though."

I raise my eyebrows at her, skeptical and curious. "And why's that?"

Holly arches her back and sits up straighter, placing her dainty hands on her hips. "Why, because of Super Kim, of course! Just the hero that this town needs."

My cheeks flush but I end up giggling and rolling my eyes. I can't even begin to think about the little weird things happening to me every so often.

"She is pretty handy with a bat," Owen remarks, already finished his wrap. In the absence of his inclusion, he managed to finish his lunch before Holly and I made much of a dent in our meals.

I give Owen a peculiar look until I recall that I did almost swing at him. Not my proudest moment.

"Oh, have you seen her at the cages?" Holly presses. "Gretchen said she saw her once, apparently she gets really in the zone."

"Gretchen saw me?" I say. Despite it being very public, I'm still surprised that people take that extra moment to notice me in the cages. I guess when nobody else is there, I'm an uncommon occurrence.

Holly nods, and before I can add anything, Owen saves my blunder and says, "Yeah, I've seen her there."

"Work hard, play hard," Holly says.

"Minus the working hard," I joke. The homework for my classes so far is a farce, and I'm hoping it stays that way. I might just do better in university than I did in high school.

"Smile!" A small and preppy voice shouts in the cafeteria, and Brit appears out of nowhere, holding a camera to our faces. The camera is so huge that it nearly hides Brit's head, except for her voluminous blonde locks. Marla is lingering behind her, chowing down on her own half-eaten wrap, being careful not to ruin her meticulous dark lipstick.

"No!" Holly yells in kind, cowering quickly and frantically trying to fix her hair.

"You look great," I say, but still find myself running my fingers through my own hair. I'm usually on the other side of the camera, and I'm a little surprised that I'm so willing to be photographed.

Brit drops the camera to reveal her rolled eyes. "You all look great. Just let me take a picture."

"What's it for?" Owen asks as Holly and I sneak in closer towards him.

"Photography," Brit says, raising the camera back into view. "Mr. Wolfe wants us to get lots of pictures of the students because it's a new university and whatever."

"What for, like, a yearbook?" I question, forcing a smile.

"Kind of." Brit leans closer. "Owen, put your arms around the girls." I can see her partially hidden grin, but I'm not sure why she's smiling. Owen takes a deep breath before draping his arms across my shoulders and around Holly, tugging us in closer. "Perfect."

"Do I look okay?" Holly asks, teeth clenched in a tight smile.

"You always look beautiful," I respond, and Holly quickly snaps her head to me, mouth gaping.

"What?" she says, shocked. "That was so nice."

I eye her cautiously before recalling the conversation we'd had before. We weren't so lucky as to escape high school unscathed. Maybe we really do have the same scars. We both smile gently, and suddenly I don't have to force my smile. I feel like I have friends, *real* friends. It's an amazing feeling.

"Over here," Brit says, and before either of us can process the camera lens we're staring into, she takes a photo. A few, actually. Brit stands up and smiles, Marla gazing around the room, only holding the napkin remnants of her burrito. She looks unsettled. "Perfect. I love it."

"Guys!" Cam's voice echoes in the cafeteria, followed by his frantic footsteps. Owen takes his arms back and we all turn to sprinting Cam, who halts next to our table. Her nearly trips in his skater shoes, and uses the benches as support.

"What?" Holly sneers.

"You need to see this," he says, panting. He searches all our eyes before his own widen and he throws his hands in the air. His face is red, he's out of breath, and he looks downright scared. "Right now!"

Before I can even bother to question Cam, I'm hopping out of my seat and trailing behind him, abandoning my hardly touched meal. Owen, Holly, Brit, and Marla are right on my tail, muttering amongst themselves. Cam halts before a large group of people, all of us crowded around a bulky raised flat screen TV. I've never been in the connecting foyer for the cafeteria, and I certainly didn't know there was a television here for students to watch.

"What's going on?" I ask. Cam shakes his head and starts to fight his way through the sea of students. He extends his arm, offering the invitation, and we all wiggle around the stressed teenagers until we have a suitable view.

"What the hell?" Brit mutters, clutching her camera close to her chest. She quickly glances down, as if she needs the reassurance that her Kodak is there, even though her hands are wrapped tightly around it.

Our eyes fix to the TV.

It's a news segment, showcasing several police officers standing around behind some yellow tape, all staring at the same dug up hole in the ground. The volume is turned off, the subtitles on, but I can't concentrate enough to read them. My eyes are stuck on the banner at the bottom reading, "young woman found dead, suspected student of Seven Oaks."

"Oh, my god," Marla says, her hand finding its way to rest on her posh lips.

"This is so fucked up," Brit states, and I'm not sure whether it's more for herself or for the people around her. She leans into her girlfriend, and Marla instinctively wraps her arms around her. "What's even happening?!"

"Who is it?" Holly's voice is quiet and meek, something so foreign that I even turn to her as she speaks. I can't place the expression on her face, but my best guess would be...realization.

"I don't know," Cam says and crosses his arms over his chest.

"I don't understand," Brit urges.

My ears tune out the confused statements of my friends, and my eyes travel over to Jay and Carolyn. She's circled in his arms, head burrowed into his chest, as if she can shut the world out, Jay's letterman jacket the barrier between her and reality. Given the few students who can't bear to stomach what's on the screen, everyone's eyes are absorbed on the TV before us. The subtitles are moving quickly and jerkily, giving me a headache when I try to comprehend them.

My eyes soon fall onto Mason's. He's standing near some of the football team, but he's staring off at nothing in particular. His head is slightly cocked to the side, eyes narrowed and harsh. As if he senses me, his eyes shoot up and meet mine so abruptly that I stumble back a little. My body sways just briefly against Owen's, and he instinctively steps closer to me. A small sound escapes from Owen's lip, a subconscious comfort, but I'm still stuck on Mason.

The horror on his face is not from what's being shown on the screen, the shallow grave of a potential lifelong resident of Seven Oaks. A life that's been cut short.

He looks more shocked that we are looking at each other more than anything.

I stiffen and face forwards once more. Mason has something to do with this, or he knows something, or...*something*. This can't all be a coincidence. It just can't. Out of the corner of my eye, Mason slips back into the masses, disappearing from my sights.

The news camera on the TV zooms in closer to the recently revealed burial, appearing to be in some kind of forest. A flash of colour pops from the grave, a bright yellow garment, and the students collectively groan, some looking away.

"Oh, my god," Holly says.

I look around for Georgina, for Patricia, but neither of them are here. My heart starts pounding at the fact that someone I know could possibly be dead. My eyes grow teary, my breathing not coming to me so easily.

The idea that I just potentially stared a murderer in the eyes sends me into a panic, but I clench my fists and take a deep breath.

Breathe, Kim. You're going to need to try to keep a level head for this.

All at once, everything becomes real. The bubble pops, and my view on everything I thought I knew in this town is skewed. The seedy underbelly and restless hearts of this town are really starting to shine through. This world has tipped sideways, and those rose-coloured glasses are long gone.

Welcome to Seven Oaks.

About the Author

Kaitlyn Johnson is a young Canadian author, based out of Vancouver, BC. She first started writing when she was 14 years old, and has since published a short story, Cake and Coffee, a poem, Sail, and a novel, The Time It Takes. Seven Oaks is her second novel, and her first dive into series writing.

Made in the USA
Monee, IL
04 November 2019